PENGUIN BOOKS
LOVE IN THE

Carol Clewlow was a jour____ _____ _____ ____ ___ _____
and the Far East. She published her first novel in 1988, the
highly acclaimed *Keeping the Faith*, which was nominated
for the Whitbread First Novel Award. Her second, *A
Woman's Guide to Adultery*, followed in 1989 and was a
great critical and commercial success. It is also published
by Penguin. *Love in the Modern Sense* has been serialized on
BBC Radio 4's *Woman's Hour*. Carol Clewlow lives on
Tyneside.

CAROL CLEWLOW

LOVE IN THE
MODERN SENSE

PENGUIN BOOKS

PENGUIN BOOKS

Published by the Penguin Group
Penguin Books Ltd, 27 Wrights Lane, London W8 5TZ, England
Penguin Books USA Inc., 375 Hudson Street, New York, New York 10014, USA
Penguin Books Australia Ltd, Ringwood, Victoria, Australia
Penguin Books Canada Ltd, 10 Alcorn Avenue, Toronto, Ontario, Canada M4V 3B2
Penguin Books (NZ) Ltd, 182–190 Wairau Road, Auckland 10, New Zealand

Penguin Books Ltd, Registered Offices: Harmondsworth, Middlesex, England

First published by Michael Joseph 1992
Published in Penguin Books 1992
1 3 5 7 9 10 8 6 4 2

The quotation on page vii from *And our faces, my heart, brief as photos* by John Berger,
published by Granta Books, is reproduced by permission

The quotation on page 228 from *Intercourse* by Andrea Dworkin is reproduced by kind
permission of Martin Secker & Warburg Ltd

Printed in England by Clays Ltd, St Ives plc

To Stuart White, with thanks

In one sense what happens between women and men in love is beyond history. In the fields, on the roads, in the workshops, at school, there are continual transformations: in an embrace very little changes. Yet the construction put on passion alters. Not necessarily because emotions are different but because what surrounds the emotions – social attitudes, legal systems, moralities, eschatologies – these change.

Romantic love, in the modern sense, is a love uniting or hoping to unite two displaced persons . . .

John Berger,
And our faces, my heart, brief as photos

Thursday Afternoon . . .

1

SHE WATCHES HIM from the window. Surprising herself. Beginning to like him.

Poking apart the slats of the blinds, she spies on him, his head back, feigning sleep.

Last week there were three of them, the week before that six, and at the beginning so many that they blocked the street with their cars and their vans and their paraphernalia, so that Gerald next door called the police.

He was the first of them to appear on her doorstep.

When he said the name, she felt the past and the present collide in her head.

'Bernard?' she had echoed at him blankly.

Later the same day, he had appeared silently at her elbow as she put the rubbish out. She had not realized he was there until he stepped forward from behind a wall murmuring her name, so that she looked up to find herself staring into a pair of eyes, watery blue and bloodshot and full of a weary ironic determination which seemed to say to her, 'I know . . . I'm too old for this . . . but still, nonetheless . . .'

Lowering her head and jamming down the lid upon the dustbin, she heard his feet scuffing gently and awkwardly upon the gravel as he let fall phrases, practised and comforting, about how she might help him, at some financial gain to herself and yet without loss of honour.

She shook her head in bewilderment as the phrases fell about her and, without speaking, turned sharply, pushed open the garden gate and clashed it noisily behind her.

Soon there were more of them, all murmuring the same name, all clicking and snapping and smiling and performing small unctuous genuflections at her when she opened the door.

One even tried to give her flowers.

He held them out to her on the doorstep. For a moment she stared at them mesmerized, before slamming the door in outrage so suddenly that a bright red beheaded carnation fell with a melancholy plop on to the hall floor.

After that she took no notice when the doorbell rang. She unplugged the phone too, so that eventually, one by one, the small persistent tide began to seep away.

Now all that was left was him, him and his photographer, who sat, one knee crooked up beneath the steering wheel, talking continuously and polishing a lens with loving and relentless care.

One day, peering like this through the blinds, she had seen them argue. She had seen him throw his head back in an angry ejaculation, had seen him tear open the car door to stride a short way up the street, where he stopped and hurled himself, head back, against the trunk of a tree.

As he leant there, shoulders hunched, hands thrust gracelessly into the too-tight mackintosh, a black plastic bag scuttled past him, rising up and dipping as if doing mock obeisance before sweeping on its way. But he did not see it. He was staring up at her window. His thinning hair lifted in the wind, his shoulders twitched in a shiver and on his face was a look of absolute despair.

And that was when she almost drew up the blinds and unlatched the window and called down to him, 'All right then. Since you've stayed so long. Come up and I'll tell you about Bernard O'Donaghue.'

2

I T WAS PUNISHMENT of course. Being stuck here. Outside her house. For what? Oh God, for what? For getting old, for growing fat, for going bald. For these and all those other crimes against the state.

This morning Bullerman had said what he said each morning. He said, 'You've had two warnings, Crane.'

The three-warning system. A masterstroke of industrial relations from their new editor. They still called him the new editor although he'd been with them for over a year now, since the day of the *putsch* when the old one came in one morning to clear his desk and leave by the back door with only a quarter of a million pounds for company. Strange how the price for failure got better the higher up you went.

Several weeks later he and Malone were called down to head office. They were sitting with the rest of the old men from the districts surrounded by the children from head office when Sally appeared and sat down beside them.

'They're so young,' he said to her, wrinkling his brow, looking around him.

'So young and so ambitious,' she said, a grim smile on her lips. 'It's the way *he* likes them.'

He tried to be fair.

'We were all ambitious, Sally,' he said.

'Not like these,' she said, jerking her head. 'They'll do anything. Morality? They don't know the meaning of the word.

'Look in their eyes, Crane,' she said, 'There's nothing there. I think they turn them out somewhere in the basement.'

Later she said, 'You have to understand. They're from the top of the pile. They're the new super-race. They belong to the new ruling class and they know it. They're young and they're arrogant and they're well educated and the only thing that means anything to them is money. Their job, as they see it, is to write crap for the proletariat: that's what they're paid to do, and they're paid very well, so as far as they're concerned the proletariat is only getting what it deserves.

'Wait,' she said, 'till you meet our new leader.'

They heard him a hundred yards away, his shoes clicking aggressively along the corridor. Then the double doors crashed open and there he was before them, a dwarf in a motorcycle jacket trailing two accountants in dark glasses like Tontons Macoute.

Bouncing up and down on the balls of his feet and stabbing a finger in the air at them, he told them the way it was going to be.

'Forget the fucking union,' he told them, spitting at them, the East End accent scything the air. 'It's personal contracts from now on. More money,' he said, leering at them, smacking his lips over the words, 'for those who earn it, for those who deserve it. And for those who don't,' he said, swivelling his head from side to side, catching them all in his piercing stare, 'free warnings and yer out.'

Hiding himself behind the person in front of him, he had lowered his head behind a hand and started to laugh. 'Free warnings,' he whispered to Sally. 'Isn't that nice.'

'A problem in translation,' she said. She wasn't laughing.

'He's a barrow boy,' she said and then she strangled her vowels in imitation of the editor. ''E 'ates blacks and queers and dykes and anyone who don't speak English.'

Her face was a mask of scorn.

'You may feel,' she said, 'that this is already beginning to show in the paper.'

Before them their editor was reaching his finale. His eyes and his cheeks bulged, and the way he bounced and flapped made him appear like some bizarre blow-up doll being inflated with a bicycle pump.

'What I fucking want,' he screamed at them, 'is fucking can-do people and those who fucking can't do should get the fuck out of here.'

And then the man was gone, taking the Tontons with him; the only evidence that he had ever been there the double doors still clashing crazily together behind him.

By his side Malone sat hunched up in his old car coat shaking his head at the space where the editor had stood.

'A call to arms, Malone,' he said airily, clapping him on the back, 'Stirring, certainly, but not, I think, quite attaining the poetic resonance of "Once more unto the breach, dear friends".'

They laughed, the pair of them. But not Sally.

She said, 'He's insane, you know?'

They smiled. They shrugged. 'Well . . .?' they said, a 'well' that said, 'well . . . insane . . . in our business . . . so what?' But she bit back at them.

She said, 'No. You don't understand. I don't mean

he chews the heads off daffodils at parties. I mean the man is *clinically insane*.

'It's OK for you two,' she said, 'stuck up there, but here, here in London, it's like . . .' and she searched around for the word. 'It's like Babylon,' she finished.

Around them, as she spoke, the room was rising to its feet. The children were putting on motorcycle jackets just like their leader's.

'Can-do people?' he said to Sally, trying to cheer her up with a smile. She gave him a long look.

'Cannon fodder,' she answered coldly.

Yes, it was clever, all things considered, the three-warning system. All you had to do to get rid of someone was to send them out on three impossible stories. Each time they failed, you warned them. Come number three, bingo: nicely, neatly, *legally*, they could be fired.

In his case it had been even simpler. They hadn't needed three stories. They had one which would do the job perfectly. The Alice Potter story. Almost certainly the most ungettable story on which a poor unfortunate hack had been despatched in the history of popular newspapers.

Yes, all he had to do to save himself from the dole queue was to persuade right-on, card-carrying leftie feminist writer Alice Potter to share the most intimate secrets of her marriage to Bernard O'Donaghue with him, Jim Crane, a representative of probably the country's most rabid, most right-wing, most deter-minedly sexist Sunday newspaper. No problem, right? In professional terms, a piece, one might say, of the proverbial piss.

And so, each morning, as if somehow it might have slipped his mind, Bullerman said to him, 'You've had two warnings, Crane.'

To annoy Bullerman, he would not answer, merely continuing to slit open the morning mail so that eventually Bullerman had to say to him, 'Editor wants you round at the house again, Crane.'

Again he would leave a silence and then he would say coolly, with deliberate calmness, 'It's a waste of time, Bullerman. She won't talk.'

And so their conversation every day became a set piece with Bullerman saying, 'Offer her money, Crane,' and him sighing, 'You know I've offered her money, Bullerman,' and Bullerman saying nastily, his temper straining, 'You're in trouble, Crane, you know that?' and him answering, finally, disdainfully, 'I know that, Bullerman.'

Yes, of course he was in trouble.

Warning number one, in a curt memo signed by the editor, arrived after the first week, number two after the second. And this was the third week, so he could expect the last and the final one at any time, next Tuesday probably, waiting for him in the office after the weekend. And after that, it was all over bar the haggling, as some embittered, emasculated union man went into battle with the Tontons to get him some decent redundancy money.

One thing was for sure and this he knew. Alice Potter wouldn't talk.

In the three weeks he had staked her out, he had knocked at her door, phoned her and waylaid her on the street. He had even written her a letter. Naturally enough though, she would have nothing to do with him; as, indeed, she would have nothing to do with

10

any of the pack who had congregated upon her doorstep, those lucky individuals unlike himself who had been allowed by their newsdesks to admit defeat and so had drifted, one by one, away.

During the three weeks she had done her best to ignore him, putting down the phone when she heard his voice, staring right through him and walking on when she saw him in the street. Except, strangely enough, for this afternoon.

He had been wandering around the back of her house when he had espied her coming out of her gate.

Hiding behind walls so that she did not see him, he had shadowed her all the way to the shops. He had played the gumshoe, coat collar turned up. Diving into a shop doorway when she looked about to turn, he had landed fair and square on an old woman coming out. Her arms were full of brown paper bags which split, cascading apples, oranges and onions on to the pavement. He was scrabbling around in the gutter, breathless with apologies, when he heard a sound he knew could only be Alice Potter laughing.

Ahead of him an orange rolled merrily down the street. He made a dash for it, reached, felt it run like a well-held cricket ball into his hand.

Rising to his feet, dizzy from the effort and from his success, he tossed it nonchalantly into the air. But then his eyes caught hers, full of laughter, caught the brightly gloved hand at her mouth and he laughed too, dropping his catch which rolled away, a second time, into the gutter.

Later, outside the supermarket, he waited for her like a bored husband, the flat of his foot against the wall.

On the way home, he hip-hopped after her, kicking stones that skittered through her legs.

'Look,' he told her enigmatically, 'it's me they're after, not you.'

She walked on with her head down but he pressed on behind her.

'I know what you think of us,' he said. 'You think we're scum and probably you're right. You're sick of the sight of me outside your house. I know that. But if you'd only talk to me. For ten minutes. For five. Throw me a titbit. Tell me anything about him. The silliest things. A paragraph would do. Then they'll pull me out of here and you'll never have to see me again.'

They'd reached her back gate by then. She took a large old-fashioned key from her pocket.

Over her shoulder, she said, 'You're quite mistaken. I'm not tired of you at all.'

Twisting the key in the lock, she turned to face him. Her eyes were green – no, not green, something else, yes, aquamarine. Pools of aquamarine. They stared up at him, flecked with laughter like foam.

'Actually,' she said, 'I've got used to you. As a matter of fact I think I'd quite miss you if you were gone.'

And then she was away, inside the gate.

Walking back to the car he found himself laughing. She'd quite miss him if he were gone. That was a good one. Well he'd be gone soon, that was for sure.

He thought it would be a good one to tell Malone.

Then he remembered Malone was dead.

3

*B*ULLERMAN LIKED TO sound threatening on the phone. It was part of the vision he had of himself, this caricature of a man sweating and swearing and chomping on his cigar in Manchester.

Bullerman's life was spent inventing himself, turning himself into what he thought a man of his calling should be, a man who asked nothing better out of life than to be laid beneath a slanting tombstone engraved with the words, *Robert Bullerman: The best Northern News Editor ever*.

This morning, though, the threatening voice was hollow somehow and unconvincing, full of a bluster that betrayed an underlying panic.

'You're not just making trouble for yourself, Crane,' he said. 'I'm getting it in the neck from London because of you. You're a selfish bastard. You know he's looking for any excuse to get rid of the lot of us.'

It was true of course. The editor had a neat idea for cost-cutting. He liked to share it with the staff in London, who chuckled dutifully as he bellowed it, cackling with laughter, across the newsroom.

For all those useless wankers in the districts were worth, he liked to say, you might as well take a knife, cut the country across the middle north of Watford.

Fucking good idea that, he liked to say, cupping a musing hand to his chin.

And so, hearing the bluster in Bullerman's voice,

he, Crane, could hear too the over-ambitious mort-gage, the time-share in Spain, the child maintenance from the first marriage and the feed-bill for the current step-daughter's wickedly voracious pony. And, hearing it, he smiled with grim pleasure.

'You too, Bullerman,' he said to himself.

But then he felt the muscles tense in the back of his neck at what Bullerman said next.

He said, 'Don't think I don't know why you're being so bloody-minded, Crane.'

Refusing to answer, he forced Bullerman to speak again. When he did so he could hear him making an effort to sound reasonable, attempting to inject some understanding into his voice.

'I know how you feel, Crane,' he said. 'Malone was a mate of mine too, you know. But for God's sake he was fifty-seven years old. And it wasn't as though he didn't get decent redundancy. I mean most people would have been glad to go.'

A huge rush of distaste at what Bullerman said welled up in his throat, preventing him from speaking, so that at last there was an explosion at the other end of the line.

'They didn't kill him, for Christ's sake, Crane,' said Bullerman.

They called it afterwards, with a wry smile, 'The Night of the Long Envelopes'.

They were pushing the chairs back beneath the desks when one of the Tontons had returned. In a cold unraised voice which nonetheless managed to reach the four corners of the newsroom, he informed them that personal letters from the management

14

awaited all of them in the office of the editor's secretary.

They looked at each other, the three of them, he, Sally and Malone. Then Sally shrugged and, reaching into the bag over her shoulder, sat down again and with deliberate calm lit a cigarette.

'Might as well let the crush subside,' she said.

So he and Malone sat down too, and together they began to laugh too loudly and talk with too much animation, determined to show that they had only what they spoke of in mind. But then the children began returning, chattering like parrots, clapping each other about the shoulders and throwing congratulations and cheerful jibes about the room, and though they tried to ignore them their conversation became thin and stringy, and in the end they rose to their feet unhappily and walked out through the double doors and along the corridor to join the queue, which had lost all its confidence by this time, and its gaiety, and contained only the morose and the apprehensive, to which they knew now, each one of them, that they belonged.

Shuffling along in it like naughty schoolboys, they finally reached the door of the secretary's office and, peering in, saw her behind her desk, her face blotchy with tears, a bamboo letter-opener snapped in two pieces on the blotter before her.

Tearing open his envelope, he took out the letter and stared at the words but found he could not read them and, looking up, saw Sally close her eyes and let out a breath of relief.

Dropping his eyes again, he saw that he too had cause to be grateful. Before he could stop it, the same pure selfish sense of deliverance that he had seen on

Sally's face washed over him too, but then, looking up a second time, he saw Malone's expression and his relief turned to fury.

Rising up out of his blind rage, he saw again the editor's face as it had raked their own upturned before him, the eyes bright and child-like with the sheer delight of the exercise of power, the lips salivating at the fear he could taste in the air around him.

'Some of you will probably be leaving us,' he had sneered.

Screwing his letter up into a hard little ball, he hurled it into the corner where it came to rest with the half-dozen or so others.

The secretary started to cry again, not discreet silent tears but great gasping sobs, laying her head down on her arms upon the desk. He fell on his knees before her, touching her arms, but she would not stop weeping.

In rage, still upon his knees, he turned and began to rant at those still behind them in the queue.

'Look,' he said. 'Look what bastards they are. They don't even have the nerve to hand out this stuff themselves. They leave a girl to do it for them.'

He leapt to his feet and made a rush for the editor's office but the secretary was there before him, jumping from her desk and spreadeagling herself against the door, a paper tissue still fluttering from her fingers.

Her mascara had run, making rings around her eyes. She looked like the heroine in a silent film. He closed his eyes with the horror of it, put his hand to his forehead and, shaking his head, walked out of the door.

*

16

Later on, after Sally had gone home to her flat, he and Malone had come back to the newsroom with a handful of others. They were very drunk and, drinking some more, suddenly became full of Luddite intent. He himself had raised a bottle threateningly at a VDU screen. But as he did so, he thought suddenly of Bullerman, of a time when he had worked with him in Manchester, years ago when Bullerman had been just a reporter along with the rest.

He remembered an incident, almost impossible to imagine now, from Bullerman's wild days; from the days before Bullerman had grown ambitious and, recognizing his ambition, had begun to tame himself, preparing himself for the slow, steady clamber, hand over ingratiating hand, up the ladder of success.

He remembered how Bullerman, enraged at his own news editor, had lifted one of the heavy old upright typewriters and hurled it, with a great grunt, across the room at him, but with suitably inaccurate aim, so that the great black monster rose in an arc of astonishing grace and slowness before crashing out through the window, with great dignity, to its death.

He remembered how they had gathered round on the pavement four floors below, gazing at its remains, collecting up the mutilated fragments, strangely appalled and silent, as at the death of an old friend.

And so, gazing at the screen, he had realized that that was the thing about typewriters. Typewriters were old friends. They would give up their lives for you. Sacrifice themselves for nothing more than a moment of anecdotal splendour. And while smashing and wrecking might do for machinery which was old and black and heavy but still human somehow, it ill became the plastic hi-tech whimsy before him, whose brain would continue to function long after its grey little face was broken.

And so he had lowered his bottle defeated, as did the others, as if they too were thinking what he was. And, unable to find anything else to do, they sank down to drink some more and talk about the old times, and say it wasn't the paper they joined anyway, and moan about how it was all bingo and soap stars and readers' offers and there wasn't any news in it any more; till at last, talking this way, they passed out, one by one, and the room came to resemble a battle-field, full of slumped and snoring corpses illuminated in the sinister green half-light of the fire-exit signs.

He was stumbling along the corridor some time later trying to find the toilet when he heard it, an eerie, excited, melancholy moaning.

Following the sound he found himself back in the secretary's office, the door before which she had thrown herself open now to reveal the room inside.

The motorcycle jacket hung on the back of an over-sized black revolving chair which was agitating gently upon its axis, each agitation giving off a tiny squeak and revealing lying along its arm a left hand with a garish ring, its stubby fingers clutching and rhythmically releasing the over-stuffed leather.

As he stood, turned to stone in the shadows, the man's moans spiralled up into the air above his head, becoming faster and faster, running like a chain till finally they broke back over him in a howl of anger and elation and despair.

For a moment there was silence. Then from the other side of the chair there came an expiration, a humourless chuckle and finally an ejaculation, theatrical, defensive, and utterly devoid of love.

'Baaabeeee,' said his editor.

It seemed to Crane then that an apparition appeared before him, a column of brightness rising above the top of the chair and swinging up, into the air, in a glorious golden arc.

It was a girl; a woman, very beautiful, with pale creamy skin and very smooth wide lips and a waterfall of long straight hair which she had thrown, with a thin, red-nailed hand, back from her face.

Surfacing through the hair, she stared directly at him. It was too late for him to hide. He could not have done so anyway for his feet felt cemented to the floor.

She looked at him without expression, her eyes holding his, taking in, it seemed to him, everything he was. Then one perfectly shaped eyebrow raised itself and the smooth lips twitched into a long, slow, supremely triumphant smile.

It took in everything, he saw that. It was cold and entirely contemptuous. It took in the man attempting now with limp vulgarities to regain his pride. It took in him, Crane, standing, the voyeur in the shadows. It took in every man there had been in her life. It took in every man there ever could be.

It put a seal on something, that smile. It said, 'So far but no further.' It said, 'Thus it was but things are different now.'

On and on went the smile and back and back, over the small white pointed teeth. It grew bigger and wider and whiter. It grew up and down. It escaped over the lips and began to drip blood.

And then she raised a hand to him, slowly. It hung

in the air for a second, a salute from blood-red fingernails, a sinister sign. Dropping the hand, she took a small step aside, threw her head back and laughed.

He knew what she was going to do before she did it. He tore his feet up in one gigantic lunge in fear of it, hurling himself from the room, striking a waste-paper basket with a loud echoing clang as he went. But it was too late. The last image in his appalled eye was of his editor, prick nestling limply in his lap, mouth open in surprise, whirling round in his monstrous black leather chair like a child on a round-about.

He staggered along the corridor and threw himself down the stairs, taking them two, three at a time, bouncing off the walls as he went and almost falling at the bottom. There he saw a pair of double doors which he thundered through, finding himself in the basement with the dark shape of the printing presses all about him.

Seeing the toilet sign, he crashed in, banging the grey formica closed behind him.

There he lowered his trousers and fell down on to the seat and began to crap heavily.

He put his head in his hands, balancing his arms on his knees, and wondered if it was possible that he might have stumbled into hell.

4

AT THE END of the street now, she can see Rita Mountjoy running. It occurs to her that Rita looks especially frail and spidery when she is running. Her strides are light and the long arms and legs rotate like delicate pistons. The heavy hair caught in the plait is tight to her head, while her small braless breasts prick out in precise points beneath the T-shirt.

As she watches, Rita slows to a halt and then begins strange sideways leaping movements, which she performs for several minutes in the middle of the road, between the house and the car parked some way to the right on the opposite side of the street.

Flopping forward, she swings her arms and rests for a moment, then raises herself, hands on her waist, to strain backwards, face to the sky in satisfaction, before finally crossing the road and reaching a hand out for the gate.

The click of the latch makes him start and raise his head sharply. Her eye is caught by the movement. Pausing, her hand still on the gate, she raises her shoulders at him and tosses her head to throw at him, diagonally across the street, a long cold accusatory stare.

On the doorstep she raises an eyebrow in disdain, still staring at him fixedly.

'I see the animals are still with us,' she says.

*

21

Rita Mountjoy. Her best friend Rita Mountjoy.

She and Rita are like sisters. They discovered their genitals together, anointing each other innocently with creams and cotton wools stolen from their mothers' bedrooms, provoking thus by delicious accident strange ripples of new and mysterious pleasure.

At twelve years old, she took her half-crown pocket money and made her way with Rita across the moors to the dyke, to the spot above the weir board beneath the weeping willows where Rita pressed the coin, and her own as well, into Tommy Harrington's hand to persuade him to take down his trousers, so that, together, they might make close inspection of the object which lay beneath.

Tommy Harrington, beautiful black-curled half-gypsy, slowly and lovingly unbuttoned himself and, standing like a statue, eyes staring straight ahead, endured with quiet dignity their chill uncharitable examination.

Stretching out with cool and unembarrassed hand, Rita lifted up a frayed and grubby shirt, at which the flabby oddity trembled, shook itself, straightened, rose and danced a little as if attached to Rita's fingers by a thread.

Around them the wind made admiring whishing noises in the grass. Rita rose and pursed her lips and nodded and, grasping Tommy Harrington's hand in comradely farewell, was gone.

Many years on she saw that there above the weir board, beneath the weeping willows, Rita had seen all she would ever want to see of male genitalia.

On a sunny Saturday, some time later, they went back to the same spot where Rita opened up her saddle-bag and pulled out from beneath the lemonade and the sandwiches a paperback book.

Settling down on the bank, she put on her glasses and began to search among its pages. Finding what she wanted, she cleared her throat, adjusted her glasses and read out, '"Th'art good cunt, though, aren't ter. Best bit o' cunt left on earth. When ter likes! When th'art willin'!"'

Lowering the book, she said severely, 'Now you do know what "cunt" is, don't you, Alice?'

In the manner of the time, of course, their mothers told them nothing of sex.

Her own gave her only one piece of advice. She was thirteen at the time, stiff and uncomfortable in a new Germolene-pink cummerbund of a suspender belt whose constriction both elated and angered her.

She was passing the cubbyhole at the top of the stairs that her mother liked to refer to as her linen closet when she heard her name called out through the curtain.

For a moment she thought she would simply stride on noisily to her room pretending she had not heard it. She was afraid her mother might be about to tell her something which would make the skin go cold on the back of her neck, just as it had some months before when her mother put the gauzy bandage in her hand and said, accusingly, 'You'll be needing this soon, Alice,' neglecting among other things to warn her about the pain so that when it came, several months later, she thought at first that she was dying.

But when Alice put her head through the curtain her mother never turned. She merely continued to

23

fold out the sheets, flipping them over, smoothing them out.

She said, 'Don't listen to dirty jokes, Alice, it makes you cheap.'

Ever afterwards she wondered how her mother could have known. Because of course she had already heard her first dirty joke. It was about a honeymoon couple who stayed in their room all week. They told their landlady, who came to enquire after their health, they were living off the fruits of love. The landlady said that was all right but would they please not throw the skins out of the window.

Durston told her the joke, Durston small and evil and ugly, Durston on the back of the bus.

When Durston told the joke, she didn't understand it, but in the way of these things she laughed with the rest. And that was when Durston turned on her. His eyes were very cold for a fourteen-year-old. He said, 'Why are you laughing, Alice Potter?'

All around her she felt the air go thin and very tight.

He said, 'Tell us what it means if you're laughing, Alice Potter.'

She was closing her eyes with the shame of it, with the chorus howling all about her, when suddenly there she was, Rita, her Rita, Rita with the long dark plait down her back, with the thin old face and the deep eyes, towering above them all even then.

Rita's voice was chilly and contemptuous. It speared Durston to his seat.

'Really, Durston,' she said. 'Do you think Alice doesn't know about Durex?' Which of course finished Durston. Because Durston called them 'French letters', a namby-pamby name for a boy, namby-pamby himself beneath the bullying.

The truth was that Durston didn't really know anything about Durex and suddenly the whole bus knew it. But Rita knew, because Rita had made it her business to know about such things and the whole bus knew that as well. And from that day forward, Durston became 'Durex' Durston.

Ten years later when he took a bend wide on his motorbike and ended up embedded in the grille of a tractor an old schoolfriend stopped her on the street.

'Did you know Durex Durston was dead?' she said.

Durex Durston till the day he died.

Durex Durston, the man who dared tangle with Rita Mountjoy.

Side by side now, she and Rita stare out of the sitting room window across the street.

'Really, it's appalling,' says Rita. 'The way they're allowed to harass people. Make them a prisoner in their own house.'

As Rita speaks, she, Alice, feels a small but distinct tightening of her jaw. Why is it, she wonders, that since the beginning of this thing she has felt that Rita's disapproval somehow encompasses her? Why is it that she has come to feel that the presence of these reporters on her doorstep is somehow her fault?

'Well it's just the two of them now and really they don't bother me. They don't even come up to me any more. They just seem to sit there, that's all.'

She is annoyed at her own voice which is not only placatory but mildly defensive.

To her further chagrin, she experiences a sharp

stab of guilt as she realizes she has no intention of telling Rita that today she has spoken to him for the first time.

5

IN THE CAR now he shakes his head and pushes it more firmly into the seat in an attempt to dispel the sound that still lingers in his brain.

When Alice Potter's friend had thrown them That Look across the road, he had hunched himself down in the seat knowing what would come. His whole frame had tensed itself waiting for it and come it did: a long, liquid nasal expiration, sibilant, polysyllabic, composed of many strains, the squeal of brakes, say, of a 125 pulling into a station, the hiss of steam from an overworked geyser.

'Wassamattawiverven?' said Gibb, the hand that endlessly agitated imaginary dust from the camera lens for one brief moment stilled.

Once, a long time ago, in the way of these things, in the way in which human nature will seek to find excuse for its own failure, the grumble was that the Geordie mafia held the shop floor of the country's popular newspapers in its nepotistic grip. In those long-gone days there was a certain cachet in being our man from the North. Walking through the newsroom in head office was a slow progress of hailing hands and slapped backs and exchanged football scores that extended from the humblest minion right up through the highest echelons of power. But now times had changed. Now the voices that counted contorted their vowels in a different way. Now Essex man was the one in control. Now the newsroom in London was full of editor clones, a swarm of black-jackets who seemed to have hatched out overnight, who bounced like him on the balls of their feet and jabbed their fingers in the air and parroted, with raucous respectability, the same appalling racist, sexist views. Like Gibb for instance.

Gibb worshipped the editor as only another Essex man could. Spoke of him in hushed tones. Recounted his latest editorial outrage with an admiring chuckle.

God how he hated Gibb.

Often, sitting like this with his head back, he would muse on the inadequacy of words like 'hate' and 'loathe' which failed to express what he felt for Gibb, an emotion best summed up in the desire he felt now to turn to the man, put his hands around his throat, press very hard and then twist, closing him up like a paper bag, cutting off for ever the stream of offensive inanity that he, Crane, had had to endure every day for the last three weeks holed up here in the car with him.

Gibb despised him, of course, in the way that the ambitious always despised those they saw were on the way down. Gibb also blamed him for his exile from his homeland.

Every day he moaned down the phone to the picture desk in his, Crane's, hearing. He sat with his Reeboks up on Malone's desk, chewing gum. Once, when he thought that he, Crane, was safely out of the room, he called him a useless wanker, chortling in shared scorn with another Essex man on the other end of the line.

He told people, when they asked, that Gibb was a

cocky bastard. But that wasn't enough. Gibb was *the* cocky bastard. If cod-pieces came back into fashion, Gibb would have one by Armani.

Of course he was jealous. He knew that. He was jealous of Gibb's hair, the hair that hung in rich black trembling spikes over his forehead. He was jealous of his tight little ass and the shirt that did up over his belly. But most of all he was jealous of the bustling little cock that bulged comfortingly out from between the stocky blue-jeaned thighs.

Oh, he knew Gibb was a moron. Of course Gibb was a moron, and he knew that knowing that was supposed to make him feel better. And most of the time it did. But then occasionally, just occasionally, rationality let him down and he wished, God forgive him, that he was more like Gibb. Like now, for instance, as he contemplated That Look which Alice Potter's friend had flung them from the gate.

It was a special look, That Look. He knew it and he hated it. He hated it but he had grown used to it now.

Once upon a time when they asked you what you did for a living you could tell them and you could see their eyes light up with old misconceptions, with memories of old movies. But now things were different. Now their faces froze in unfriendliness. 'Press,' they said, the esses hissing in disgust. Now they gave you That Look, the look that told you that the world had changed, had halved and split, that there were two sides now and you, the looked-at, belonged on the other.

Yes he knew That Look and furthermore he knew at fifty yards who was going to give it to him. Who? Oh the *Guardian* readers, the gay-righters, the third-worlders, the anti-apartheiders, the save-the-whalers, all those thoroughly decent people with standing orders for thoroughly decent organizations which his newspaper liked to regard as a threat to the security of the state.

Janet had given him That Look.

'Don't you *care*,' she used to say when they were together. 'How can you *work* for that rag?' Janet always used italics when she spoke from the moral high ground.

He hated the two questions – the way they were always harnessed together, the way they were like bar stools that he slipped drunkenly between. The way sitting on one denied him for ever a seat on the other.

Did he care? Yes he cared. He cared like everyone else. He cared about nuclear weapons and apartheid and Aids and people sleeping in the street. He cared about famine and pollution and the hole in the ozone layer. He did, by God he did; he cared about all of these things just the same as anyone else. But how then could he work for that rag? The million-dollar question.

There was a simple answer of course. Not one though that anyone asking the question wanted to hear. They wanted a serious answer. They wanted there to be some deep, decent, meaningful or at least Machiavellian reason why he did it: a wife and six children to support, say, his grandmother's hip replacement operation to pay for. At the very least he should have the decency to be saving to buy the freedom to write a first novel.

As always, the truth was much simpler.

'What are we doing here?' he had said to Sally as they shuffled forward to the secretary's office.

She snorted. She said dismissively, 'We're here because we've always been here. Because it's what we do.'

Then abruptly her attitude changed. She turned to him. Her lips were curved in her usual mocking smile, but staring into her eyes he saw something new. It frightened him. It looked like desperation.

'The official story,' she said, 'is that we're here because we don't want to send out press releases for the Gas Board or retire on our reputations to some tin-pot weekly in the country to serve out our time as the office drunk.

'Unofficially,' she said, 'we're here because no one else wants us. Because we're stamped with the mark of the beast now and hanging on here is all that we have left to us.'

And, of course, she was right.

Occasionally overcome by the guilt of it all, despising the paper and everything it stood for, he had made vague attempts to find jobs elsewhere. The curt rejection letters not even calling him for an interview had sent cold frissons of fear down his back.

'You're a hack,' Janet had said to him once very coldly.

'Of course,' he said, coldly back. 'But then I don't consider "hack" a pejorative term.'

And he didn't. Still. Despite everything. He was a hack. Of course. That was it. That was what he was. He was not a journalist. Journalists interviewed prime ministers and got caught in cross-fire. Journalists brought with them their degrees from Oxford. He brought the memory of that first Thursday night, the first time he saw the line of papers warm and still wet snaking towards him with his name on the front of every one.

Yes, he was a hack, a reporter, a foot-in-the-door merchant, he was your singing parrot man, your saucy stag-night correspondent. He was an old-fashioned newspaperman with 'Press' in his hat.

And when Gibb said, 'Wassamattawiverven?' for one wicked infinitesimal moment he did not want to do what he always did, which was to sigh, to gather together all the reserves of contempt and sarcasm that were so wasted on Gibb. He did not want to say what he did say, which was, 'Perhaps she's sick of having us on her friend's doorstep for three weeks. Do you think that could possibly be the reason she looked at us that way?' No, for that one wicked infinitesimal moment he wanted to sit easy for once, park himself squarely on one of the stools. He wanted to turn to Gibb, dig him in the ribs, wink at him and smirk, man to man.

He wanted to say to Gibb, Gibb whom he loathed and despised, exactly the sort of thing he loathed and despised him for, exactly the sort of thing that, of course, Gibb did say, lowering his head back over his lens.

'Stupid fucking bitch,' said Gibb.

6

YES, SHE AND Rita are like sisters. But the truth is that, like sisters, they have grown apart.

What does Rita really think of her? She wonders this now, smoking a sly cigarette at her desk, hearing from along the corridor the sound of the shower running and the restrained tones of Rita's beloved Radio Three.

What does Rita really think of her? Something, she suspects, that corresponds to an affectionate, slightly superior smile, to a small raise of the eyebrow, to a sigh and a shrug and the faintly amused 'Oh Alice' which spans the length and the breadth of their friendship.

She knows that Rita thinks her — what should she say? — to be kind; charming, yes; lovable, certainly; essentially, though, untidy in her life and her work.

And next to Rita she *feels* untidy, not just in the way that she looks — although naturally enough her size-twelve body always seems a little overweight and out of condition compared to Rita's, her clothes always a little too tight — no, it is more than that. Next to Rita her very thought processes feel undisciplined and ill fitting. She is ashamed of the way that she wavers in an argument, sees the other point of view. She knows she has no clarity of purpose compared to Rita, who she knows thinks her weak and insufficiently radical.

And the problem is that somehow, faced with

Rita, she becomes even weaker, even more indecisive. As with the smoking, for instance. Many times she has attempted to give up. Sometimes she will go a whole day, even two, without a cigarette. But then Rita commends her in her warm, faintly school-marmish fashion and before she knows where she is she is halfway through another packet, and worse than the sore throat and the sinus problems are the loving remonstrances of Rita.

For she loves Rita, she knows that. She loves the long plait, still the same thirty years on; loves the dark sunken eyes and the thin, long, brittle sports-woman's body.

There is something, she thinks, unearthly about Rita, something eerie in the beauty of the spare, over-exercised frame. There is something detached in her way of living, some curious coolness that spreads to the four corners of her life. Somewhere in the back of her head she has an idea for a novel in which a woman like herself has a friend like Rita whom she discovers is not human at all, but specially assembled to live life on earth as a female and report back to a distant, ineffably superior planet.

Once, hiding as a child beneath the overhanging tablecloth on the cake stall at the village fête, she heard them say that Rita Mountjoy could not belong to Gwen and Ernie Mountjoy, that Rita Mountjoy must have been left one night by the fairies.

Perhaps Gwen and Ernie believed it. After all, Gwen was forty-three when Rita was born, their first and only child.

It always seemed to her, Alice, that there was

something of the Elisabeth and Zacharias about Gwen and Ernie. Certainly they treated Rita from the beginning rather as the grateful and astonished parents of John the Baptist might have treated their infant son, with a lack of familiarity, even a respect, as if she might not really belong to them, as if she might truly be a gift from on high. She could still remember the expression of faint bemusement that would cross Gwen's face when she looked at Rita, the small sideways glances she would throw at her as if attempting to work out exactly how it was she came to be among them.

When Rita tried to kill herself, their bemusement mutated first into a tragic confusion before disintegrating finally into open, unashamed incomprehension.

Visiting Rita in hospital, she looked through the window of the white-tented room and saw them sitting either side of the bed, Rita sleeping peacefully between them.

They sat perfectly still, pictures of humility both, staring at her with faces heavy with the sorrowful acceptance of the cruel trick that fate had played upon them in bequeathing to them a being beyond their understanding. The only movement in the room came from one of Gwen's fingers which she stroked in gentle nervous agitation over one of Rita's bandaged wrists.

Exactly what prompted Rita to attempt to take her own life, no one was ever to know, not even her best friend Alice Potter.

It was a serious attempt, not a cry for help. She was found, quite by chance, by a room-mate who was supposed to have gone home for the weekend.

From the first moment when Rita opened her eyes to discover she was still alive, though, she refused to discuss it.

'Rita . . .?' she, Alice, had said awkwardly, taking her friend's hand in her own. 'If you want to talk about it . . . If something's happened . . . If there is someone . . .'

Rita, however, withdrew her hand gently but with great dignity. In her eyes there was a fierce un-approachable pride.

'Thank you, Alice,' she said politely, 'but I don't want to talk about it. I was stupid. I made a mistake. It's over now. There's nothing more to say.'

They were eighteen years old at the time. Rita was in her first year at Cambridge. She, Alice, still at home and working in a solicitor's office in the nearby town, had recently lost her virginity to Clive and, believing herself in love, believed also, with the inno-cence and the arrogance of youth, that something similar must have happened to Rita.

A decade or so later, when Rita had been pursued by some of the finest specimens of manhood that Oxbridge could produce – including, incidentally, Andrew McCartan, the man who was to become their publisher – and had shown not the slightest interest in any of them, she revised her opinion.

In keeping with the times, she decided that Rita must be gay and for the next ten years she stood waiting for Rita to step, in her own cool, imperious fashion, out of the closet.

Every time Rita's face became especially serious, every time she began a sentence, 'Alice, there's some-thing I really must tell you . . .' she, Alice, felt a deeply virtuous and satisfied affection well up inside her. The speech that she had been preparing over the decade rose in her throat. 'Rita ... my dear ... it's whatever you want, whatever will make you most happy ... that's the only thing that matters to me.' She prepared to clasp her friend to her bosom and, in joy, prepared to feel her grateful tears on her shoulder.

Only it never happened. The closet door remained firmly closed, till, finally, thinking one day of Tommy Harrington, it came to her that Rita was no more interested in women than she was in men, that she wasn't gay in the same way that she wasn't heterosexual, because she simply wasn't interested.

And so it was no surprise, in the end, when Rita produced her book on celibacy.

She, Alice, read the book from cover to cover and in fact much admired it, which all in all she thought was rather ironical.

For faithfully, each time one of her own books was published, she had given a copy to Rita, inscribing each with a loving message, as in, 'To my darling Rita without whom etc. etc.'

Each time Rita received it with her own special cool hug.

She would say something very suitable like, 'You are clever, Alice. I can't imagine writing a novel,' which she, Alice, thought was probably true. Then Rita would put it up on her bookshelf, from which spot the author was sure it never came down.

In company Rita enthused about her friend's work. She had even written warm reviews of it for feminist periodicals. It hurt somewhere though, in the deepest reaches of her soul, that Rita – and of this she was certain – had never actually read one of her novels.

It hurt a little too, she could not deny it, that *Celibacy: The New Sexuality* had forged Rita's reputation in a manner hitherto denied herself, and, indeed, had sold more copies than all her novels put together. It hurt too that she had a sneaking suspicion that at least part of the reason that Andrew McCartan continued to publish those less than successful novels was that they were blessed with a generous and influential lobbyist in the person of Rita.

Despite all this, to her own shame, in those selfish secret reaches of her soul, she allowed herself the luxury of referring to *Celibacy: The New Sexuality* as 'Rita's feminist hip and thigh diet.'

Rita's argument, essentially, was that celibacy was not asexual, celibacy was not non-sexuality, celibacy was a sexuality all of its own.

She, Alice, understood all of this. She saw how celibacy could be regarded as a positive force, as a radical redeployment of resources. Indeed some part of her passionately admired Rita's argument. Some part of her wanted to be like Rita, to have a life clean and clear-cut in this manner, free from the awful confusion of sexuality.

She had tried to talk about it when Bernard left. She knew that Rita longed for her to have learnt some lesson from the experience, longed to see her slice away from her own life, in consequence, what she, Rita, saw as the muddy extraneous matter of love.

'But it's not for me, Rita,' she said to her imploringly, trying to explain. 'It's right for you. It's the way you are. But I can't do it. I'm different.'

And she was. She couldn't tidy sexuality away like Rita could. She couldn't drop it in the 'out' tray, file it, feed it into the shredder.

'My life is a muddle, Rita,' she said humbly. 'It's mucky and cluttered and all of a jumble and I know that. I make mistakes. I get into trouble. I suppose it's a bit like the front garden, all overgrown but the way that I like it.'

And what did she get in reply?

The affectionate slightly superior smile, of course, the small raise of the eyebrow, the shrug and the sigh and, of course, the faintly amused, 'Oh Alice.'

And so she, Alice, kissed her and turned away to wonder; to wonder what she had wondered many times, what she wonders now hearing the shower run.

She wondered about Rita's suicide attempt, not why she had done it, but why, given everything she was, she should have chosen the method she did.

She wondered if the decision to slash her wrists had been peculiarly significant, whether it had been designed as a gloriously out-of-character finale, the one and only defiantly messy thing she had done in her life.

And more especially she wondered whether the sterile antiseptic existence her friend called 'life' was somehow her penance, whether she went through it now like some Lady Macbeth, forever washing her wrists in it, trying to wipe away what the world saw only as hairline scars, but what she saw forever as the mucky, intemperate, irrepressibly spurting blood.

7

ONCE, AS A matter of fact, he thought he might actually kill Gibb.

He had been sitting, as he sat now, with his head back, trying to ignore the stream of banality that washed past his ear, when he heard Malone's name.

'Nice old bugger 'n' all that,' he heard, 'but past it, of course, as a photographer.'

They never made Malone Photographer of the Year. Never exhibited him. Never turned out glossy coffee-table books of his work. But he loved Malone's photographs.

Often now he would drive round to Malone's house, let himself in as he had done so often before, walk up the stairs to the study, pour a whisky from the decanter, sit down on the old leather chair and stare at the pictures.

They were old, certainly, many of them, but that was why he loved them. He liked the certain dowdy dignity, the models in chaste chainmail swimsuits, the footballers in long shorts and the politicians in impossibly unglamorous overcoats.

They were all there on Malone's wall, the train crashes, the crippled tankers, the fires and the flash floods, the blizzards and the buildings blown apart, explosions from an age of innocence when all that was to blame was leaking gas.

Yes, they were all there, the murderers and the grieving mothers, the sex fiends and the saints, pools winners learning to live with money, runaway heiresses learning to live without it.

And in the middle, the man himself, Malone, astonishingly young but already old, in baggy suit and soft felt hat, clutching a cumbersome plate-glass monster, smiling, awkward and embarrassed, into someone else's camera.

When Gibb said what he said, the fury swirled around inside him. It made him tremble, made his fingers curl and uncurl with the impotent desire to smash, to punch, to pulp.

He could not fight. He had tried once when he was very young. A fight had erupted suddenly in a pub where he was drinking. Next to him a burly labourer had thrown a punch. Seeking to protect himself, he'd thrown one back. It flew wildly in the air and glanced off the side of his assailant's head. For a moment they stared at each other and then the man reeled away to flail drunkenly at someone else.

But the memory stayed with him. All his adult years since he had lived in fear of finding himself in a situation where it became necessary, as a matter of honour or survival, to have to try the same thing again.

Now he said, 'How fucking dare you?' appalled at the banality of the words.

He turned to Gibb and told him that he, Gibb, was an ape crawling on all fours at the dawn of civilization compared to Malone who was a prince among men. He told him, furthermore, that he, Malone, had

41

more talent in the tip of his shutter finger than he, Gibb, had in the whole of his body.

He spat sarcasms at Gibb. Lashed him with his fierce disgust. He told himself, as he did so, that words were better. That fists were no substitute for well-turned scorn. In his heart though he did not believe it.

In his heart he knew he longed for blue-black flesh and spitting teeth and blood spurting over a shirt front. And so it was in disgust at himself more than at Gibb that he flung himself from the car, his anger eating down inside him.

Striding in fury up the street he could still hear Gibb's propitiations ringing in his ear.

'Sorry, mate . . . no offence, mate . . . didn't realize he was such a mate of yours, mate . . .'

Leaning against a tree and gazing into the middle distance, he saw himself, for the first time, with great clarity.

He saw that while he liked to think of himself as late thirties he was in fact forty-two. He saw that while he liked to think of himself as putting on a little weight he was in fact fat. He saw that while he liked to think of his hair as thinning the mirror told him he was bald. Worse than all of these things, while he liked to think of himself as cautious he was in fact nothing better than a coward.

In short, it occurred to him at that moment that he had not turned out to be anything which in his mildest dreams as a young man he might have hoped he would be.

Pushing his head back into the trunk of the tree, he had closed his eyes and given himself up to despair.

8

WHY HAD SHE not told Rita that she had spoken to him this afternoon? Because she could not face the small raise of the eyebrow, the shrug and the sigh and the faintly amused 'Oh Alice' – that was why.

Leaning towards a crammed and overspilling filing basket with a grimace, she draws out a piece of paper hidden cleverly among the chaos.

Unfolding it slowly upon the desk-top, she begins to read it, hunched over it guiltily.

For all the same reasons, she knows, she did not tell Rita about his letter.

When she had first picked it up from the mat and read it, she had thought there had been some mistake, an extra zero laid down like a wild card in error. The amount that he was offering her for her story had quite literally taken her breath away. She had put an astonished hand to her heart and sunk down upon the sofa. Then she fell to musing, as she had continued to do since, what they thought she could possibly have to say about Bernard O'Donaghue that could be worth all that money.

She stares first, as she always does, at the signature.

Signatures, she knows, are supposed to say a lot about a person. As if to confound the notion, his appears studiously ordinary, not egotistically large nor yet obsequiously over-small. Free of extravagant flourishes, it still retains a certain dash, bespeaking a man of mildly Bohemian inclination. It does not, though, masquerade behind indecipherability, but is firm and definite, as if intent on making it clear that it has no shame in identifying the man who chose the words 'Yours sincerely' as the one who signed himself beneath them 'Jim Crane'.

She has read the letter so many times that she can recite one of the paragraphs from memory. Still, she rereads it again, as if hunting in the spaces between the words for something she has not seen before, for some clue to the piece still undiscovered.

'I can see,' she reads, 'that what has happened over the last three weeks has been anathema to you and I should like to apologize for the way we have intruded upon your life. The harsh facts of the case are however that this is a mercenary world, and that there is now a financial value on the story which you could tell about yourself and Bernard O'Donaghue, should you wish to do so.'

Reading what comes next, she grimaces. It was impossible, she had found, once having read it, to forget it. It was rather like The Fall. Impossible to turn back the clock on that first impulsive bite. Impossible to cover with any amount of fig leaves an exposed and naked greed.

'As far as this newspaper is concerned,' she reads again, 'we estimate the value of your story to be something in the region of £30,000.'

As her eyes strike the figure, she closes the page up abruptly, as if, in doing so, she can wipe out its memory. But this she knows, with a sigh, she cannot do. For, from experience, she knows that it jiggles up and down in the back of her brain all the time now, poking its head out like Mr Punch when she is pretending to think of other things.

Yes, it swings in the air, this £30,000, flashes on and off and glows like neon. And now that the Pandora's box has been opened, it is quite impossible not to contemplate what one might do with it, not to speculate, for instance, how it would perfectly solve the pressing problems of her beloved Tanglewood.

She bought the house with her grandmother's money, ten years ago now, when she, Alice, returned from abroad. Much of the heavy old furniture, too, belonged to her grandmother so that she thinks of it in some way as *her* house, not just because of the money and the furniture, but because of the house itself, which is younger than the rest of the street, and skittish somehow, and a little wayward, and has a certain whimsical dignity, and in all of these things is reminiscent of her.

Her grandmother walked alone up Shooter's Hill during the zeppelin raids on London, and did not scurry for shelter but went on walking, waiting, watching, looking upwards into the night for a glimpse of one of the silent, cigar-shaped monsters.

They talked about it the day that she, Alice, left for her travels. She said to her, 'Weren't you afraid?' and her grandmother said 'No' quietly at first, thoughtfully, and then 'No' again, more forcefully this time, and then, finally, 'No', a third time, shouting it out, eyes glowing, one hand clamped knuckle-white around the arm of the wheelchair.

Unable to bear the pain of leaving her, she waited for her to die and when she did not, knew she could wait no longer.

'Afghanistan, Pakistan, India . . .' she said to her, holding the names up for her, like jewels, to the light.

When the moment came for parting, when it could be put off no longer, her grandmother picked up the cane, discarded now by the wheelchair, and waved it in the air at her in short loving stabs of farewell.

'Go,' she said, and then, 'Live, live. Don't be like your mother,' crying the words out urgently, angrily, like an order, like a command from the front, so that she fled from the room without kissing her goodbye, crashing into a chair and turning it over, weeping all the way to the train with love for her.

She was in Hong Kong when she got the letter from the solicitor telling her that her grandmother had died. She read it first in the post office which was noisy and hot and full of altercation. Then afterwards she read it again to Céline.

Céline did not try to comfort her. Instead she shook her head slowly at the sadness of it all and poured out a beer and rolled a joint and laid her forehead against hers in solemn, silent, consolation.

Later they went to the temple together and lit joss sticks before the gods. And she set alight, too, in the Chinese manner, small bundles of make-believe money, ensuring that her grandmother would be as well placed in the afterlife as she had made her grateful granddaughter in this.

For that night she told Bernard whom she had only just met but with whom she was already in love. And he lifted her hand and kissed it on the palm making something shift very far down inside her, while at the same time looking very deeply into her eyes in a way she was afterwards to see him do on the television. And then he said, as she had known that he would, 'I think we should go home to England together, Alice.'

And then he kissed her, leaning against the railings

46

of the Star Ferry, with the Hong Kong harbour night like velvet all around, and the neon blood-red on the water and the lights shining out from the Peak like diamonds.

And as she closed her eyes receiving his kiss, she saw the money curling up in flames in the temple, blackening at the edges and sending smoke up into the eyes and the nostrils of the gently grinning god. And she said to him, to the god, 'I know ... I know ...

'I know, I know,' she said. 'But it's what I want.'

*I*T WAS BERNARD who found Tanglewood.

They had come north when he landed a job with the local repertory company. He never explained satisfactorily at the time how he happened to be in Tanglewood's part of the city. Years later she discovered, quite by accident, that he'd been having afternoon sex in a bedsitter nearby with a stage manager called Becky.

During the viewing Bernard trod heavily on the floorboards and struck the panelling with a suspicious air.

'Needs a lot of work,' he said knowingly, and so they got the house cheaply, thanks in some small part to his performance, but, in the main, to the undisguised rapacity of the owner, a wrinkled over-tanned woman who had inherited it from her great-aunt, and who wanted the money quickly so that she and her faded silent husband might winter in their favourite spot in Majorca.

'Spinster,' the woman said of her great-aunt, pursing her pink-caked lips meaningfully and fluttering her heavily over-mascaraed lashes.

'Wouldn't have a thing done to the place,' she said, this avaricious magus, whom she, Alice, had imagined carrying pragmatic unaffectionate gifts of talcum powder and tiny pocket handkerchiefs each Christmas and birthday, to lay beside the manger of Great-aunt Myrtle's will.

She knew Tanglewood had to be hers the moment she saw it.

She loved the Gothic glory of the place, the huge roof sweeping up to the towering oversized chimney stack, the casement windows and the imposing iron-bound front doors. She loved the jungle of shrubs from which the place had taken its name, the lily pond, the mossy birdbath and the overgrown smirking cherub. But most of all she loved the ivy, the ivy that clambered all over the house, cladding it deep and rich and green, twining around the eaves and the guttering, crawling right up over the roof to the chimney.

Standing that first time, looking up at the place from the gate, she noticed some guttering had come away pulling the ivy with it. A long stem lifted in the wind. The leaves shivered and shook. They were like fingers, green and ghostly. They swayed towards her. She could have sworn that they beckoned.

Left alone for a moment during the viewing, she had stroked the panelling lovingly. As she did so she thought she heard a sigh, from Great-aunt Myrtle or from the house itself she could not tell, but she thought she felt something too, an infinitesimal lowering all round her, as if the very frame of the place had been holding itself rigid with fear but felt it could relax now, safe in the hands of someone it knew was going to love it.

It was a performance, of course, what Bernard did when they viewed the house. He knew nothing of do-it-yourself nor had any desire to learn. It was she, therefore, who stripped the floorboards and the panelling, uncovered the fireplaces, papered and painted and tiled, over the years restoring Tanglewood to its former glory.

Everyone loved Tanglewood now and that included Gerald.

Over the past three weeks he had been deeply sympathetic about her predicament. 'So appalling, Alice . . . Hounding you like this, Alice . . . A prisoner in your own home, Alice . . .'

She knew though that Gerald coveted Tanglewood, liked its corner site, its large gardens front and back. It occurred to her that beneath his solicitations he nursed a tiny hope that her harassment might encourage her to sell Tanglewood.

Yesterday, for instance, he had coughed and cleared his throat. He had said, 'Of course, Alice, we'd hate to see you go, Marion and I. But if you should ever decide . . .'

She said, 'You'll be the first to know, Gerald.'

It was Gerald to whom she had turned, as had become her custom, when the roof started to leak.

She had been sitting at her desk working on her novel.

A scatter of rain flung against the window made her glance up. At the same moment she heard a loud reverberating plop. Looking down she saw the words on the sheet of paper in her typewriter roller streaming away in a rivulet of black.

The builder whom Gerald brought pursed his lips in the way of builders.

'It's your ivy,' he said.

And so it was. She saw it when he showed her, the ivy she loved so much, clambering and clawing, gnawing away at the same time into the stone and the slates and the concrete, eating away into the very heart of the house.

'You need a new roof,' said the builder. 'And your pointing's gone and as for your gable end . . .'

50

'It's bulging out,' he said, taking her into the garden. 'Look, you can see it.' And so she could.

Back inside, he reached up in her study and gave a gentle tug to the wallpaper, a great tear of which came away in his hand. Behind it, stretching from floor to ceiling, was the most enormous crack.

'One high wind and the lot could come down,' he said.

'Yes,' he said, mournfully. 'Basically it's your ivy that's your problem.'

And so it was. She was sure of that. It was her ivy that was the problem.

She pushes her chair back abruptly and gets to her feet, pacing restlessly, without purpose, up and down.

Walking to the window, she stares thoughtfully out at the road, at the white rectangle left behind, like a reminder, by the parked car.

The road is black now from the light drizzle which falls on to the birdbath and the murky pond and the fallen cherub, covering them with a fine mist of diamonds along with the tangle of shrubs, bare and branchy now in the late autumn twilight.

'Enchanting,' the television director had said.

He had stood, he and the cameraman, staring up at the front of the house, holding their hands up in strange shapes and peering through.

It was several weeks ago, just before this thing had blown up about Bernard.

They had come, the pair of them, with a researcher and an interviewer, to do a short piece on her for the local arts programme when her last book had won the feminist novel award.

They asked her to stand at her study window, which she did, feeling foolish. Below her the cameraman heaved his camera up on to his shoulder and stepping backwards on the lawn, began to pan up the front of the house, tracing the ivy slowly and lovingly, from its knotty roots, up to her study window where it caught her staring with stony embarrassment out through the casement.

They filmed her at her typewriter too, and reading from the novel in her grandmother's rocking chair.

As she read the camera nosed around her study, a smooth, sinister, disembodied eye. It scrutinized her pictures and her posters and her books rising on their shelves to her ceiling. It travelled over her rag-rolled walls and her stripped pine floorboards, resting for a moment on her elegantly restored marble fireplace. It took in the trailing pot plants and the painted bird cage, the wind-up gramophone and the tailor's dummy. And after staring at all of these things, it turned its attention to her.

Up her arm it went, across her rings and her silver bangles, inspecting her earrings and her scarf before ploughing on mercilessly over the washed-out, unfashionably tight scoop-necked T-shirt, the Oxfam waistcoat, the Indian cotton skirt with its glimpse of antique petticoat and the sensible flat-soled boots.

The interviewer, who was also the show's presenter, was very pretty with very black hair and a very short skirt and reminded her of Madeline.

She sat before her, a clipboard on her knee, smiling a warm, bland, obfuscating smile.

For five minutes they talked about her life and her work, she, Alice, ranging a little too wildly, a little too grandiosely over the influences on her writing, the issues with which she dealt in her books.

The interview was drawing to a close and she had begun to relax when she noticed the interviewer's smile had hardened and become unignorably sardonic.

'Your novels are all very much standard feminist fare, aren't they?' the interviewer said.

There was no reason to feel insulted and yet the words entered her heart like a smart deft little barb.

Caught unawares, she retreated into what she hoped was amusing self-deprecation.

'Oh absolutely,' she said. 'Standard feminist fare certainly. Mothers, best friends, first sexual experiences, all that sort of thing.'

She knew she was in trouble. The smile now was inflexibly pleasant and there was a steely glint in the eyes that stared out at her.

'You see some people might say,' the young woman said, 'that this sort of novel is, to put it bluntly, old-fashioned, that in the post-feminist era the whole idea of an award specifically for women's writing is out of date.'

She did not answer well. She rambled, became defensive and tiresomely serious. Watching herself two weeks later, she screwed up her eyes in embarrassment and winced and drove nails into herself running it over and over on the video.

'So you have no fears about still calling yourself a feminist?' the interviewer had finished, the smile now quite openly mocking.

'No,' she had answered. 'Absolutely not.'

There was a small pause. They waited, the cameraman, the director, the interviewer, for her to repeat herself. It was a trick of the trade, she saw afterwards, for of course she did, condemning herself out of her own mouth.

'Absolutely not,' she said again.

And so the camera held her in its final shot, earrings and scarf and bangles, smiling awkwardly, defiantly, her skirt scrunched over her knees, until the picture faded, and there was the interviewer again, but back in the studio now, all very long legs and perfectly bobbed hair and with that same sardonic smile.

'Alice Potter,' she said gravely, like a valediction.

Oh how she reminded her of Madeline.

Watching herself, that first time, she had seen immediately that something was wrong. Rewinding the video and playing it a second time, and then a third, and then over and over again, she saw that what was wrong was that everything was completely and utterly right.

She saw, as she watched, that she lived in exactly the right sort of house, a house of precisely the right Gothic perfection, decorated in exactly the right fashion, scattered about with just the right sort of junk-shop bric-à-brac, with the right sort of books on the shelves, the right sort of pictures and posters upon the walls.

And, of course, she saw that she looked right too. She saw that she looked exactly as a feminist novelist might be expected to look. And she spoke the right way too. She said everything she could be expected to say. She, agonizing over the right sort of issues, outlining precisely the right sort of dilemmas, used the right sort of films and plays to illustrate her points, and the work of exactly the right sort of writers.

But it was when she heard the words of her own novel read from the rocking chair that she felt the pain; not a serious pain, not a pain that took the breath away, just a small ache in her heart.

For she realized that worse than all of these things, she wrote the right sort of books, books written for the right sort of people – *female* people, she thinks, sighing now, staring down into the garden, the sort of people who will be at her reading tonight.

She saw that she wrote books with exactly the right sort of ideas in them, books with the right sort of characters doing exactly the right sort of things, books with entirely the right sort of slightly wrong ending.

Staring at herself on the screen, she could not help but feel that there was some justification for the sardonic smile. She saw that somehow she had weeded her life out, had planed it off, so that there she was, like Winnie in *Happy Days*, buried up to her waist in her own rightness, with her right hat on her right head and her old plastic bag of right things at her side. Right-on old Winnie, with an empty *trompe l'oeil* sky of rightness wrapped around her. Rightness, rightness, rightness, as far as the eye could see.

Then, listening to her own words one last time and watching the camera pan slowly slowly up the front of the house, it came to her that the ivy she so much loved, which had beckoned her to buy the house, had become a metaphor for the insidious, ever-growing rightness which had wrapped itself about her life. She seemed to see it creeping and crawling, its grip upon the house growing by the moment, shivering and shaking its head outside her window, forever tapping on it, begging to be let in, twining itself not only around the place but around herself as well, gently, lovingly, squeezing the life out of her, conspiring in her fate as the dank dark tarn conspired in the fate that befell the House of Usher.

She remembered what the builder had said a few weeks before and she started to laugh, a hollow laugh.

He was right, she thought. It was her ivy that was the problem.

Thursday Evening . . .

1

THEY SAUNTER IN around him in twos and threes, easily, immersed in conversation, bracelets jingling, earrings dancing, reaching into purses at the doorway to lay down coins and notes upon the green baize table-top.

Two choose his row, pausing before they do so to appraise him, curiously, critically, taking in what he is, what they presume him to be.

In preparation for their passing he pulls his chair in too sharply, too eager to oblige. Before his lowered eyes fingers pass, fingers full of rings with dark-tipped fingernails guarding bulging bags of cloth and basket-work. On the bags are many badges. One informs him, in passing, that all such as he must be considered capable of rape.

He had tried to reason with Bullerman.

He said, 'Look, man, don't you understand? There's no point in going there tonight. She's not going to talk to us. She hates everything we are. She's got CND posters on her wall and a Save-the-Whales sticker in her car window. She's a feminist novelist, for Christ's sake.'

Down the line had come a licentious cackle.

'Fucking dyke,' said Bullerman.

*

Was she? Who knows? And anyway, what business was it of his? She didn't look like it. But then, neither did . . . He stops. Six years. And still he stops. The fact unsettles him.

He read the word graffitied on her back gate. It was there, one morning, crawling, scrawling, rising in a silvery green arc. The next day it was gone and the gate freshly painted.

Dyke.

He grimaces now, saying the word in his head, as he would have grimaced had he said it to Malone, sitting, as they always sat, like bookends at the bar.

He hated the word in the same way that he hated Bullerman. The two were connected in his mind, the word and the man. He knew that he, Crane, could not use such words naturally, that they felt awkward in his mouth.

He wasn't Bullerman, after all, with his beer belly swelling over his belt, his half-moons of sweat beneath his arms and his appallingly dirty jokes.

There was something bizarre about Bullerman and his dirty jokes. The more disgusting they were, the more gynaecological, the better he liked them. He used them as an initiation rite, trapping new members of staff in a fawning semi-circle around his bar stool, fixing his stare upon them, reviewing his collection for the filthiest, like a jeweller selecting his rarest gem.

When Bullerman started in on his strange tale at the funeral, he was only half listening for he thought it was just another of the man's disgusting jokes.

He hadn't wanted Bullerman to come to the

funeral. Malone had loathed the man as much as he did. But Bullerman always went to the funerals of old-timers like Malone. It was part of the vision he had of himself, that he and whoever it was who had died went way back together, that the two of them belonged to some golden age unknown to those who came afterwards.

At the Indian restaurant where they went to eat, Bullerman brushed aside the menu offered by the waiter and ordered a vindaloo, complaining, when it arrived, that it wasn't hot enough.

It was there, in the restaurant, that he discovered what he disliked most about the man: not his vanity, not his stupidity, not even his disgusting jokes, no, the way he ate, shovelling and sweating, swilling down the food with mouthfuls of the mediocre, overpriced wine.

He had gone to the gents to get away from the sight of him. He was standing before the urinal, his eyes closed in disgust at the memory, when he heard the sound of the door, and opening his eyes found Bullerman unzipping his flies in the mirror beside him.

Peering at Crane through eyes pink with drink, Bullerman thrust his head forward, launching immediately into the story.

There was this woman he'd been having an affair with. In the village where he and his wife lived. He'd called round. Unexpectedly. The back door was open. So naturally enough . . .

At first, said Bullerman, he thought there was no one there. Then he heard a sound in the bedroom. He thought he would surprise her. He crept upstairs. Opened the door quietly. They were on the bed. Four of them. She and her friends. Naked.

61

It was only then that Crane realized it wasn't a joke, for Bullerman's voice which had begun boldly had dwindled almost to a whisper. Beneath the great curve of his belly, his hand was still as his eyes bored into Crane's. There was confusion in them, outrage, and something else which looked like fear.

'Crane,' said Bullerman, a drop of perspiration running down his forehead into the bush of an eyebrow, '*they were sucking each other off.*'

The words seemed to him the crudest he had ever heard. He turned away from the force of them. They stood out in the air like the sweat on Bullerman's forehead. They seemed starker than the white tiles, brighter than the bleached glare of the strip lighting.

Before him Bullerman's mouth hung open. As he stared he licked a small drop of spittle from his lips. For a moment the two of them looked at each other in absolute silence. Then Bullerman moved abruptly, shaking himself and zipping himself up with a defiant thrust of his shoulders.

A smirk appeared about his lips; grew wider, more self-satisfied. He could see the man was making an effort to salvage some of his old jauntiness.

'Dykes,' said Bullerman.

Still staring at him in the mirror, Bullerman lifted the crook of his fleshy white arm in its rolled-up shirt sleeve and jabbed it viciously sideways. He felt a sharp pain below his bottom rib as it dug into his flesh.

The eyes, red-veined and sweaty, gave a monstrous wink as Bullerman gave a last heave to his belly.

'That's all half of them are these days, eh Crane?' said Bullerman.

2

WHAT AFFECTED HER most was the misappropriation of the word. Its taking without consent. Its stealing.

The writing had not been going well with all the fuss about Bernard. Unable to concentrate, she'd given in for the day and decided to clear out the attic. She'd pushed open the skylight for air and was standing on an old trunk looking out when she saw Harold coming up the alleyway. He was swaggering, hands in the pockets of his new denim jacket. One pocket bulged out suspiciously.

He stopped a few yards from her gate, about here, where now she stands waiting for Rita to reverse the car from the garage. It was his manner that caught her attention. He hunched his shoulders like an old man and looked around furtively.

She saw him take something from his pocket but she could not see what. Walking further in towards the door, he disappeared from her view. Several seconds later she saw him scurrying on down the alley.

Half an hour or so later when she opened the door to put some rubbish out, there it was, staring out at her, fresh and new, from the peeling paintwork.

The evidence was purely circumstantial, of course, but still she smiled mysteriously, refusing to be drawn when Gerald tut-tutted, as was his way, and blamed the yobbos on the council estate.

'That's the trouble with *Guardian* readers like you, Alice,' he said. 'You just can't accept that all some youngsters need is a bloody good hiding.'

She merely continued to smile. She knew that beneath it all Gerald liked her liberal bleeding-heart credentials. She knew it gave him some cachet in his own mind, this stalwart of the local Conservative Association, this managing director of the family carpet firm, to live next door to someone with political opinions so diverse from his own.

'By the way,' said Gerald, 'it's Harold's Bob-a-Job week so if you do have anything that needs doing around the house . . .'

'Oh I think I can find something, Gerald,' she said.

She caught Harold as he was passing in his uniform, calling to him through the window.

Taking him upstairs and into her study, she asked him to be kind enough to fetch her dictionary from the shelf, the dictionary her mother had given her to start grammar school, patched and pasted, thirty years old now, too old to deal in slang.

Requesting him then to look up the word 'dyke', she asked him why he had chosen to spray the term for a ditch or a watercourse upon her back gate. Receiving only silence in reply, and a beetroot-red flush, she said with some sympathy, 'I'm sorry, Harold. I saw you from the window.'

She produced for him then a pot of paint and a brush and asked him to be so kind as to put a fresh coat on the back gate, a task he carried out with all speed, his face growing even redder. When he had finished she gave him a pound and as he disappeared at a gallop up the front path throwing his farewells over his shoulder, stuck her 'Job Well Done' sticker in the window.

He did a good job despite his speed, she thinks to herself now, inspecting the paintwork in the car lights.

She had said as much to Rita, telling the story, laughing. Rita, however, was outraged.

'Well now you know what they teach him at that nasty little private school he goes to.'

'He's twelve years old for God's sake, Rita. He's just experimenting with words. I mean what the hell does he know?'

She meant it too. Perhaps she should have been outraged. But the silence and the beetroot face and the galloping goodbye stopped her. Rita, though, would not be placated.

'I would have thought it was perfectly clear what he knows. One of your problems, Alice, is that you have never faced up to the sheer unadulterated hatred of women that exists in certain areas of our society.'

It wasn't true. She had of course. That day. How long was it now? God, six years or more. That day at the airbase with Madeline.

Standing, that day, nose to the wire with the other women, she had stared deep into the soul of a soldier, who stared back at her, face blackened, beret pulled low over his eyes.

As she stared, she saw his lips move and tighten, passing on to her a message through the diamond of the wire. It came to her clear and low and unmistakable, through the singing and the chanting, a message from this man, this child, young enough to be her son.

65

'What you need,' he said, 'is a bloody good fuck.'

The words seemed to pierce the steel slowly and firmly and with great determination. She shivered with them because she saw that for him, for this boy-child, this, fucking, was punishment.

After that he began to whistle very softly, a tune she knew. He smiled at her as he whistled, holding her eyes. Then he began to sing the words in a low sweet boy's voice.

It took several moments for it to register that the words were not those of the song. It took several more for the sickness of them to permeate her brain. When they did she turned away shivering with the hate of them, shook her head from side to side as if to shake them off, as if they had settled on her like maggots on a corpse.

Early in the morning the female priest came with the bread and the wine, arriving with the late-night party-goers returning home.

And so, as the cup and the wafer passed around, the air became thick with blaring horns and whistles and jeers and with the sharp sting of obscenity.

'Slags,' they said, 'slags,' chortling, the word chewing up their faces with pleasure.

And then one, hanging so far out of a car window she thought he must fall, screamed, 'Go fuck a Russian,' so that she thought that this must be the way it always had been, that this must be what they always had shouted, this thing, this 'Go fuck'. Go fuck. Go fuck a Greek or a Trojan, an Arab or a Jew. Go fuck a Hindu or a Muslim, a Protestant or a Catholic, for so they would shout, she thought, go fuck a Martian if it came to a War of the Worlds and the women had a will to protest.

She asked herself then what dark unspeakable resentment simmered beneath the surface of the sexes to throw up, upon demand, this obscenity?

What had they, women, between their legs, that made them reach for it, these men, blindly, instinctively, in rage and in fear?

What, she asked herself, turned the world this way?

3

IN THE INDIAN restaurant, sitting beside him at the large round table, Sally bent her head intimately to his. She was drunk. But then so was he.

She said, 'Tell me, Crane' – she slurred her words a little – 'I always wanted to ask you. What exactly did happen between you and . . .'

'Janet,' he said. 'Janet.'

When Bullerman had said he was coming to the funeral with Sally, he had known what he was supposed to understand. He imagined Bullerman's lips wet with delight at the end of the phone.

During the day, though, Sally all but ignored Bullerman.

She swept across the platform in a cherry-red coat, her black hair catching the shafts of wintry sun shining through the station roof. She looked large and very handsome. Behind her Bullerman staggered, already a little unsteady, from the train.

Reaching him, she laid her smooth olive-skinned forehead against his, beginning to walk with him, her hand on his arm.

'I'm so sorry, Crane,' she said.

It was always 'Crane' with Sally.

Only once during the day did Sally acknowledge Bullerman's presence.

· He leant over to her in the pub after the service

and tried, proprietorially, with vulgar jocularity, to pull down the skirt of her sweater dress. Without looking at him she struck his hand away with a cool contemptuous slap.

Later she insisted that he accompany herself and Bullerman back to the hotel. He was too drunk and too unhappy to say 'No'. And besides, he never said 'No' to Sally.

Snatching the key from the check-in desk, she strode across the foyer leaving Bullerman to sort out the formalities. In the room she went immediately to the fridge, jamming the key in fiercely and swearing softly as at first it refused to open. Stooping, she took mixers from inside and, rising, slapped them down harshly upon the fridge-top. Suddenly all her drunkenness had dropped away, as he had seen it drop away when he worked with her, one minute tipsily raising her glass in the bar, the next clambering stone-cold sober into a taxi to a bomb-blast or a riot or another sectarian killing.

'They're trying to get rid of me, Crane,' she said.

He slipped the coat from his shoulders and sank down into a chair.

'They're trying to get rid of all of us, Sally,' he said.

She whirled on him then, her face a mask of fury.

'No,' she said. 'You don't understand. They're trying to get rid of me. Of *me*. Sally Hardwicke.'

She turned back to the fridge, dipping down to pull out the ice-cubes. She dropped them slowly, thoughtfully, into the glasses.

She said, 'I was the first woman sent to Northern Ireland, Crane.'

He said gently, 'I know, Sally.'

She said, 'They gave me an award for Christ's sake.'

He said, 'Yes I know, Sally.'

Her head was bowed. Her hands rigid as they grasped the fridge-top.

She said, 'I saved your life once, Crane.'

He said, 'I know, Sally, I know.'

He had been new there. It had felt like war and the feeling felt good. He went looking for trouble and he found it halfway up the Shankill. The whole street was ablaze, the army and the rioters red-black devils in the firelight. He was standing watching with his back against a wall when suddenly, without warning, he was surrounded.

Their faces were very thin and their eyes very hard and they hissed it at him, the accusation, the ends of their lips turning downwards in pleasure at the acquisition of the word.

'Press,' they said.

Staring back at them, making hollow gestures with his hands, he saw that he was in a foreign country, that he didn't speak the language and he was frightened.

And then, all of a sudden, there she was, beside him. His mouth fell open as she began shouting at him, the unfamiliar vowels distorting her face. He was her boyfriend. *English.* She tossed her head, waved a hand for all to see. She had told him to mind his own business. She had told him to stay at home. But would he listen. Would he shite.

She slapped him, then, heavily, upon his cheek. Around her they nudged each other, began to snigger, laughing, finally, out loud. Continuing to berate him, she led him away while all around him they raised their eyebrows as he passed, pursed their lips and winked at him, becoming one with him suddenly, in solidarity, with his predicament.

Out of sight, around the corner, she introduced herself, shaking hands. Later she took him home and afterwards to bed, so that almost immediately he was lost in love with Sally Hardwicke.

Many times after that, descending from her stool, throwing her fur about her, Sally would say, 'My place. Crane will cook a spaghetti,' and more often than not he would, scrabbling around in her grime-encrusted cupboards for tins of tomatoes and dried-out garlic and pasta escaping from packets.

Fumbling among the unwashed dishes and pans, he would hear Sally laughing in the lounge. He learnt to smile as she appeared at the kitchen door with a glass of wine.

'For the chef,' she would say, eyes too bright, face too flushed, giving him a cool kiss upon his cheek.

'It's so wonderful,' she would say later, before the others, pursing her lips red from the sauce in an outrageous moue, 'to have a man around the place.'

She was older than him, five years older, and he fell in love with her too quickly. It had rushed over him and borne him away before he realized it.

One night, tired, drunk, he had crawled into her bed with the sounds of the Saturday-night party beyond the door. When he woke, some hours later, the bed was still empty. Searching her out, he found her standing by the sink looking out of the window into the yard. Her cigarette was low, close to her lips, and she sucked on it noisily as he entered.

The room was in darkness but the light from the streetlamp caught her dark lips and the curve of her breasts in the tight polo-neck sweater.

'What's the matter, Sally?' he said.

She did not start. She had known he was there. She said, 'Go back to bed, Crane.' Her voice was low and flat and very angry.

He said, 'Is something wrong, Sally? Have I done something to upset you?' He heard the nervous whining tone in his voice and was ashamed.

In return she laughed a short, high-pitched laugh and stubbed her cigarette out hard upon the draining board.

'Oh for God's sake, Crane,' she said.

'If you want to know,' she said, 'I'm pregnant.'

The first thing he felt, in his folly, was a surge of joy.

'Sally,' he said, moving towards her.

'Don't,' she said, stopping him in his tracks. She turned back to the window.

'Before you say anything there's something you should know. There's no reason to presume that it's yours.'

The pain went straight to his bowels. His legs went weak from the strain of it and he dropped down on a spindly plastic-covered kitchen chair.

He brushed a hand back and forward over the table-top as if pushing away imaginary crumbs.

He said, 'There's someone else?' at which she turned on him her face full of wrath.

'Of course there's someone else,' she said. 'There's always someone else, for Christ's sake.'

There, then, in the night, with the darkness comforting about him, a certain madness came upon him and

72

he said many things; many things which, afterwards, he preferred to forget; things that skewered his heart and were the worse for being true.

As he spoke them he was filled with an absurd joy.

'It doesn't matter, Sally. We could get married anyway, Sally. It would be just like mine, Sally. I love you, Sally.'

As he spoke the words, he saw himself sending her flowers, many flowers, roses, every day, and enigmatic telegrams. All of which as a matter of fact he did as though, he thought afterwards, some pact had been drawn up with a God of Love who was also, at the same time, a God of Absolute Betrayal.

He sent these things, these flowers, these telegrams, even after she said what she said, raising her face to him, shaking her head, smiling at him sadly, arms crossed inflexibly across her breasts.

'Don't be such a fucking romantic, Crane,' she said.

4

THEY CALLED HER first novel 'dazzling'. But then they called all first novels 'dazzling'. They called it 'poignant' too, and 'unflinching' and 'a candid account of a coming of age'.

Rising to her feet upon the platform clutching the book in her hand, the adjectives had stared up at her derisively from the back cover.

Now the words of the novel falling ponderously upon the air seem to mock the accolades further. They sound hollow to her ears and clichéd, trembling on the very edge of pastiche. She is not reading well, of course. She can hear that. She has no rhythm. She stumbles too, makes it hard to make sense of the words by pausing in all the wrong places.

Perhaps, she thinks, it is he who disturbs her.

Pushing open the double doors as they hurried in, Rita had let out an exclamation of disgust.

'I'll get rid of him, Alice,' she said.

'No.' She had spoken sharply. A small frown appeared between Rita's eyebrows.

'It's a public event,' she said. 'He's entitled to be here.'

Seeing her enter, he had half risen, but she refused to meet his eye and swept on past him to sit down on the platform. He looked round, as if for a discreet means of escape, but the room had gone deferentially quiet for they were late, and so he sat down again with a small shrug, thwarted.

She had tried to ignore him. But lifting her eyes to turn the page she found her glance, against her will, falling on him. For a moment their eyes caught, and now even as she reads the words the image of his upturned face gazing up at her is imprinted in the corner of her retina.

She wonders if it is him sitting masculine and heavy and out of place who makes the words seem so fatuous and unconvincing.

It was so rare to see a man at her readings. Just occasionally one would appear, attending with his girlfriend in a demonstration of matchless solidarity, dressed in black the same as her, with more earrings and even more feminist zeal.

Reaching the end of a chapter, she looks up and smiles to take a small break. A shiver twitches her shoulders. The room is chill through disuse, the one-bar heaters on the walls glowing dully as though already defeated. Long faded velvet curtains at the window give off a musty smell. A flake of paintwork of pale institutional green peels off before her eyes and floats down from the wall. Before her, the audience shifts too and tries to readjust itself on the rickety old-fashioned fold-up chairs. She sighs. In such rooms, she thinks, are benefits for Women's Aid Centres held.

She turns the pages and, looking up, forces a smile. 'We move on a little now,' she says brightly. 'The heroine is growing up now. She's fourteen and her mother has agreed to drive her to the fair.'

'You can have an hour,' she said, parking the old Austin Seven at the gates. When I looked back from inside, her head in its little dark hat was already bent over her book.

I wore a wide dress with large orange roses on it and a cloud of net petticoats and white shoes whose high heels sunk down into the spongy ground.

I stood by the dodgems and watched the young men, dark greasy angels, dancing lightly from car to car, swinging on the poles, bending low over the heads of candy-floss hair.

In my ears was the sound of music, country music, beautiful and sweet and overwhelmingly serious.

As I stood there, one of the angels came up to me and held out his hand and led me to the car, where he stayed with me, from that time forward, leaping on and off, taking my money sometimes, sometimes not, bending to whisper mildly wicked suggestions in my ear.

Sometime later, some long time later, in a dream, eyes closed with the glory of it, I heard my name spoken sharply and looking up saw my mother on the side of the rink.

Walking back to the car she berated me for staying so long. Her voice was tight with unspoken accusation. She said, 'And I don't like the way you've begun to dress either.'

I can still remember the shame when she said it. It prickled on my skin like the petticoats, ran ice-cold down my back and up over my throat and face like fire.

Walking back to the car, I stared down at the flattened grass beneath my feet, at the chip papers and the used tickets and the drink cartons and all the other flotsam of the fair.

*

It was not long after that I heard them arguing.

They were picking blackberries in the garden. I was behind a hedge and they did not realize I was there.

My grandmother said, 'You're bringing the child up wrong, Addy.' Her voice was blunt. The blackberries dropped into the enamel bowl with an approving plop.

My mother's voice came back sharply from the other side of the bushes. 'She's my child. I'll bring her up the way I want.'

There was a moment's silence while the plopping continued. Then my grandmother said, 'You're too strict with her. It's unnatural. You're taking things out on her, things that happened to you. You'll end up making her like yourself.'

My mother said, 'Oh no,' very slowly. I could tell by her voice she had the strange bitter smile on her face.

'Oh no,' said my mother. 'She's not going to be like me at all. She's going away. She's going to university. She's going to be free and independent. She's going to do all the things I never did.

'Believe me,' she said. She was whispering it now, reciting it, like a mantra. 'She's not going to make the same mistakes I made.'

Only it didn't work out that way. Because five years later I stood before her, fists clenched, face white with determination.

'I'm not going to university,' I said. 'I'm going to stay here and get a job.'

She had just finished a lesson and was standing by the side of the piano. As she spoke, her eyes narrow with disgust, she crashed a hand down hard on the keyboard.

'You fool,' she hissed, the room ringing with the harsh discordant chord.

'You fool.'

I was eighteen and the night before I had lost my virginity.

He was ten years older than me, short with a shock of red hair, with red hair too on the backs of his hands. He was proud of the hair and of the curve of his belly, already a little swollen with beer.

He played the guitar and sang in the market-place and knew about painting and plays and music, and drank and smoked marijuana, and swore easily and went on marches and despised people, like my mother, who voted Conservative.

He lived in a tumbled-down house in the country with others like himself, men with long hair caught in bands with silver bangles and bright beads and leather knotted at their necks and their wrists, who called their girls 'my old lady'; such girls, brown girls, girls with long earrings and great sweeps of hair, with babies on their backs, girls who wove and baked bread, who moved gently and smiled sweetly in their sacred secret Xanadu in the soft Somerset hills. Oh, how I wanted to be such a girl.

On the night of my initiation he bought a half-bottle of whisky and stood it beside the bed. I stared at it and at the moonlight catching the naked globe of his belly.

Penetrating me, he caused me enormous pain, a pain that seemed to me to be the heart of me tearing.

I told my mother, 'I love him. I'm going to live with him.'

'Love . . .' she said, slamming a saucepan down on the Aga top.

'Love . . .' she repeated, drawing out the word, her lip curling in disgust.

5

B EHIND HIM NOW, the door opens noisily, turning heads all around him. The sound makes Alice Potter pause momentarily, mid-sentence. She raises her eyes to throw a quick glance down the hall, before lowering them again to continue. Turning too, he sees the familiar figure and sighs. Stanley. Stanley Smithson. Stanley who had been there at the beginning pursuing Alice Potter for his newspaper as he, Crane, had been pursuing her for his. Stanley who had gone away and whom he had dearly hoped would not return. Stanley, this same Stanley, stands now in the doorway, his gaze swivelling around the room.

As their eyes meet, Stanley gives a small grimace. He begins ambling towards him with a carelessly unsoft tread and, when he reaches the end of his row, drops down in the seat beside him where he stretches his long legs out beneath the chair in front. Folding his arms across his chest, he leans his head in conspiratorially.

'Couple of spare pricks at a wedding here I'd say, Crane,' he whispers loudly.

Sally was right. He was ridiculously romantic. He had presented himself to her in a parcel marked 'fidelity' without first checking if fidelity was what she wanted. And, of course, it was not. And of course there was someone else. What he had never been able to accept was that that someone should have been Stanley Smithson.

For several weeks after she had told him it was over, he was drunk. The flowers and the telegrams went unanswered. There was no answer at her flat either, and when he called her office a strange voice told him she had gone back to the mainland for a holiday. Then, several weeks later, walking into the bar, he saw her, from the doorway, with Stanley.

Stanley was good-looking in those days and much sought after by women. He'd been the youngest reporter ever to be taken on by his newspaper and was very much the rising star. Like all rising stars of the era, he shuttled around the triangle of the world's trouble spots, Vietnam, the Middle East and Northern Ireland, during which time he developed an attractively cynical war-weary air and a flamboyant dexterity with chopsticks.

But time had been no kinder in the long run to Stanley than to the rest of them. The Vietnam War ended, or ended at least as far as the Americans and therefore the Western media were concerned. The conflicts in the Middle East and Northern Ireland subsided into attrition, and eventually Stanley's paper, along with others, succumbed to soap stars and bingo and thrusting naked breasts.

Most of them had put on weight with the years. Only Stanley had grown thinner. He was tall, a full head taller than him, Crane. His thinness as a young man had been sensuous, poetic. Now though, with age, he had become spidery. The floppy jet-black hair which in the old days had given him a dashing appearance had greyed and come to look dusty. When he was young, women had loved to run their fingers

81

through it, so that later, growing older, he could not part with it and still wore it long, which aged him further and, what was worse, gave him a slightly seedy appearance. In the last few years he had taken to wearing a small moustache, which did not suit him, and, all in all, now had the air of a salesman about him, the old-fashioned sort, the sort, Crane thinks, who might open up a case of brushes on your doorstep.

Casting sideways glances at Stanley, he tries to summon up the sensation of just how it had felt to be jealous of him and fails. And yet jealous he had been, so jealous, that night he had stood in the doorway staring at the pair of them, that a great ball of it had risen inside him, making him tremble, freezing him to the spot, stopping the words that he had been speaking to his colleague dead in his throat. And with the jealousy had come a coruscating self-mortifying anger as he remembered a night a week or so earlier at Sally's when Stanley had raised a tumbler of red wine at him, a plate at his lips, mouth reddened with sauce.

'Great spaghetti, Crane,' he had said, grinning.

And so, as he had stood in the doorway, Sally had smiled at him from her table in the shadows in the furthest reaches of the bar, a cool, pleasant smile that set him at a distance and told him that what had been was exactly that, told him there was no need to approach.

But of course he did approach, when he was drunk, very drunk, trying to talk to her, trying to push in at their table.

'Sally . . .' he said, swaying a little, not sure what it was he wanted to say.

Beside her, Stanley had uncurled his long thin frame and stood up. There was triumph in his eyes as he looked down at him, coupled with an amused and merciless pity.

'Drink, Crane?' he said languidly.

Friends led him away in the end. Put him in a taxi, patted him on the shoulder, told him to cheer up, that things would be better in the morning.

Not wishing to return to his hotel, he asked the driver to drive around a little which was how, together, they had come upon it.

It was late, past midnight, in a part of the city where it would have been wiser not to be. The road was almost in darkness, one solitary streetlamp, unshot-out, still burning.

The driver saw it first. He said, 'Mary Mother of God,' jamming a foot down hard on the brake, slewing the taxi to a halt and throwing his head forward from the spot where it had been resting, eyes closed, on the back of the seat.

It hung forward from the streetlamp, perfectly still, gleaming in the light, a mass, oily and shapeless, suppurating with the blackness, like an oversized evil embryo.

In the taxi he and the driver sat staring as if turned to stone. As they watched, there was a movement. Through an open window they heard the small rattle of chains. Before them the shape raised itself; became a body, legs, arms and finally a face, prised open an eye and then another and stared back at them through the windscreen.

Slowly, slowly then, so slowly it seemed to take for ever, the lips opened, dripping ebony, began to agitate, to pull, to widen as the head fell back very slowly like a dog about to howl. Out of the mouth formed now in a perfect O came a long, slow, entirely silent scream.

She wasn't the first. She wasn't the last. She was seventeen years old and she had been to bed with a British soldier.

He watched impotently as they cut the chains away from her, disgust at everything, including himself, boring down into his belly.

'Witches,' said the fireman, sawing away at the chains.

'Frightening, isn't it?' he said. 'Women did this.'

Later, when he tried to file the story, he found himself unable to pronounce the words for the lump in his throat. He banged his hand down hard upon the phone cradle and laid his forehead against the bedroom wall. He tried to force some brandy inside him from a bottle by the bed but his lips chattered so much the liquid spilt over on to the counterpane.

He got under the covers but could not stop shivering. He felt a yearning to cry but it seemed to him that his eyes were gummed together with the horror of what he had seen. Sometime later he called a doctor who pursed his lips and looked at him hard and wrote out a sick note for nervous exhaustion.

He was packing his bag when Sally tapped on his door.

She sat down on a chair and pulled out her cigarettes.

'I just came to say goodbye, Crane,' she said, but he turned from her, looked out of the window.

She got up then, came up behind him. Her voice was urgent but there was kindness in it.

'Don't make a big thing of it, Crane,' she said. 'I know what you're like. You're such a fucking romantic.'

Her voice became harder then.

'More than likely it wasn't yours. It was impossible to tell and it doesn't matter anyway.'

She laid a hand on his arm. It felt cool and friendly and overwhelmingly self-confident through his shirt.

'I'm thirty years old, Crane,' she said. 'Old enough to know my own mind. I don't want children. I've never wanted them and I never will want them and that's an end of it. That's my right.'

The phone went then so he had to turn to answer it. It was the reception desk to tell him his taxi was waiting.

Sally stubbed her cigarette out and picked up her coat. She threw it over her shoulder like a man and came to him, standing before him and holding his upper arms in her hands. She gave him a long sad look and, leaning forward, kissed him on the cheek.

'I like you, Crane,' she said. 'I'll always like you. But it would never have worked. You're too nice.'

And that was when he learnt about 'nice'. That nice was a two-edged sword. That nice was not always a compliment when it came from women.

It was true, of course. He was nice. He knew that. He was the one who didn't presume, the one who offered to sleep on the sofa when the last bus had gone. He was the one who *liked* women.

'Equality,' he liked to say. 'Of course. Who wouldn't be for it? Pass me the standing order. Show me where I sign.'

Because he had tried. By God he had tried. He had tried not to be like the Bullermans and the Gibbs and the Stanleys of this world, and it had always pleased him, at parties, to be found in the company of women. But lately it seemed to him that something had changed. He could not say what it was or when precisely the change had come about, but it seemed to him that some support on which he had relied had been withdrawn; that because of it, through no fault of his own, he had found himself, as in the car this afternoon, fallen unhappily between faiths, lost in a no man's land between what he was and what he felt it imperative to try to be.

He had said all this once to Malone.

'I try, Malone, I really try,' he said. 'I try to be different, but I don't see them beating a path to my door either.'

It was during one of their long Sunday lunches. It was a grey day, the sort of grey day he loved in this city, his city, the city where he was born.

They sat in the window, their drinks in their hands, staring out over the roofs to where the great grey-green span of the bridge disappeared into the blank colourless sky.

'I'll tell you about "nice", Malone,' he said, his brandy glass suspended in the air.

'I've seen "nice" in their eyes. Nice is respectable, nice is unadventurous, nice is guaranteed not to stir the blood. Nice is what they think is waiting for them when all else fails. For nice read dull.'

Malone cleared his throat, adjusted the old tortoise-shell glasses.

'You know what I think about nice, Crane,' he said.

'I think nice is what women want to want but know in their hearts that they don't.'

6

'DON'T FEEL YOU have to wait to the end to ask questions,' she had told them smiling, in the embarrassed ingratiating manner she found herself adopting at readings.

The arm had unwound almost immediately in the air, releasing a shoal of silver bracelets which ran down it like water. She had hair that stood up upon her head like the crest of a cockatoo, pale lips with a shy smile and dark-rimmed eyes that were mistily self-conscious.

'Is it autobiographical?' she asked.

She was used to the question. She had been expecting it. Naturally enough, she prevaricated.

'Well that's not really the way writers work . . . I mean it's ideas that novelists tend to take from their own lives rather than actual events . . .'

It was pure obfuscation of course, camouflage, a blatant attempt to cover her tracks.

Her first novel was about her mother. And why not? Mothers, after all, were the stuff of which first novels were made.

And where would feminist writing be without mothers?

'Go then,' she said. 'Go and live with him. If that's what you want. Go ahead. Do what I did. Ruin your life for a man.'

And so I went upstairs and packed a small bag, just some jeans and T-shirts and some books, nothing which would mark me out as anything but a believer in the Xanadu of beads and brown rice and brotherhood to which I was going.

Several weeks later we were busking in the marketplace, he and I. We had the open guitar case before us. He was playing and I was singing, the only song I knew right through, which was 'Silver Dagger'.

Busking was still unusual, considered even a little daring in this conservative country town, so that a small knot of people had gathered.

I was on the second verse when suddenly there she was, framed, the other side of the square, in one of the stone arches.

I have a small sweet soprano voice which carried clearly, thin and sharp, across the cobbles. As we stared at each other, I stumbled, faltering at the awful pertinency of what I was singing.

> 'All men are false,' I sang, 'says my mother,
> They'll tell you wicked loving lies . . .'

'She didn't have to be unhappy,' my grandmother said.

We were washing up. We had buried my mother that afternoon.

When everyone had left, when the last cup and saucer had been put away, my grandmother suddenly slapped the tea-towel down angrily upon the draining board.

'It was the war,' she said. 'Nobody cared.'

She turned decisively to the sideboard, opened a drawer and took out a brown envelope which she thrust towards me.

'Here,' she said.

Inside was my parents' wedding photograph. It was six years after the scene in the market square. I was twenty-four years old and it was the first time in my life that I had seen it.

I have the picture still. It stands beside my bed: the bridegroom, a tall rakishly handsome naval officer standing, cap beneath his arm, too sharply to attention; the bride, all dark crêpe dress and jutting hat, one hand clutching a large bouquet of dark roses too tightly, the other tucked unhappily into the arm of this stranger now her husband, whom the camera has caught, with its customary cruelty, with shards of regret in his eyes.

My father was the best-looking young man in the village, according to my grandmother, when he celebrated a weekend away from the war by walking home from a dance one Adeline Selway whose pigtails ten years before he had pulled at school.

I've tried, over the years, to imagine how it happened. My father, talking in measured fashion at the gate. Kissing my mother's hand so courtly in farewell that it ensnared her heart. Persuading her sometime later, all against her better judgement, to commemorate the end of hostilities with him in a pretty patch of shade on the banks of the dyke that drove like an arrow through the low dank moorlands surrounding our village.

When three months later my mother was unable to dispute the mounting evidence that she was pregnant, my father, it being the custom of the time, was constrained to marry her. This he agreed to do, not manifestly against his will, according to my grandmother, with a certain young man's sense of disappointment for what might have been, yes, but in the main with a decent heart and a determinedly philosophical view of the future.

Not so Adeline Selway.

Adeline Selway was heartbroken. She was heartbroken because she was ashamed and being ashamed she decided to take revenge in the only way she knew how. She developed a stoop and a scurry to advertise her shame. For the rest of her life she would stoop and she would scurry. She would stoop and she would scurry and in doing both she would pay her husband back for destroying her dreams while at the same time paying back Life, too, for its appalling lack of romance.

When I think of my father now, I think of the traditional dark shape of which those like myself who have lost fathers in this way are supposed to think.

The dark shape disappeared around the time of my third birthday, along with the rather more buxom outline of a former land-girl called Brenda.

The village to a man, to a woman, shook its head. It would have liked to throw itself without reserve behind Adeline – Brenda, after all, being no more that an interloper in the village. But life is not that easy and there were those who felt sorry for my father, those who said he had tried, God help him, and a man shouldn't be made to feel guilty all his life for the simple sin of making a woman pregnant.

In such a way did my father disappear from my life. We heard nothing from him, or of him, ever again. A few years ago, I made some attempt to trace him through the usual agencies. I found out that he and Brenda emigrated to Australia early on in the 1950s. I traced them from Sydney to Melbourne but there the trail went dead, and I gave up, lacking the interest to pursue it. It gives me a strange feeling sometimes, though, imagining this whole other half of me, step-brothers and -sisters, living in a land of sunshine, unaware, more than likely, of my existence the other side of the planet.

When my father left, my mother put a postcard in the window of the village shop advertising piano lessons. At the same time she agreed with the licensee of the White Lion to play at weekends in the lounge bar, the very place where her husband had fallen for Brenda's charms.

My enduring memory still is of my mother sitting stiffly behind the pub piano, a glass of orange squash on its top, the fluid movements of her fingers failing to cause the smallest shift to the rigid line of her shoulders.

Permitted to go down to the pub for half an hour each Saturday night, I would watch her, face empty of all expression, staring over the heads of the customers, dressed in the familiar chaste twinset and pearls, hands dipping and rising, playing for her public upon demand, exquisitely but without the minutest display of enthusiasm, the finest love songs ever written.

7

O N THE SEAT next to him now, Stanley has succumbed to a surfeit of gin and tonic and fallen into a deep sleep. His chin is on his chest above his folded arms, and with each sleeping breath his head slips a little further downwards towards his, Crane's, shoulder. Lifting his elbow he gives a sharp jab into Stanley's chest. Stanley wakes with a small 'harrumph', shakes his head grimacing blearily. He stares at Alice Potter for a few moments as if trying to recall who she is. Then his eyelids begin to droop and, within seconds, he is asleep once again.

He has some sympathy with Stanley. The truth is, Alice Potter's novel does not fall naturally on his own ears either. It is too delicate for him, too over-refined. He would prefer something, well, a little more robust. A good thriller, say. A Forsyth or a Higgins. He's a philistine of course, he realizes that. At least that was what Janet used to call him. The first time she said it was in the early days when such arguments were still genial. He had wanted to watch *Bullitt* on one side on the television, she *The Spirit of the Beehive* on the other.

'Philistine,' she had said, with fond superiority.

But then, later, the superiority changed and became open contempt.

'Oh God, not Hemingway *again*,' she would say.

He'd been a Hemingway man since he was seventeen, since he swaggered with *For Whom the Bell Tolls* sticking out of his duffel coat pocket. *Qué va.* Another romantic.

Mostly though, he read non-fiction: biographies, military history. World War Two, Korea, Vietnam.

'What is this thing you men have with war?'

He can still see the thin cold indulgent smile on her face.

He had refused to treat the question lightly, scoured his brain for the words. In the end all he managed to come up with was the oldest and the corniest, the words that his father had used.

'I suppose,' he said carefully, 'it's something to do with the comradeship.'

The photograph on the sideboard. The hat at a jaunty angle, clinging to the side of his head. The smile of absurd bravura. Gunner Crane. Quite impossible to grasp that this boy was his father.

'Comradeship.' A clumsy old-fashioned word. A word from another time.

'We fought a war . . .'

'Oh God, don't tell me, for people like me . . .'

The first of the fights between Janet and his father.

'Aye, actually, aye now you come to mention it. For people like you.'

God, he had felt so sorry for his father. The foolish hurt look on his face. The finger flailing impotently in the air. He felt sorry for him and despised him at the same time. The worst possible combination. And for a moment he hated Janet.

'You didn't have to . . .'

'Oh for Christ's sake . . .'

The first of the words going nowhere.

It had occurred to him that Janet might be here tonight. It amazed him, how it was possible not to meet in so small a city, how it was possible to disappear so entirely from each others' lives. Would they still recognize each other after six years? Perhaps not. Still, he looked around him when he came in, checked the door each time it swung open. Because after all, here was the sort of place she would probably be. Here, with this sort of people. People like Alice Potter.

'It's a funny thing, you know, Malone,' he said. In his head, he still went on talking to Malone. 'Alice Potter . . . she doesn't seem . . . you know. I mean this afternoon, for instance . . . when she laughed. And her hair . . . Would you call that red, Malone, or gold? And she doesn't wear those . . . you know . . . Doc Martens and stuff. And her ankles. I'll tell you something, Malone . . . at the risk of sounding old-fashioned, there's something about a well-turned ankle . . . *Oh God.*'

Smiling to himself at the old expression, staring into space, he had found someone staring back. Widening his smile automatically, he had received in return a look of seething dislike which hit him like a handful of hail in the face. It was her friend, sitting next to her on the platform, the one who had given him That Look, who now had caught him leering at Alice Potter's ankles.

He drops his eyes, puts his hand to his mouth, coughs and rummages around on his person as if in pursuit of something of such importance that without it he will be unable to continue his evening. Inside the jacket pocket, two fingers close like scissors upon something hard, a card perhaps or a ticket, no, something else, something square and smooth. He eases it up across the lining and out through the flap into the open. Ah yes. He had forgotten it was there. The photograph of Vera.

She sits upon a stool, hands clasped about her knees, leaning towards the camera.

The silk dressing gown, tied modestly, still manages to suggest the divide of her breasts. Below the waist, its folds frame her legs which are long and exposed to the tops of her thighs, where they disappear beneath a glimpse of lace knickers.

The eyes which stare directly into the lens are questioning, a little nervous, empty of any suggestion of allurement. The stare is myopic, the stare of one asked, as a special favour, to remove her glasses and indeed, there they are, behind her on the sideboard.

Her hair is dark and closely curled in the style of the times and there is a shy uncertain smile upon her face.

It is the smile of someone unused to such posing, someone, though, determined to do her best, someone making an effort to be recorded this way, with absolute pleasure, for someone else's very private posterity.

Vera. He knew she was called Vera. Malone had written it on the back.

When the solicitor told him that Malone had left his savings to his wife, he said, without thinking, 'No. That's not possible.'

The solicitor, a young man, a little pompous, jerked his head back in surprise.

'I can assure you . . .' he began, stiffly.

He had flushed immediately beneath the man's stare, feeling foolish and defensive.

'No,' he said, 'I'm sorry. You misunderstand me. It's just that I never knew. I mean Malone and I have known each other for ten years – more – and I never knew he was married.'

The solicitor nodded. His fingers, surprisingly thin for his plump frame, searched among the papers before him.

'I gather it was a long time ago,' he said. 'The lady divorced Mr Malone and eventually married again.'

He gave him her name and address. It was a long name with many Ss and Zs. The address was a small town in Minnesota.

At home, he got a number from directory enquiries. When he rang it, though, it rang on and on with the peculiarly empty single ring that seemed to belong to America. He sent an invitation to the funeral anyway and, although he knew it was impossible, half expected to see her there, at the cemetery, a woman all in black, black-veiled, black-umbrellaed, standing beneath a dripping tree. But of course she wasn't there and anyway, the sun shone the day they buried Malone.

Two weeks later he got a letter from her. It was short and courteous in a careful, slanting, old-fashioned hand. She thanked him for his invitation. She was sorry that it had been impossible for her to be there. She had been away visiting her daughter and son-in-law in California and anyway she found it difficult to travel. She sent him kindest condolences on the death of his friend.

Struggling, after the funeral, to put a name to what he felt, he found that it was hurt. He had thought that he had known Malone. He had been proud of the depth of their friendship. It had seemed to him to be one of the small triumphs of his life. Now he found that he was not 'Malone' at all, that he was 'Charles', 'Charles' in a slanting old-fashioned hand.

He stared at the name trying to match it up with the man. And then, searching in Malone's desk for some papers for the solicitor, he came across the envelope.

It was a large envelope, heavy and brown, lying in the bottom of a drawer. Inside were letters tied up neatly with tape and the photograph bound in with them. There was a book too. Poems. Kid's stuff. He could make no sense of it. On the flyleaf, though, he recognized Malone's hand.

You shall have my chairs and candle
And my jug without a handle . . .

To Vera, with Great Affection, Charles Malone

He lifted the letters several times from the desk, plucking at the tape before dropping them again. Finally he untied them and opened them out and began reading.

Before him tortured enigmatic phrases limped stiffly, with great dignity, across the page.

'I know there are difficulties . . . I would hope with time . . . All I want is to make you happy.'

He read the letters slowly, lowering them at intervals and closing his eyes to allow for the bursts of pity.

When he had finished reading, he laid them down on the desk-top awkwardly, unsure what to do with them. He must have sat over them like this for half an hour or so, just staring at them, for when some time later he glanced at his watch he found he was already late for the solicitor.

He'd gathered the letters up in a rush and pushed them back in the drawer with the poems. Finding the documents he needed in another drawer, he had reached for his coat and had been halfway out of the door when he spotted the photograph on the floor.

Snatching it up, he stuffed it into his coat pocket, which is where it must have lain, tucked into the lining, ever since.

Staring at the picture now cupped in his hands he thinks he sees something he had not seen before, some shadow, some darkening in her face. Something in the eyes, yes, behind the myopia, something taking shelter in the shy uncertainty of the smile. Confusion, was it? Yes. But something else, something stronger. Disappointment? Yes, that was it. Disappointment, innocent and wicked and waiting to become disillusionment.

He sees again the precise legal fingers picking through the papers.

'The marriage was brief and there was no issue. Still, Mr Malone left explicit instructions making provision for his former wife in his will.'

Before him the letters rise up.

'I'm sorry I couldn't be the man you wanted me to be,' Malone had written.

'I'm sorry too,' she wrote by way of reply.

'I love you, Vera, you know that,' he had ended his last letter.

'It's not enough,' she answered. 'I wish it was. God bless you. Goodbye.'

8

*I*N THE MIDDLE of the hall now, Harriet Robinson drags her hair back from her face. She clutches the strands in her fingers which she drops, after a moment, to lay thoughtfully upon her lips.

'I suppose what I'm trying to say, Alice, is . . .' she says.

God how she has come to dread the obligatory question from Harriet Robinson.

Harriet's questions, she has noticed over the years, are not questions at all. Instead they're restatements of Harriet's manifesto, long, overdrawn and almost completely unintelligible; the jargon that she loves so much laced together with names from the lexicon of the feminist great and good, thus: 'As Gilbert and Gubar have shown us . . .' or 'Thanks to Kristeva we can now see . . .'

'I'm assuming, Alice,' she had started tonight, 'that you're familiar with Foucault . . .'

Listening to her now, she thinks Harriet Robinson the worst sort of academic, hot on dogma, cool on genuine, open-hearted delight.

Once, peering through the wired rectangles of the windows of the lecture-room doors at the university, she had seen students daydreaming and doodling in Harriet's lecture. At the back she had seen a couple fondling each other, on the brink of making love, none of which had been noticed by Harriet. There were students, or so she had heard, who after a year of Harriet's tutorials showed all the signs of being brain dead.

Harriet was so dull. Highly intelligent, yes. Academically unimpeachable, yes. But oh so terribly, terribly dull.

The sad thing about Harriet was that she actually concerned herself with important business: the construction of gender; patriarchal language; the exploitative nature of male fiction. More often than not her arguments had a great deal of rightness about them. But she pursued them, as now, with such dogged determination to such entirely life-denying conclusions that eventually they collapsed, losing every last scrap of their validity.

She was entirely without humour too and yet, despite all of these things, or perhaps even because of them, she had been commissioned on several occasions to produce critical books in her chosen field: late twentieth-century fiction, male fiction, Fowles and Amis and McEwan. Naturally Harriet only wrote about people she abhorred.

That Harriet is a fan of her work disquiets her. She has no shame, she knows that. She is willing to stretch the net of her approbation to breaking point to encompass those who will only say something nice about her books. But Harriet Robinson, she thinks now with a sigh, confounds even her determinedly elastic approach.

As Harriet continues to circle round and round, weaving elaborate word patterns like ribbons in the air, her voice is pierced suddenly by the long discreet squeak of a door being opened with care. A briefcase pokes through, then an expensive lace-up brogue followed by the heavy tweed cuff of a Hugo Boss over-coat.

Andrew has made it after all.

She had felt the familiar sharp frisson of embarrass-ment when she heard his voice on the phone.

'I'll be in Edinburgh during the day so I'll stop off for the reading,' he said. 'I might be a bit late but I'll be there.' There was a small pause. 'It would be nice to see you, Alice.'

The 'nice' was cool and friendly, pronounced, it seemed to her at the time, in a determinedly neutral way as if he were anxious she should not misconstrue it. It reaffirmed that faint sense of shame she felt now in her dealings with Andrew.

In her saner moments, she told herself not to be absurd. It was not as if anything had happened. She had got a little drunk, that was all. Deep in her heart, though, there lurked the uncomfortable truth, that when last they met, she had thought she was going to go to bed with Andrew McCartan.

The idea seemed ludicrous now, of course. It had seemed ludicrous from the moment she had woken up the following morning with a most appalling hang-over.

She had gone down to London to receive the feminist novel prize. Probably, she thought, it was this that had done it, sitting at dinner surrounded by people whose job it was to say nice things about her.

She had dressed up for the occasion, a new pair of shoes with heels slightly higher than those she was used to, an antique silk camisole beneath the dark thirties suit she found in the second hand shop, the pearls that had belonged to her mother. She was feeling . . . well . . . feminine. Probably it was that which had got her into trouble. Or perhaps it was Andrew himself; Andrew her publisher, but that night forced into the role of consort. Whatever it was, the praise that night ran like wine in the tight, lonely, dried-up rivulets of her veins. She got drunk on it, and then drunk on the wine as well.

She did not know now what could have persuaded her that there was the remotest possibility that she and Andrew would have made it to bed; how she could have erased from her mind the fact that since the moment he set eyes on her at university Andrew McCartan had been irreversibly, albeit quite hopelessly, in love with Rita Mountjoy.

She had wondered, many times, what the words 'in love' might mean to Rita and Andrew, how being 'in love' might manifest itself between them. One of those large cold expensive flats perhaps, with shared bills and a double futon and an abstract over the bed. Bedside tables piled with books and topped with identical pairs of reading glasses. Let us not to the marriage of true minds admit impediment. Oh no. Indeed not.

Rita and Andrew's relationship had always been a mystery to her. Certainly Rita was fond of him. She treated him in all respects like the good friend she clearly felt him to be. They spoke several times on the phone each week. She often stayed with him in London and they went to the theatre together and to concerts. Acknowledging now his raised hand with a faint smile as he drops down on to a seat at the back of the hall, she, Alice, has no doubt that it is Rita whom Andrew has really stopped over to see.

It has always seemed to her that Rita and Andrew are perfectly matched. She doubts that Rita's lack of interest in sex would prove a difficulty for Andrew, because, after all, he has that same coolness about him, that same air of not needing what the rest of the world required, as if he too belonged to that same distant planet. Yes, he and Rita might have a very fine marriage, one that would survive many years, perhaps even for the rest of their lives, being free, as it surely would be, from the messy complications of sex.

It irritates her that, quite against her will, ten years on since they first met, she is still intimidated by Andrew.

He shares the same fearsome intellect as Rita. In his case, though, it is laced with a certain audacity, an audacity which catapulted him with indecent haste straight from Cambridge into his own publishing company.

It was to Andrew that Rita sent her when she returned from Hong Kong, hand in hand with Bernard, with her first novel burning a hole in her suitcase.

Yes, she felt awkward in Andrew's presence even then. To her annoyance, that awkwardness grew worse four years ago when Bernard left, and she became, officially, a single woman again. She told herself such awkwardness was quite unaccountable. Which of course was nonsense. It was perfectly accountable. The truth was that despite his coolness, maybe even because of it, she had always been rather reluctantly attracted to Andrew McCartan.

After the official dinner, they had gone back to his house for a brandy. There he had flattered her, drawn her out, praised her oddities and her idiosyncrasies.

As he did so she felt herself swell in his hand, felt herself glow, felt her facets turn in the light. And so her voice became too loud, her hands began to wave too extravagantly in the air as she began to talk too warmly and with declining modesty about her work. Insidiously, wickedly, for absolutely no good reason – except the obvious ones, loneliness and desire – she began to assume, with some pleasurable anticipation, that she and Andrew McCartan would soon be in bed together.

At what point it was when it began to dawn on her that it was not to be, she cannot now remember.

She remembers only that, sometime after midnight, sitting upon his hearthrug, she upset her wine for the second time and realized, in that moment, that she was very drunk but more importantly that Andrew McCartan was not.

Looking into his eyes then she saw a chillness, a clarity that frightened her, and seeing this felt a great bitterness lift up through her limbs from the floor and lodge itself, black and angry, in her brain.

She saw suddenly, staring into Andrew McCartan's eyes, that she both delighted and offended him, that while as her publisher he welcomed with open arms the emotional disorder which had produced her books and which he had encouraged her, in his professional capacity, to lay at his feet, as a man he would shun it to the very depths of his soul.

She saw that Andrew McCartan would not want such dishevelment licking away at his loins, would not want doubt and distress like an aftertaste on his lips. Andrew McCartan would not wish to explode with Rochesterian abandonment bollock-full into her feminine bewilderment, would not wish to wake to all that bitterness and black mist beside him in bed.

'"A woman moved . . ."' she said. She was very drunk.

'I'm sorry?' said Andrew.

'"A woman moved,"' she said. 'Shakespeare. *The Taming of the Shrew*.' And then she recited it for him.

'"A woman moved",' she said, getting up and walking theatrically, unsteadily, to the back of the sofa,

> '. . . is like a fountain troubled,
> Muddy, ill-seeming, thick, bereft of beauty,
> And while it is so, none so dry or thirsty
> Will deign to sip or touch one drop of it.

'Trust old William,' she said, bitterly, 'to get it right.'

As she left, her taxi throbbing in the street, he gave her a very chill kiss on her cheek.

He drew back, holding both her arms, charming and friendly, his eyebrows rising in surprise.

'My goodness,' he said jovially, 'you're freezing.'

She drew back from him. Gathered her loneliness and her desire like dignity around her.

'More than likely,' she said.

9

WHERE TO CATCH her, that was the question.

She was sitting talking now to the guy who came in late, a smoothie if ever he saw one. Best to leave it till she had finished with him. There were a couple of girls too, hanging about with books to sign, and that awful woman who had asked that long-winded question.

Strangest thing, he had thought at the time. To hear someone speaking something you recognized as your language and yet be completely unable to understand it.

She'd said this thing. He'd been half asleep at the time and the words took a few seconds to penetrate. 'Most women,' she'd said, 'have now taken on board the notion that the ideology of the orgasm is fundamentally patriarchal.'

It was, he supposed, pretty much what Janet had said a great deal more clearly on that last night.

The word 'orgasm' had suddenly, miraculously, jolted Stanley out of his coma too. He snorted, shaking his head, blinking his eyes furiously.

'Here,' he said, leaning over to whisper loudly, eyes bright with delight at his own irrepressible humour, 'is she talking dirty?'

'Hard to tell,' he had answered with a cold smile.

'Now where to catch her, Malone, that's the question.

The door. Whaddya think? Yeah. Why not? Head her off at the pass so to speak. You know what amazes me, Malone? Twenty years in this business and my stomach still churns when the moment comes for me to approach them. You know how it is. The obsequious phrases turning over in your head: "Excuse me, I wonder if I might . . ." or, "I'm terribly sorry to bother you, but . . ." or that well-known top-of-the-range model complete with hangdog, self-deprecating expression, "Look, I realize that you don't want to have anything to do with me and I understand that but I'm just going through the motions . . ." '

Next to him, Stanley has uncoiled himself and risen, speaking as he does so.

'Sorry?'

'I said are we going to get this dyke or what?'

'We don't know she's a dyke.' He is surprised, slightly embarrassed at the edge to his voice. So is Stanley, who cocks a questioning eyebrow.

'I mean we've only got the ex-girlfriend's word for it,' he, Crane, says, shrugging his shoulders, straining to be casual. 'And let's face it, she doesn't exactly sound like a reliable witness.'

'Thinking woman's crumpet, you know?'

'What?'

'O'Donaghue. That's what they call him.'

'I wouldn't know. I'm not a thinking woman. And anyway I've never watched him.'

'Well, you're a lucky bastard then. I had to get a second telly just to get away from the man. Women, you know. They love him. Twice a week the house grinds to a halt. Can't get so much as a cup of tea. Her and the daughters, all of them, glued to the box. Make a sound and you're dead. And they watch the omnibus version again on Sundays. Can you believe that? The girls have got his bloody picture all over their bedroom walls. I'm surprised she doesn't stick one up in our bedroom as well. I mean, I ask you. Mothers and daughters lusting after the same man. And a bloody priest as well. Is that disgusting or what?'

'I wouldn't know. I told you. I never watch it.'

Stanley blows through his mouth, shakes his head glumly like a motorized toy winding down. Then a small wicked grin spreads slowly over his face.

'Hey, speaking of thinking woman's crumpet . . .'

Stanley's voice is easy but the eyes are very sharp and very clear and very full of self-satisfaction.

'I hear old Sal's knocking off Bullerman now . . .'

What astonished him as he sat drinking in the hotel room with the pair of them after the funeral was that Bullerman seemed to want him to stay as much as Sally. He pressed drink on him forcefully.

'Come on, man. For fuck's sake. It's a wake. It's for Malone,' he kept saying.

Malone had loathed Bullerman.

Both Bullerman and Sally were very drunk, as indeed he was too. He suspected that they argued a lot when they were drunk and this was why Bullerman wanted him stay. Against his will, he began to feel sorry for him. His shirt and trousers strained heavily against the beer gut and his face was florid, even in the soft bedroom lighting. Several times he caught him casting uneasy sideways looks at Sally.

Left alone in the bedroom, they listened to the

sound of him sluicing and belching behind the bathroom door.

Sally grimaced. She lay with her legs stretched out upon the bed.

'He has some say, you know,' she said.

He looked away. He could not meet her eyes. He wanted to shout at her, 'For God's sake, Sally. It's not true. You know it's not true. It's the accountants who decide.'

And so it was. He had wanted to shout at them too, the Tontons, when they had sacked Malone, scream into the empty screens of their dark glasses, 'This man turned in every day for thirty years like it was the first day and now you're getting rid of him.'

So when Sally said what she said about Bullerman, he just mumbled, saying nothing.

For a moment there was silence and then she said, 'He's no trouble, you know?'

He said, 'Don't, Sally.'

She smiled, an awful smile, a smile that struck fear into his heart.

'Can't get it up if you want to know the truth,' she said, reaching across to the bedside table to grind a cigarette down hard in the ashtray.

'Don't, Sally,' he said again.

But she would not stop. She put her whisky glass to her lips and stared at him over its rim.

'What about you, Crane,' she said, 'can you still get it up?'

Her smile stripped him bare along with her eyes. He shivered, wondering that once he had been young enough and courageous enough to make love to this woman.

He said, 'I have to go, Sally,' and he got up, lifting

his mac once again from the bed.

This time she was there beside him picking up her coat as well.

'I'll come with you,' she said.

For a long second they stared at each other, then he said, 'We can't turn the clock back, Sally.'

The words were banal and he was ashamed of them as soon as they were spoken. Before him he saw her lips curl with disgust, her eyes go black with anger. She tossed her coat back on the bed.

'Don't give me that shit, Crane,' she said.

She strode to the fridge and began to throw another drink together viciously.

'Do me a favour, Crane,' she said, her voice ice-cold with fury, 'tell the truth for once in your fucking miserable little life. Say what you really want to say, which is "No thanks, Sally Hardwicke. Thanks for asking but no thanks I don't think I'll bother." But don't give me crap like we can't turn the clock back. Because we can do what the fuck we want to do. You just don't want to that's all.'

He put a hand wearily to his forehead. He said, 'I'm sorry, Sally,' at which she finally erupted.

'Jesus,' she shouted, rounding on him. 'You really don't get it, do you. You don't have to be *sorry*.'

She spat the word out at him.

There was silence then between them. She looked away breathing deeply.

Finally she shook her head. 'For Christ's sake,' she said, smiling grimly, all her anger quite gone. 'Stop being Mr Nice Guy, Crane.'

10

A ND NOW HARRIET, grasping earnestly for
the words she requires, stares down at the floor while
at the same time plucking a forefinger and thumb
thoughtfully across the bridge of her nose.

She takes a deep determined breath. 'I'm not sure
what I mean here, Alice, but . . .'

Around them, the small semi-circle – Rita, Andrew,
some girls who have bought books for her to sign –
stands frozen in mid-movement as if turned magically
to stone by the sheer dead weight of Harriet's words.

She had been sitting mutinously silent before Andrew
when Harriet had begun to hover nearby.

She had moved steadily and inexorably closer with
tiny agitations till at last she was quite impossible to
ignore. 'Alice, I'm sorry to bother you again but I'm
writing this paper for the *New Feminist Review* and I
wonder if I might . . .'

Before she could answer Andrew had jumped to
his feet.

'Of course, of course,' he said with a dazzling smile
at Harriet. 'We've quite finished, haven't we, Alice?'

They hadn't of course. They hadn't finished at all.
But they were talking about money and it was clear,
from his alacrity, that Harriet's interruption could
not have come soon enough for Andrew.

The same day she got the letter from Jim Crane,

she also received one from Andrew. The contents were similarly easy to recall.

'Dear Alice,' said the letter. 'Thank you for the manuscript of *Winter is for Women*, which I have now read and enjoyed enormously. It is a rich, mature novel and one, it seems to me, which marks a further stage in your development as a writer. We envisage publishing the novel next autumn. Accordingly I should like to offer you an advance of £3,000; £1,500 upon receipt of the revised manuscript and £1,500 upon publication. Kindest regards, Andrew McCartan'.

The letter ran over and over in her head as she sat before Andrew, hands clasped in her lap like a school-girl.

'I just can't believe it, Andrew,' she said. 'I have two novels behind me and a book of short stories. From what you've told me you appear to think *Winter is for Women* is a good novel, a further step forward etc. etc., yet all you're willing to offer me for it is a paltry three thousand pounds.'

The embarrassment she felt at the circumstances of their last meeting had given way to a raw anger. She found it difficult to discuss money with Andrew. Most authors had the same problem with their publishers, she had noticed. No matter how many times you told yourself sniffily that money did not equate to excellence, still the notion persisted like some ancient pagan belief that would not die. Because of this discussions about money had an unpleasant habit of becoming distressing. Conversations that should have been distant and matter-of-fact and unemotional began working themselves, against your will, danger-ously close to your core.

112

For these reasons, she had decided after her first novel was accepted to find herself an agent. Unfortunately she made the mistake of mentioning her intention to Andrew.

'By all means look for an agent if you wish, Alice,' he had said loftily, 'but frankly, I really don't think you need one at this stage. I'm sure we can handle everything for you quite adequately.'

He gave the impression, cleverly she saw now, that she had in some way offended him. Because of this, being still a new author, and like all new authors desperately grateful to have been published at all, she abandoned the idea.

Sitting opposite Andrew tonight she had seen clearly for the first time that he not only knew about her difficulty in discussing money but that he was prepared, quite shamelessly, to use it to his advantage. Money was a subject he avoided at all costs with his authors. Forced into a discussion of it against his will, he deflected their ire, for more often than not they were very very angry, with his own particular brand of sweet reason, clever, gently barbed compliments spoken in a smooth soothing voice, accompanied by a deeply patient smile. It was a winning combination guaranteed to leave the guilt-ridden author feeling there was something altogether vulgar, not to say faintly reprehensible, about having raised the matter of money at all.

Tonight the smile had been even more saintly than usual, the voice undiluted honey. The expression on his face told her that anything he had to say to which she might take exception was said more in sorrow than in anger.

'You know I consider you one of our most original

113

writers, Alice,' he said. 'One of our strengths, I feel, as a publisher, is that we are deeply committed to bringing out work like yours which is, shall we say, outside the mainstream.'

Shall we say? Of course we will say, she thought. For the phrase had been a dagger to her heart. For 'outside the mainstream', she knew, read 'doesn't sell'.

'You see, the problem for us, Alice,' he said, 'is that things just aren't easy at the moment. In a recession, you know, things like publishing are the first to suffer.'

She had been rebellious. Childishly belligerent.

'I thought we weren't in a recession,' she said. 'According to the government . . .'

'Oh . . . well . . . the government . . .' He waved a white elegant hand dismissively in the air. 'I think we all know about the government,' he said.

He leant forward then, conspiratorially, and stared down at his hands which he had clasped between his knees.

'You know, Alice,' he said, slowly, as though he were sharing with her some very special thought, with which he was sure, upon consideration, she could only agree, 'my primary concern has always been for our authors. For me, they're the people who matter. And the truth is that, aside from the financial consideration, I simply don't believe in large advances and the reason for that is that I don't think they're good for the writer.'

He raised his eyes to her then. They were clear and unashamed and in them she could see the audacity for which he was famous.

'To be frank with you,' he said, 'I wouldn't pay large advances even if we could afford them.'

Staring at him, she had felt the bile rise up inside her, up through her belly, through her throat to her head where it seethed and bubbled and forced itself against the inside of her skull.

She wanted suddenly with great passion to be a man. She yearned for it. To be the worst sort of man, old-fashioned, violent, chauvinistic; a Welsh poet, say, an Irish playwright, a drunk, a womanizer, anything, but a man able, by virtue of his masculinity, to put a decent fear of God into his publisher.

Christ, she had thought, how she would leap up from her chair, how she would stand there sweating and foul-mouthed, how in a moment rich in colour for her biographer she would drag Andrew to his feet by the collar of his Hugo Boss overcoat and shout gloriously, furiously, full in his face: 'You fucking mean bastard, McCartan.'

Above her now Harriet Robinson jiggles her glasses on her nose.

It seems to her, Alice, staring up from the chair, that Harriet's words and phrases are growing up around her like the plucked branches and woven undergrowth of a stockade. She hacks away at them, trying to make sense of the sentence, forcing her way through 'diverse determinants' and 'perpetually shifting configurations', through 'female subject positions' and 'particular representational strategies'.

She feels lashed to the chair by the invisible threads of Harriet's words. Life seems to have faded away around her. All that is left in the world, it seems to her, are Harriet's lips, Beckettian lips, demented, disembodied on a black-curtained stage, prioritizing and inter-textualizing, spewing out the eternal mysteries of over-contextualization.

She had always thought Harriet a fool, but it comes to her now in a rising tide of anger as she listens, that Harriet's grinding impenetrability bespeaks something other than folly, a hubris, yes, a hubris, that was it. For what else but hubris could prefer the isolation of this ugly unintelligible private language to the rich communication of ordinary everyday speech.

She makes a small sharp impatient move with her head. It unsettles Harriet who jiggles her glasses defensively, takes a breath and finishes in a rush.

'Of course I love your work, you know that, Alice, but what's not clear to me is whether your writing is, for want of a better word, conventional, or whether it is something more complicated, actually self-deconstructing.'

Naturally enough there is a small several-second delay before the sense settles in her brain. But when it does outrage floods her soul.

Rita, though, is there before her.

'Alice,' she says hastily, 'I think it's time . . .'

Andrew too edges in to forestall the moment.

'I think so, Alice, yes . . . Time to eat.'

Without looking at either of them she rises to her feet, at the same time holding up a magisterially restraining hand.

'I'm feeling my way here, Harriet,' she says, her voice, even to her own ears, like chips of ice. 'But would I be correct in thinking that what you are actually asking is if my writing is cliché-ridden by accident or whether I'm actually doing it on purpose?'

'Alice . . .' says Rita warningly.

'Um . . . Alice . . .' is the best Andrew can do.

116

'Harriet?' she says, mercilessly ignoring them both, her eyes boring into hers.

Harriet's hand has flown to the bridge of her nose. She throws small desperate glances about her.

'Well . . . let me think now . . . yes . . . I suppose in a manner of speaking, Alice . . .' she says unhappily.

Deep inside her, now, the fury is a long thin column of steel, piercing her soul like a vampire's stake. The dreadful irony of it. That it should be Harriet, stupid vain Harriet, who had confirmed her own worst suspicions.

She lifts her handbag from the chair and puts the strap over her shoulder, before turning to face her.

'Then why the fuck don't you say so, Harriet,' she says, her voice calm and very cold.

And with that she is off down the hall, her feet striding along in time with her fury.

He is at the swing doors when she catches him, a hand outstretched to push his way through.

She taps him on the shoulder and he starts. When he turns he sees to her surprise the anger she can feel in her own eyes mirrored in his.

For a second or so they stare like this at each other. As she stares she sees the anger begin to die away in his eyes, to be replaced by an expression of bemusement.

'OK,' she says, 'I'll do what you want. Just get me out of here.'

Friday Morning . . .

1

AND NOW HE stands as he thinks he must have stood half his life, a phone jammed into his neck. Times change though, for in his ear Vivaldi plays, a cold mechanical Vivaldi, thin and over-bright. Outside the window, branches newly bare clack and tap and beckon him towards the steel-grey river, while here, in his hotel room, synthesized shepherds dance, bringing in the spring.

'The Four Seasons', the first piece of classical music Malone had played him.

It was not long after he had moved back from Manchester, after he had got over what everyone, himself included, was too embarrassed to call a breakdown.

'I'm more a Doctor Hook man,' he had told Malone, apologetically, riffling with respectful fingers through the line of classical LPs on the shelf. 'I'm afraid this sort of stuff has always been rather unknown territory for me.'

'Try this then,' Malone had said.

He had sat entranced with the sweet, stirring, yearning tones of the thing and had gone out and bought a copy the following day.

'Crane.'

His own name, oily, almost caressing, breaks in on his thoughts. He knows that it is spoken this way for the benefit of the acolytes around the throne, whose only business is to listen and enjoy.

'Bullerman.'

'How are you, Crane?'

He does not answer. He is not supposed to. He knows this for the words are rich and slow with savoured sarcasm.

'Now it's like this, Crane. I'm staring at a copy of your morning newspaper, as indeed I do every day at this time, but today, well, today is different, because what do I see today bang in the middle of the front page but a picture of my district man playing the white knight with the dyke novelist whose doorstep he has been standing on without result for the last three weeks. So bearing in mind, Crane, that I've been trying for the last couple of hours to raise you at home and in the office without result, perhaps you would be good enough to tell me, considering that I am, after all, your northern news editor, what the fuck is happening?'

It was extraordinary. He had been leaving. Chucking it all in. Fuck everything, he had been thinking. Fuck Stanley, fuck Bullerman, fuck the whole damn business. And most of all, fuck Alice Potter.

As Stanley had said what he said about Sally, he had uncoiled himself and risen languidly to his feet. Stanley's eyes were bright with the assumption of shared masculinity. When he saw it he, Crane, made to move away, afraid of what Stanley would say next. He was too late, though. Because Stanley said it. Immediately. Before he could turn away. 'Bit of an office bicycle now, I'm afraid, old Sal,' said Stanley.

And so, for the second time in less than a week he felt it, the same sickness he had felt with Gibb, the sickness that rose up inside him, curled and uncurled his fingers and tightened his jaw.

Yes, he had felt sick with it, sick with Stanley for what he had said, sick for Sally, for Sally who had saved him, sick with a life that allowed this thing to be said, but sick most of all with himself for his own sickening lack of gallantry.

For he did not answer Stanley. He did not scream back obscenities for what Stanley had said. He did not seize him by the lapels, hurl him against a wall. As with Gibb, he simply walked away.

He did not answer Stanley because he had nothing to say. Striding away from him, jaw working, hands clenched, he had felt the same appalling sense of despair he had felt that day with Gibb, only this time it was worse for this time it had a sense of utter finality about it.

He told himself that it was all over. Whatever it was, he told himself, it was finished. He was out of it. He was throwing in the towel. If life was a game, then he had lost. He was getting out of there now. He was going home where he would get very very drunk. If he was lucky he might not wake up in the morning. All this he was saying to himself pushing his way out through the door when he felt the tap on his shoulder.

His immediate thought had been that it was Stanley. He thought either the man had something to say which would further enrage him or else he would be about to apologize. Either way it did not matter. He turned in fury. To find himself staring full into the face of Alice Potter.

When she said what she said, he could not believe it. He just stared at her, furrowing his brow, unsure that he had really heard the words. So confused was

123

he that he was unable to think of anything to say, just stood there looking at her, so that eventually she stamped her foot petulantly. 'For heaven's sake,' she said. 'It's what you want, isn't it?'

He said, 'Yes,' but still did not move. 'Yes,' he said again, and then, shaking his head, said, 'but why?'

'Oh God not *now*,' she said, the word almost a scream, and with that she gave him a sharp shove that pushed the pair of them out through the swing doors.

Grabbing his arm, she began dragging him along the corridor. Behind them, as they ran, he heard the double doors clash open and a woman's voice call out in anguish. 'Alice!' it said. 'What are you *doing*, Alice?'

'Come *on*,' she hissed.

Then the doors crashed a second time and the voice was a man's. 'For God's sake, Alice,' it said, sharply reproving.

As they turned the corner, he had thrown a look back down the corridor where he had seen her friend, the one who had given him That Look, hurrying after them, her head bent in to the smooth man in the fashionable overcoat who half ran beside her.

'Faster,' snapped Alice Potter.

He was panting by the time they emerged into the foyer. Groaning, he saw Stanley standing, arms folded before the revolving door, a they-shall-not-pass expression on his face.

'Tut tut, Crane,' he said jocularly.

You had to admire Stanley. He must have reconnoitred the place beforehand, so that by exiting from the doors at the other end of the hall he had somehow managed to get to the front door ahead of them.

Stanley's face changed then. His brow darkened. His voice deepened and became theatrically urgent.

'Alice,' he said, 'if you don't want to talk to my newspaper, I respect that. That's fine. But don't, please don't, I beg you, go with this man.'

Next to Alice Potter, he, Crane, had sighed.

'You don't think you're overdoing this slightly, do you, Stanley?' he said. But Stanley had not finished. Slowly he raised an arm, extending a finger to point it at him in the manner of one embarking on a dramatic, unflinching *j'accuse*.

'This man, Alice,' he said, 'has the most appalling reputation. This man has broken hearts before.'

He had shaken his head wearily, put a hand over his eyes. 'I can't believe I'm hearing this, Stanley,' he said. But Stanley was in full flow by now.

'This man,' he said, 'promises money and never pays. This man fabricates quotes. This man would stitch up his own grandmother for a story.'

It was an absurd performance, of course, but the extraordinary thing was, it had had an effect on Alice Potter. He could see her faltering. She glanced nervously over her shoulder. At the sound of the running feet she let out a desperate, 'Oh God.' Stanley, encouraged, laid a hand, fetchingly, upon his heart.

'Look, Alice,' he said, 'it's like I said, it doesn't matter if you don't want to speak to me. That's fine. But don't, whatever you do, go with him. Let me take you home. Get you away from all this. Away from him.'

It was a great performance. He had to admit it. He'd begun to smile against his will.

'Very good, Stanley,' he said. 'Collect your Oscar from the desk. Now if you've quite finished, perhaps you'd allow us to be on our way.'

He'd taken Alice Potter's hand then. Felt it cool and hesitant and a little damp in his as he drew her forward. Suddenly though, as they made the move, the foyer dissolved into chaos, on one side of her, her friends who had emerged from the corridor, the pair of them gabbling at her, 'You can't do this, Alice . . . This is quite awful, Alice . . . Think what you're doing, Alice . . .' and, on the other side, from nowhere, the woman who had asked the long involved question, apologizing for something it seemed, flapping her hands in the air, 'I'm so *sorry*, Alice . . . I really didn't quite mean that, Alice . . .' Then of course, by this time, there were the handful of hacks from the local papers who'd been waiting for Alice Potter in the bar, reporters and a couple of photographers clicking away. There was no sign of Gibb. It was typical of the man, of course. The only time he was ever needed he was nowhere in sight, still in the bar probably, chatting up the barmaid, which was what he had been doing when last he, Crane, had seen him.

Beside him, Alice Potter had put a hand to her head, turned her face into him as if to get away from the noise. Taking her hand from his, she clutched it instead on his arm. At the touch he looked down at her and found himself staring into two sea-green pools, misty with confusion and with an appeal for help in them that struck him like a stab to the heart.

He seemed to stare into her eyes for a very long time. As he stared, it seemed to him that the mêlée around them faded away, and all there was in the world were those eyes.

At first, as they ran along the corridor together, he had been annoyed at her, the way, in this absurd fashion, she had thwarted his plans. It had occurred to him to tell her the thing was off, to tell her to go and find Stanley because he wanted nothing to do with any of it any more. But as he looked into those eyes, everything changed.

'It's all right, Alice,' he said.

Turning to Stanley, he said in his sternest voice, 'Right, Stanley, enough is enough.' Stanley, though, didn't move so he, Crane, laid a hand on Alice Potter's back, 'This way, Alice,' he said.

As they began to walk towards Stanley, the confusion fell away and people parted respectfully. As they walked, he and Stanley stared at each other, fixedly, like two gunfighters at the OK Corral.

The grin on Stanley's face grew wider the nearer the pair of them got. He didn't move; just stood there, with his hands across his chest.

They were almost upon him when he, Crane, made his move. His eyes still boring into Stanley's he lunged suddenly, grasping the edge of the revolving door and giving it a huge heave. It let out a groan as if making a gigantic effort, then it creaked and clunked and began to spin.

As it began to move, he lunged forward a second time, giving Stanley a sharp jab in the middle of the chest.

The push took Stanley totally by surprise. He toppled backwards and as he did so was sucked into the revolving door like a fairgoer on the Wall of Death.

The last they saw of him, jumping into the next compartment behind him, was a nose flattened against the glass, a pair of bulging eyes and a long thin body spreadeagled like a spider. The next minute they were staggering out on to the steps together.

Feeling her about to fall, he had encircled her waist with his arm. Instead of steadying her though it pulled her a little more off balance towards him, so that they ended up crushed together in an embrace, her chin upon his shoulder. Thrusting his own face round to enquire after her, he found himself about to lose balance himself, so that he stuck out a hand in front to steady himself, and it was then that the camera caught them.

He knew the photographer who took the picture. He worked for the local paper and he was lazy and mean and more than likely skulking on the steps figuring out ways to go home.

For a moment they were mesmerized by the phutter of the flashes but then, as one, they leapt forward and, in perfect step, ran down the last of the steps to the taxi rank. As the cab pulled away, he turned to look out through the back window and there saw Stanley taking the steps three at a time and screaming at the taxi that had drawn up in the spot from which they had left.

As Stanley hurled himself in, his taxi lurched forward and was upon theirs almost immediately. He, Crane, leant forward to his own driver.

'There's a fiver in it for you,' he said politely, 'if you can lose the cab behind.'

Their driver was young and stocky with a scrubby moustache and many tattoos.

'Be a pleasure,' he said.

In the mirror, a broad smile drew back over bad teeth as he changed down a gear with ominous calm.

They took off like a space shuttle with booster rockets firing. He and Alice Potter were hurled back against the seat with the momentum, but the solid shoulder of the driver in front of them never moved.

For what seemed like half an hour then, but was actually little more than a couple of minutes, they bounced around in the back, straining against their respective windows and clinging to their straps like drowning men.

They ducked and weaved in and out of the traffic in an attempt to lose Stanley's cab but without success. It sat firmly on their bumper.

They were taking a corner on two wheels, when the radio crackled into life and a plaintive voice began requesting them to report their position.

'Debbie,' their driver said to them conversationally over his shoulder, with a nod of what seemed to be satisfaction.

'Lovely girl, our Debbie,' he said.

At that moment they screamed to a stop at a set of traffic lights, Stanley's cab drawing up beside them.

As one man, the two drivers turned their heads to glare fixedly at each other, easing out their clutches as they did so and pressing their feet down hard on their accelerators so that the two cabs eased forward, bucking gently like horses straining at the reins.

. 'Gives her a hard time, our Debbie,' their driver had further ventured, his eyes narrowing in the direction of the rival cab, Which is when it had come to him, Crane, that there was a worrying degree of bad blood between their two drivers.

As if to confirm his suspicion, their driver pressed his foot even further down on the accelerator, the deafening crescendo of revs making the pedestrians crossing on the lights scuttle for shelter. It was then that he, Crane, had sneaked a look at Alice Potter. He was disconcerted to find her looking back at him, her face white and her eyes very wide.

He had been giving her in return what he hoped was an encouraging smile while at the same time preparing, in his mind, some words of reassurance, when the lights had changed and their cab had leapt forward across the pedestrian crossing in a small arc.

With its milli-second start it was able to cross the path of Stanley's cab and veer off sharply to the left. But Stanley's driver caught the change of direction in time and did the same and together they tore on to the urban motorway.

For a mile or so they raced, neck and neck, their cab in the fast lane, Stanley's beside them in the slow. He, Crane, had turned his back with determination against the glass to cut out the sight of Stanley's face, gloating at him, a few feet away on the other side of the window.

He did not choose now to conjecture what speed they had reached. Inching forward at one point to look over their driver's shoulder, he had seen the speedometer needle easing confidently towards the hundred mark, at which point he had drawn himself discreetly backwards to subside on the seat and give himself over to prayer.

The end had come when their driver had pulled off the motorway in a manoeuvre which he, Crane, thought it unlikely he would ever forget.

They were driving at full speed when their man suddenly dropped his foot from the accelerator and swung the cab sharply in behind Stanley's.

Alice Potter, taken by surprise, was flung from her side of the back seat leftwards to land on top of him. He in turn lost his grip on his strap and felt himself, as if in slow motion, slip with her downwards in an uncontrollable heap of limbs.

His face crushed into what he thought were probably Alice Potter's breasts, he felt the brakes begin to jam on and the cab begin to slip in a dangerous S to the left.

As before, it seemed to happen slowly, so that he had time to reflect that here, on Alice Potter's bosom was more than likely where he was going to spend the last moments of his life.

A series of bumps beneath their tyres proclaimed that they had struck some rough verge or other terrain not expressly designed for the motorist. He was thinking that this must be The End when by some miracle he felt the cab begin to right itself and gain control once more. By way of confirmation he heard a victorious hoot from their driver.

He tried to draw himself up from Alice Potter's torso but the cab was still rounding bends at speeds which served to flatten him back against her.

Then the brakes went on again.

Slowly, gently, inexorably, he felt the pair of them slipping downwards towards the floor.

He tried to struggle but to no avail. By the time he felt the cab draw finally to a stop, he and Alice Potter were wedged solidly in the gap between the back seat and the front.

He was still trying to extricate himself and her, while at the same time apologizing profusely, when there was a cheery, 'Where to now then, man?' from above him.

2

IT WAS NOT until he had dragged both himself and Alice Potter back up on to the seat and was staring into the enquiring eyes framed in the oblong of the driving mirror, that he had realized that, having succeeded for reasons he could not deduce in capturing his quarry, he now had not the least idea what to do with her.

'Right ... yes ... ummm,' he said vaguely and unhelpfully to the driver.

Turning to her in the small hope that she might be able to help, he found to his acute discomfort the same look of enquiry upon her face.

'Well,' he said, 'I imagine Stanley will be waiting for us at your place.' He made a clicking noise with his tongue. 'I suppose we ought to go to a hotel.'

He was aware, as he spoke, of the taxi driver's smirk.

'Fine,' Alice Potter said stiffly.

They tried four city centre hotels unsuccessfully before he spotted the yellow 'Forward into Europe' signs. He groaned to himself. Oh God, a conference. In a city notoriously short on hotel space.

'Let's think,' he said.

In the front the taxi driver slumped back in his seat whistling softly and flicking ash out of his open window. In the back beside him Alice Potter studied her nails steadfastly. Then suddenly it had come to him, which was how they had ended up at the King's Head.

He booked from a phone box.

'I think you'll like it,' he told her. 'They're quiet because it's out of season. We've got the nicest rooms, overlooking the river.'

He had settled back into his seat and was beginning to breathe normally again, when he remembered Uncle Arly.

Uncle Arly. Fat old orange Buddha of a cat.

The first time he'd gone to Malone's house – how many years ago was it now? Twelve, it must be – he had been lowering himself on to a chair, eyes fixed on the man's photographs on the wall opposite, when he hit something soft which squawked like a parrot and shot like an arrow across the room. It was standing in the corner ruffling its fur at him and glaring balefully with its great yellow eyes when Malone came in with their whisky.

'I'm sorry,' he said. 'I didn't see it.'

'"He", Crane, "he",' said Malone. 'Meet Uncle Arly.'

Uncle Arly moped now that Malone was gone and there was nothing that he could do about it, because the truth was that he moped as well.

'I'm sorry,' he told Alice Potter, ordering the taxi to make a detour. 'I have to feed him for a friend.'

He put three large plates of food down, made an unsuccessful attempt to stroke him and said, 'See you Saturday, Uncle Arly.'

Drawing away from the house Alice Potter said politely, 'Your friend? She's away?'

He said, 'No,' wanting for no good reason he could think of to shock her.

'It's a "he" actually,' he said. 'And he's dead.'

But she wasn't shocked. Or at least she didn't appear it.

She did not look away. Instead she held his eyes firmly. 'I'm sorry,' she said.

She said, 'That's a wonderful name for a cat. He must have loved Lear.'

'Lear?' he said.

'The poet,' she said.

'Oh yes,' he said. 'Kids' stuff.'

'Perhaps,' she said. 'Some people don't think so. Some people think it's love poetry.'

'Oh really,' he said.

There was silence then between them for many miles. He was lost in thought about Malone so that when she spoke again he had to ask her to repeat what she said.

'I was just thinking it's a long way in a taxi. I just asked you if you drove?'

They were approaching a roundabout. In the orange lights he could see her eyes, light, bright, friendly.

'No.' He said it shortly, turning to look back out of the window.

She didn't stop though. She said, 'That's unusual, isn't it? I thought doing your job you'd have to drive.'

'You do,' he said.

He hated to tell people. To admit it. It was embarrassing. Sooner or later, no matter how hard you fought against it, you found yourself making excuses.

'I'd only had . . . Well really I wasn't that much over . . .'

Staring out into the darkness, it occurred to him,

remembering her eyes, that perhaps he could tell her why it was he did not drive. But then he felt again that certain harshness, that lump of anger in his throat, and he abandoned the idea, instead drawing himself away from her into his own corner of the seat, to go over again, in awful detail, his recollections of the night he had been breathalysed.

It was his penance, he knew that. His Hail Marys. He was doing it again here now, remembering, the receiver still in his hand, Bullerman's voice still ringing in his ear.

They were like beads on a rosary, his memories. He told them over and over to himself, or perhaps more like nails, yes nails, that was it, nails that he drove as punishment into his flesh.

'It's important to be positive,' he told Malone, Malone who had fished with him so many times on this river bank, *their* river bank, this bank that stared back at him emptily now, the other side of the window.

His sin, the sin for which he punished himself, was that he had refused to believe Malone was dying. He had refused, in his arrogance, even to listen properly to what he was saying. He was soothing, oh so soothing, oh so Mother-knows-best. Oh no, Malone, he said. Don't worry, Malone. It can't be, Malone. They need more tests, Malone.

He said, 'You're just depressed, Malone. It's the redundancy. It's set you back. Got you down. It's to be expected. And this flu is a bastard.'

Only, of course, it wasn't flu. And Malone knew it. But since he was Malone he just smiled and nodded courteously, because already he'd reached the place that people like him did reach, people who above all were well mannered by nature, who possessed a certain grace in living that the rest of the world lacked, those *gentlemen* of the planet who would pretend for friends, so as not to distress them, that they weren't in fact dying.

He had grown irritated with Malone, that was the truth. He had grown tired of the fact that he was not getting better. He wanted to say something brisk to him, something for his own good, something like, 'Snap out of it, man.' Which was why he came up with the idea of the pub.

'Our redundancies, Malone. You've got yours and we all know mine's coming. We could afford it easily if we sold our places as well. Somewhere in the country. Buy a place cheap. Turn it into the sort of place we'd want to go. Somewhere like the King's Head.'

He'd been excited about the plan. He was proud of himself. He'd booked the best restaurant to tell him, insisted on picking him up in the car.

Revving the engine ostentatiously at Malone's gate, he watched him turn his key in the lock. For some reason the way Malone looked caught at his heart. He had on his best suit and the old car coat. He seemed suddenly very small.

Once in the restaurant he, Crane, tried to pile delight upon delight upon him, the best food, the best wine. It annoyed him mildly when he saw Malone eating without pleasure.

'Me in the kitchen, Malone,' he said, rubbing his hands together. 'You behind the bar.' He wanted Malone to be enthusiastic. He stretched out his hand, lifted his glass in a toast.

But Malone did not raise his glass with him and so he lowered his slowly. Malone cleared his throat.

'Look, old man,' he said. 'Would you mind frightfully if I had a whisky?'

He said 'No' immediately, over-warmly, clicked his fingers in the air.

When the whisky was before him, Malone said, his voice apologetic, 'I know this isn't the sort of place but . . .' and he brought out, from beneath the tablecloth, his tobacco tin.

He, Crane, hadn't wanted him to roll up. The memory of that now ground into his heart. But the fact is that he didn't want his best friend to make a roll-up in that over-priced joint with the flunkies flapping napkins around him. And because he didn't want him to, he said, 'No, of course not, man,' flamboyantly and, 'You go ahead and smoke, man,' in that forced voice used by those who make an effort to acquiesce to something of which essentially they disapprove.

Assembling the roll-up quickly on the table, Malone said, 'They say give it up.' He pulled a face.

'They say give it up *now*,' he said. His voice rose gently in derision. He put the roll-up between his lips and reached for his lighter. Flicking it and inhaling, he said, 'It's a good plan, old man. I like it. But there's a problem. It's good for you if you understand me. But for me . . . well . . . frankly . . . it's a bit late.'

He had misunderstood, of course. He would. He jumped in, immediately, pooh-poohing him. 'Nonsense, Malone . . . life begins at fifty-three, Malone.'

Malone pursed his lips, stared down at his plate. He looked awkward, as if he must say something which did not reflect well on himself.

137

He said, 'No . . . old man . . . it's not that. You see there's a problem, old man . . .'

He'd refused to believe it, of course. Malone had told him the truth, that he was dying, but it hurt too much, it was too hard to take, it inconvenienced his life with its sheer, honest-to-God impossibility. And so he drove him home with an air of displeasure, as if he, Malone, had committed some indelicacy which he, Crane, in his decency had decided to overlook, refusing to meet his eye and saying goodbye to him with determined jocularity at the gate.

He had started to shake at the end of the street.

By the time he had turned on to the motorway he was banging on the wheel.

The flashing blue light appeared in his mirror fifty yards from his door.

Breathalysing him, making him breathe into the bag, well, that was a formality really. They knew all they wanted to know when he opened the car door and fell out at their feet.

As a matter of fact, and it wasn't just an excuse, he really *hadn't* had that much to drink. The reading showed that. Even the police were surprised.

'It's the car you see,' he told them, feeling foolish. But so it was.

His car. His pride and joy. He wasn't a car bore. Frankly he wouldn't know a twin camshaft if it dropped off in the road, but he loved his car, a 1963 MGB roadster, British racing green, wire wheels, chrome bumpers, lovingly restored and lavished with all the attentions the world of auto repairs could offer.

The problem was that he had bought the car fifteen years ago. It was a young man's car. When he bought it, as well as being younger, he was also thinner and considerably more spry.

To get behind the wheel now, he had to lower his body gently, tilt back till his legs shook with the strain, and then free-fall till he hit the seat. And getting out was worse. The only way he could manage that was by setting up a rolling motion from side to side that eventually propelled him out of the door.

When he saw the light in his mirror, he had pulled off the road. Anxious to appear as accommodating as possible, he had tried to get out in a hurry. In his panic, his rolls had gained an extra momentum which catapulted him too far, out through the open door and into a heap on the tarmac.

The car was grounded now, parked in his underground space beneath the flats, its gleaming silver grille glaring at him balefully. He, meanwhile, had to suffer the indignity of being driven everywhere in Gibb's XR3i, a model of car he particularly despised.

Gibb's car, and the way he drove it, was another reason why he loathed the man. He drove like all young men of his ilk, one foot Araldited to the accelerator, a finger twitching the horn, willing, positively willing, the driver in front to make a mistake, so that he might rev up behind him then roar past, blasting the horn and calling down obscene curses upon his head while jabbing two fingers furiously in the air.

The truth was that, all things considered, he wasn't sorry there had been no sign of Gibb when he and Alice Potter had emerged into the foyer to face Stanley. He would not have wished to drive up here with Gibb. He was glad that they had had to take a taxi.

Not so Bullerman. There were no congratulations at landing Alice Potter.

'For Christ's sake, Crane,' was all he had spluttered. 'Taxi must have cost a fortune. Where the fuck was Gibb?'

'Ask Gibb,' he had answered piously.

Bullerman never missed an opportunity to rub in the loss of his licence. This morning was no exception.

'Of course, if you hadn't got done, Crane . . .' he said.

'But I did, Bullerman,' he replied as he always replied. 'And there but for the grace of God, as I have said before, go you as well.'

Bullerman put on his patient, disillusioned father's voice then.

'But what am I supposed to do with a district man who doesn't drive, Crane?' he whined. 'How am I supposed to defend you to London?'

'Oh, defend me the same way you've always defended me, Bullerman,' he said easily.

'Defend me the same way you defend all your district men who have fallen out of favour.

'Defend me the same way you defended Malone, in your traditional gutless, self-interested fashion.'

3

THE PHOTOGRAPH EMBARRASSES her. Buttering her toast, she finds her eyes straying to the paper lying beside her on the coverlet. Toast in hand, she leans back against the pillow and lifts it up with a sigh, one more time.

They delivered the paper with her breakfast tray. It was not the paper she had asked for. Naturally she had asked for the *Guardian*. Perhaps they had mixed up her order or, there again, perhaps they had just thought this one would do. She had noticed this about newsagents. To newsagents, newspapers were precisely that, just paper. She had to persuade her own not to deliver the *Daily Telegraph* if a *Guardian*, for some reason, was not available.

'But it's the same size,' he had told her once, hurt.

Naturally the picture had given her something of a shock when she first unfolded the paper. The headline read, 'Scuffles Over Soap Star's Wife'.

Beneath it, the meagre two-paragraph caption alleged that trouble had erupted in the foyer of a city-centre pub the previous night after a reading by local feminist writer Alice Potter between representatives of rival Sunday newspapers bidding for her story.

It was a gross exaggeration of what had happened, of course. In fact it was an out-and-out lie. What's ironical though, she cannot help thinking as she chews on her toast, is that the photograph appears to bear out the story.

Their faces, his and hers, are defensive, agitated, whitened by the flash. They look like fugitives flung together against the world. His arm, thrust out in front, seems to clear a path for them, seems to ward off some out-of-shot danger. The other, pulling her to him, curves protectively about her shoulders. By a trick of the steps he is much taller than her, so that his chin rests perfectly upon her hair. Beneath him she seems to nestle, yes that was the word, nestle into his chest.

Feeling again the sharp twinge of disquiet, she lays the paper back once more on the coverlet.

It had taken them some forty minutes to get to the hotel. On the way they had passed an all-night garage where they stopped to buy some necessities; a toothbrush, toothpaste and deodorant for her; razors and shaving cream for him. She had looked away as they lay there, a strangely intimate pile on the counter-top.

She took a liking to the hotel as soon as she walked in. It was old-fashioned with the sort of faded velvet and threadworn carpets that appealed to her. The dining room was closed so they ate cold poached salmon salads in the lounge, settling back in deep chintz-covered armchairs before a huge open fire.

He ordered a white wine, dry and very expensive. They were on their second bottle when he leant forward and said abruptly, 'You are quite sure you want to do this?'

She stared at him for a moment. It was absurd. For three weeks he had sat outside her house. He had stood on her doorstep, followed her to the shops. He

142

had phoned her and written letters. Now sitting before her, she had the strangest feeling he was trying to encourage her to call the whole thing off.

'Quite sure,' she said.

'Do you mind if I ask why?' he said.

'Not at all,' she said. 'Money.'

It was an over-simplification, of course, but she felt that, under the circumstances, it would do. It was unlikely, after all, that he would understand if she tried to explain that it had also to do with the general, all-pervading despair she felt about her work. What was more to the point was that she was unsure she had as yet the words to express it.

'I see,' he said abruptly.

'No I don't think so. I would doubt that you see at all,' she said.

'How much do you make a year?' she asked him.

He said, 'Oh I don't know. With expenses – thirty-five grand? Maybe forty.'

'Do you know how much I made last year?'

'How much?'

She told him then. The exact amount, quoting it from her accounts.

'It's hardly enough to pay tax,' she said. 'And I'm sick of it. I'm sick of always having to worry about money, about how much the gas bill will be this winter, whether I can afford the rates. I've got a phone I only use after six and a car I can't afford to run any more that Rita uses. Worse than all of these things, I have a house that needs twenty grand spent on it straight away to stop it falling down around my ears.'

Her voice had risen. He looked at her. There was concern in his eyes.

'I'm sorry,' he said.

'Look,' she told him, 'I'm forty-two years old. I've been writing full time for ten years. I've produced three novels and a book of short stories, all of which have been well and worthily reviewed and none of which have sold more than five hundred copies apiece. To pay the bills I do readings and reviews and run writing courses, all of which, as a matter of fact, I hate.'

She ran on, clenching her hands in her lap as she talked.

'I've been working on my fourth novel for the last two and a half years,' she said. 'Every day I go up to my study, work on it, sit there playing with the words and the phrases, sometimes just staring at a blank sheet of paper. It's about Bernard – oh, obliquely of course, because that's the way we writers do it. But essentially it's about Bernard and Madeline, the same story that you want me to tell you, only you'll pay me thirty thousand pounds which, by some irony, is precisely ten times the amount my publisher will pay. And with you I don't even have to write it. I don't have to agonize over the construction and the quality of the prose and I don't have to wonder if it's any good. I just sit down and tell it to you and you do all the work. You hash it together in flat journalese in a mish-mash of tenses and five million people will read it.'

Her voice had grown steadily more resentful as she had progressed. Hearing the bitterness in it at the end, she stared down into her glass shamefaced.

For a moment there was silence, then he coughed politely.

'I understand now,' he said. 'I do. But have you

any idea what it will be like? The sort of questions I may have to ask you?'

She looked up at him. Pulled a wry face.

'You mean *personal* questions?' she said.

She stared straight into his eyes.

'You think it's any worse than dragging it all out and putting it in a novel? Do you think, in the end, it's any more immoral or ignoble?'

She had been a little drunk by then, a little dramatic. She pulled her cigarettes from her bag.

'I suppose you could say,' she said, flicking her lighter, 'that it's better. That's what Clive says anyway.'

'Clive?' he had said enquiringly.

'Well,' he had said, later, 'at least your line of work is more civilized than mine.'

He was trying to make her smile, she could see.

'I mean at least you don't get literary hacks bothering you, door-stepping you and staking you out.'

She snorted.

'Oh really,' she said. 'Tell that to any writer who's been biographed or Ph.D.ed against their will. Tell that to J.D. Salinger.'

It took another brandy before she could broach the subject that had exercised her mind for most of the journey up.

'Look . . .' she said hesitantly. 'The thing is . . . you are serious about the thirty thousand pounds, aren't you? I mean, I didn't believe Stanley of course but . . . well . . . what I mean is . . . you wouldn't trick me, would you?'

She was ashamed of her own vulnerability. It

encouraged her to see that he looked enormously offended.

'I'm sorry,' she said. 'It's just that I don't know you.'

His face cleared a little.

'Of course you don't,' he said. 'And there's no reason why you should trust me. What you have to remember though is that you don't have to trust me. You'll have a contract which both of us will sign. I suggest, in fact I strongly recommend, that you have someone come up here, a lawyer or a friend, someone whose opinion you can trust, to go over it with you.'

She smiled. 'I've got just the person,' she said.

'That contract guarantees you the money . . .' he said. There was a small hesitation. 'With the proviso of course . . .'

'That I tell you what you want to know about Bernard.'

'Yes.'

'That's what bothers me.'

'Why?'

'Well . . . you're offering me thirty thousand pounds, right?'

'Yes.'

'The thing is . . . about him, I mean . . . what exactly is it you think I have to tell you that's worth thirty thousand pounds?'

'Ah, well . . .' Understanding was dawning on his face. 'I think I see what's worrying you.'

'I mean what are you expecting me to say? That he was a drug addict or really he fancies little boys? I mean I'm sorry to disappoint you but I guess it's something we should get straight before we start. All I've got to tell you is the story of how I met him, fell in love with him, married him and got left by him.'

'That's right.'

'That's enough?'

'That's enough.'

'But that can't be worth thirty thousand pounds.'

'It depends,' he said, 'on your understanding of the word "worth".'

He had settled back into his chair. He held his glass up before him, grimaced as he gazed into it.

'In simple terms, it's worth it to us because we can put on a quarter of a million circulation with anything about Bernard O'Donaghue on the front page.'

'A *quarter of a million?* Good God. I suppose I should have realized.'

'Yeah. But I think your main problem is not understanding our sense of the word "worth". It's not worth it in sensible, logical terms. It's not worth thirty thousand pounds like a kidney machine is worth thirty thousand pounds. It's not worth it like, I don't know, a painting is worth it, or a novel. It's not *worth* anything in those terms. In fact, in those terms, it's entirely worth*less*. But it's worth it to us, worth it with our absurd, perverted, entirely worthless system of values.'

'Why do you do it?' The question was out before she had realized it had been spoken.

'I mean you sound as though you hate it.' For so he had. His voice had grown flatter and more bitter as he had spoken.

'Oh . . .' He shrugged. Shook his head. As if he were tired of the enquiry. And indeed it appeared he was.

'The million-dollar question,' he said. 'It's my job,' he said. 'I've always done it.

'For what it's *worth*,' he said, pulling an ironical face at the word, 'I do it well.'

'Is that enough?' she said.

'No?' he said. 'Probably not.'

'It's just that –' she said.

He interrupted her, raising the glass to his lips. His voice was sharply sardonic.

'You mean how can I work for *that rag*. Don't I *care*?'

'If you like, yes.'

'It's what my ex-wife used to ask me.'

'Well I suppose it deserves a reply.'

They had had a lot to drink. Their voices had grown sharper and now the possibility of unpleasantness hung in the air between them. Then he shrugged again. Smiled, a deliberate smile to diffuse the situation.

'Well . . .' he said, putting the glass down on the table in front of him, 'I probably won't be working for it too much longer.'

'Why not?'

'Oh . . . It's a bit complicated . . .'

'So explain it.'

'Well . . . if you really want to know . . . we've recently introduced an exciting new exercise in industrial relations. Personal contracts. To take the place of the old union negotiations. Divide and conquer. The old story. Under the new contracts you can be fired after three warnings which is a neat way of getting rid of people you don't want. You get an official warning if you fall down on a job. So all you have to do is find an impossible story to send someone on and bingo, three warnings and they're out. Which is pretty much what having me sit on your doorstep for the last three weeks has all been about. Of course, they'd have liked it if you talked. But the truth is they never really expected it. If they really thought you were going to they'd have sent up some high-flier from London. No. The whole exercise really has been about getting rid of me. I've had two warnings, one each week you kept on banging the phone down and slamming the door. No doubt they've got the final one already written for next week. You've rather thrown a spanner in the works by agreeing to talk. Still, I have every confidence that when all this is over they'll find something else impossible to send me out on to finish the job and put all of us out of our misery.'

It was a long speech. He looked away from her as he spoke.

'I'm sorry.'

'Don't be.' The words came back from him sharply.

'Don't waste your pity. I don't deserve sympathy. None of us do. We know that. It's all we've got going for us, knowing it. At least we're honest. We've done very nicely out of a paper that has spent a decade consistently pissing on the unions, so we can't really complain now that it's turned round and pissed all over ours and left us all without a leg to stand on. Live by the sword, die by the sword. It's only fair.'

She said, 'Why don't you fit in? Why do they want to get rid of you?'

'Oh ... you know ... Getting old ... getting fat ... getting past it ...'

'But how old are you?'

'Forty-two.'

'But ...'

'Yeah, I know. But it's a youth culture now. They're all kids. They have to be. To do what's required.' His voice had become very harsh.

'And what is it . . . that's required?'

'Oh . . . you know . . . you know very well. What's required is the sort of thing that good *Guardian* readers like you despise. The sort of thing that makes headlines in other newspapers.'

'And you won't do that.'

'Well . . . let's just say I have some difficulty with it.'

He waved a hand in the air, ran it through his hair in a weary manner.

'Look, I don't want to make myself out to be some plaster saint. I've bent the odd quote. Grieving widows who don't say precisely what you need. Lads lashed to lampposts nude after the stag night who aren't quite as witty as we would like.'

'But you have certain standards. You don't actually make things up.'

'Yeah. That's about the size of it.'

'Good,' she said.

Walking up the wide handsome mahogany staircase by his side to bed, she had said, 'Why do people do it? Sell their stories I mean.'

He said, 'Well, there's the money, of course, and then the publicity – for the models, you know, the would-be pop stars. Then there's the Warhol factor, the fifteen minutes of fame. And then, of course, there's revenge.'

'Oh,' she said. 'It's not revenge. The truth is, like I say, I really don't have anything awful to say about Bernard.'

She thought she saw a flash of disappointment pass over his face.

It had surprised her at the time. Afterwards she

told herself it was only to be expected. He was a reporter after all. He was in search of a good story.

Yes indeed. Thinking about it again. His disappointment was only professional. Of that she was quite sure.

4

'NO,' SAYS ALICE Potter.

She busies herself about the room, lifting the breakfast tray from the bed, smoothing down the coverlet. A thin watery ray of winter-morning sunshine inches through the window, striking the red-gold of her hair as she bends.

'Look, Alice . . .' He sits before her, on the end of her bed, grinding his hands together.

'No.'

She won't look at him, arranges herself neatly in the chair before him, crossing her legs, folding her arms belligerently.

'Absolutely not,' she says.

Several minutes after he had put the phone down, it rang again. When he picked it up a woman's voice, cool, amused, said, 'Jim Crane? Octavia Eagleton. Features. I don't think we've met.'

She was clever, this Octavia. He saw that afterwards. She had that smooth persuasive affability which belonged to all the good operators in his business.

'It's absurd, of course,' she had said. 'I've told them it's quite crazy. After all, you're the one who got her to talk. But they think a woman might get more out of her and since I'm in Edinburgh on this job that hasn't worked out, they thought I might as well stop off and do it. I can be with you in about an hour.'

He was astonished at the stab of anger. Now, after he had sat on her doorstep for three weeks. Now that she had agreed to talk, *now* they were sending up the high-flier from London. It was a snub, of course. An exercise in humiliation. Another indication of how they felt about him in London. But what did it matter? Really, what was it to him, the Alice Potter story? After all, take away the pretensions and what did you have but another kiss and tell, exactly the sort of story he despised. Better all round that this Octavia Eagleton should do it.

'Look, Alice,' he says now, running a hand through his hair, feeling as always the small tremor of sadness at its loss, 'you've decided you want to do it. What difference does it make? I mean, what does it matter?'

Still she will not look at him. Her gaze is fixed over his head.

'It matters,' she says.

He tries again, gently, his hands out, palms upwards, pleading.

'They thought you'd prefer a woman,' he says.

'Well I'm sure we all know why,' she snaps.

It confuses him now, her firmness. He begins, hesitantly, 'Look, Alice . . . I don't know how to say this . . . What I mean is . . . you're not doing this for me, are you? Because of what I told you last night?'

A small pink flush rises up over her face. She looks away and when she looks back her expression is wintry and haughty.

'How typical of a man,' she says. 'To be so presumptuous. Let me put your mind at rest.' She takes a cigarette from a packet, lights it up with great deliberation before him.

'I'm not doing this because you happen to be in trouble with your paper. You told me yourself you don't deserve any sympathy and I agree with you. I loathe your paper. The fact that I'm about to make a great deal of money out of it does not alter my opinion of it one jot. It stinks. It's sexist, racist and largely responsible for keeping in power a government which I abhor. Now, I don't know why you work for it because, for what it's worth, you don't seem to me to fit in. But you do work for it and, as you say, you make a great deal of money working for it, so I certainly wouldn't waste any sympathy on you. I don't feel sorry for you at all. I do, however, trust you.'

She had risen to her feet as she spoke. Now she paces up and down before him.

'It hasn't been my pleasure,' she says, pronouncing the words carefully, 'to meet any Sunday newspaper journalists before so I have nothing to compare you with. But I must say you're not at all what I expected. Which I suspect doesn't go, for instance, for someone like our friend Stanley. I imagine he would be exactly what I expected. Now, you want me to tell you about Bernard and I'm willing to do that in return for money. That's the bargain. Frankly it's not something I'm proud of, it's not something I ever envisaged doing, but then no one ever offered me thirty thousand pounds before. Frankly, though, I don't want to be stitched up. That's the term, isn't it? I don't want my quotes "bent". And from the little I've learnt about this business, I think the best chance I've got of avoiding both these things is to do the interview with you.'

She sits down again. Stubs out the cigarette. Turns back to him.

'What I'm saying,' she says briskly, 'is I do it with you or I don't do it at all.'

For a moment he stares at her, then he slaps both hands on his knees. Suddenly, for no good reason, he feels brisk himself. Brisk. Capable. Efficient.

'Right,' he says, getting up.

He wants to say something: 'I'm pleased that you think . . .' Something like that. But her face has assumed a tight, defensive look so all he says is, 'I'll do my best to make the interview as pleasant as possible.'

Then, not realizing what he is doing, he thrusts out a hand; awkwardly, he thinks, cursing his own clumsiness, like a commanding officer to a subaltern.

But there is no formality in the way she takes it. She does not grasp it in one of those thin meaningless English handshakes, instead she takes it in both of hers, one below, one above, covering it wholly with her own hands, working it gently between them so that he can feel their warmth warming his.

'Thanks,' she says, smiling.

But then, as if she becomes aware of what she is doing, she drops it sharply, lowers her eyes, clasping both hands chastely before her.

Walking along the corridor to his room, he goes on berating himself. To have been so cold with her, so formal, when she had been so kind.

Looking up he sees himself approaching in the ormolu mirror, a man stumping heavily along, rolling his head from side to side in vexation.

Like a bear with a sore head.

Twice, in as many days, he finds himself laughing. He casts his eyes instinctively heavenward.

'What the hell's happening, Malone?' he says.

'WHY DO PEOPLE do it?' she had asked him last night. 'Sell their stories.'

'Well, there's the money, of course,' he had answered, 'and then the publicity . . .'

Clive had called her to apologize.

It was two weeks ago. She wouldn't have known about the interview but for the fact that she had gone into her newsagents to pay her bill and there on the counter was a pile of tabloids with a picture of the pair of them staring up at her, all beads and bangles and sixties hair and her in the silly peasant smock with the lace trim that she used to wear on stage.

The headline over the top said, 'Soap Star's Wife Was "Frigid" Says Comic Clive'.

At first Clive was humble on the phone. He said, 'I don't know how it happened, Alice. They got me pissed. Put words in my mouth. I thought I was there to talk about the new show.'

There was always a new show with Clive.

Clive had a show once. Six half-hours on local television shown so late that they were only succeeded by the epilogue. Ever since, according to Clive, some producer somewhere was always promising something better. In the meantime he went on crossing the country three times a week, appearing at folk clubs and festivals and anywhere else where people could still be relied upon to fall about merely at the mention of the words 'fucking' and 'farting'.

'Got to liven up the act, Alice,' Clive had said when he first started to tell jokes between the songs. They'd progressed from busking in the market-place by this time and were playing the folk clubs. Clive called himself their agent and spent all day on the phone. He insisted they have publicity material printed, including a photograph, the same one that twenty years later he had given to the newspaper.

The main topic of Clive's jokes, she soon found out, was her.

He liked to make jokes about her cooking, which was funny because, as it happened, she cooked for him every night, he being unable to boil an egg. And then he liked to make jokes about her driving, which was funny too because it was she who drove them in the van full of gear to gigs all over the country, often after a day in the office, and then home again afterwards, all this without an accident. Because, of course, Clive had no licence. And then, of course, he liked to make jokes about her love-making. He liked to say things like, 'Alice thinks fellatio is an Italian ice-cream,' and that was funniest of all because in bed he thrashed and groaned and rolled his eyes and thrust his fingers into her hair and said, 'God, no one sucks my cock like you do, Alice.'

What was deeply unfunny though was that Clive point-blank refused to return the favour.

Clive's contribution to her pleasure was a cursory pre-penetrative fidget with his finger followed by a long bout of pounding away to no good purpose inside her.

When she tried to raise the matter with him he

said stiffly, 'I'm sorry, Alice, I just don't like the smell. That's an end of it.' And so it was. For these were early days with early definitions of pleasure.

Clive said, 'Look, Alice, the fact is that the most pleasurable thing for the average male is to have his cock inside a woman's cunt. So the obvious logical assumption is that this must be the most pleasurable thing for a woman too. Because if it's not then nature must be wrong. And that can't be right. So if a woman can't have an orgasm then there must be something wrong with her.'

'But I can have an orgasm, Clive,' she said.

'No, no,' said Clive petulantly.

'I mean a *proper* orgasm, Alice.'

'Look,' Clive said kindly, 'it's not a question of blame. I'm not saying it's your fault. I mean it could be something wrong with you physically. Or there again it could just be the way you were brought up.'

'I see. So basically it's all down to my mother now,' she said.

But this was the early seventies and so she bought a manual and settled down to the study of impossibly aesthetic diagrams of impossibly attractive people attempting impossibly adventurous sex. And at the same time she also confided in her doctor.

He listened to her problem sympathetically and patted her shoulder and, reaching into a filing cabinet, pulled out a leaflet which he pushed at her across the desk.

And so it was that from that day forward Alice Potter from the typing pool worked with a frown upon her face. And those who saw it assumed that the tape she was transcribing was especially difficult. But it wasn't that at all. Alice Potter was frowning in concentration as she clenched and unclenched fiercely, in the privacy of her skirt, what the leaflet had informed her were her woefully lax vaginal muscles.

Lord knows how long, she thought afterwards, she might have continued had she not broken down in front of Rita.

'But Alice,' said Rita, 'it's the clitoris that matters to a woman.'

She stared at her best friend suspiciously.

'You do know what your clitoris is, don't you, Alice?'

Some nights later Clive was telling jokes as usual.

They had been together six years by this time although, of course, they never married. In those days it didn't do to get married.

It was the anniversary, by some twist of fate, of their meeting. It was also the first day of her period. She had helped hump the gear in as usual despite the fact that the pain took her breath away. Standing on the stage, smiling, she could feel blood from her Tampax seeping down into her knickers.

And then Clive started to tell jokes about her breasts.

She allowed the jokes about her cooking, she allowed the jokes about her driving, she even allowed the jokes about the way she made love. But the night Clive made the jokes about her breasts it was all over between them.

For by some quaint paradox her breasts were also her Achilles heel, and when Clive said, 'Poor old Alice. Her Living Bra ate her,' the stab of pain was so sharp she thought the joke must have engraved itself upon her heart. And while she was recovering, Clive hit her with another one.

'Alice's tits are so small,' said Clive, 'she has "this way up" tattooed on her chest.'

For the last time she stared out at the grinning and the howling and the guffawing. For the last time she stared out at the heads thrown back and the shoulders lifting and the beer dripping from laughing lips. Lifting her guitar slowly over her head, she walked off the stage and out through the door to the car, where she drove off, leaving Clive to find his own way the fifty miles home.

She was packing when he came in.

He was very drunk and also very angry.

He said, 'They were only jokes for God's sake, Alice,' and she slapped him hard across the mouth.

Clawing, spitting, scratching, they slithered out of the bedroom door and along the corridor like some strange amorphous creature from the deep.

As Clive became more violent she began screaming.

They were alone in the house by then except for a Zen Buddhist called Barry. She screamed, 'Barry! Barry! Help me! Help me!' flinging herself away from Clive towards his room.

With the lunge she heard the sound of tearing and, turning, saw the lace trim from the peasant smock come away in his hand.

With one last heave she was at Barry's bedroom door with her fingers around the doorknob.

As she grasped it, it turned. The door gave. And then was stopped in its track. She banged hard on it with the flat of her hand. But it was useless. Inexorably, she felt it being borne back towards her.

The last sound she heard, slipping exhaustedly down the door, was a small squeak of a bolt as Barry pushed it, furtively but with great firmness, back into its hole.

In the paper Clive said he taught Alice Potter everything she knew. But there were problems, he said. Frankly she wasn't that good in bed. He thought probably the truth was she didn't like sex.

'Why did you do it, Clive?' she asked him.

'I don't see it's any worse than you putting me in your bloody novel,' he shouted. 'In fact it's not as bad. Let's face it, that stuff I told the paper will be forgotten in a week's time. People will be eating their fish and chips out of it. But I go on for ever in that bloody book of yours.'

'But it wasn't true, Clive, what you told them.'

'Oh, you think your novel was the truth? You made me into a right chauvinistic asshole.'

'I'm surprised that you read it, Clive,' she said haughtily.

'Of course I read it,' he said. 'Fucking feminist crap.'

Friday Afternoon . . .

1

I T IS THE job of the novelist, she thinks, to spot the incongruous, the ironical, the faintly bizarre.

Were she lunching alone now in the dining room of the King's Head, at a table over there in the corner say, instead of here with the other three in the window, their party, she is sure, would catch her eye.

They do not, it seems to her sit easily together. They do not, for instance, look like friends: two couples who might have met on a foreign holiday, or on the social wasteland of a starter-home estate.

It would not occur to her, she thinks, casting surreptitious glances across the table at Octavia, to assume that they were sisters or that they had once shared a flat. And they are clearly of too disparate ages to have been at school together.

The same sense of incongruity, she thinks, clings to the two men. Something about them would tell her that Andrew McCartan and Jim Crane are not in the same line of business, that they did not meet in the office and form a friendship that overspilt into the squash club or on to the football terraces.

'I suggest,' Jim Crane had said, 'that you have someone come up here, a lawyer or a friend, someone you can trust, to go over the contract with you.'

'I've got just the person,' she had said with a smile.

When she called Rita the answer machine fired but as soon as she began to speak Rita's voice broke in on her.

'Where the hell are you, Alice?' she said.

'I'm in a hotel, Rita,' she said.

'Oh no,' said Rita, moaning.

'With a man from the Sunday newspaper, Rita,' she went on mercilessly.

Rita clicked her tongue. Her grief turned to annoyance.

'Oh what are you *thinking* about, Alice,' she said.

'I'm thinking about thirty thousand pounds, Rita,' she answered.

When Andrew came to the phone, she had him spreadeagled nicely, in an instant, over his own parsimonious barrel. She smiles, turning away from him, the memory still giving her pleasure.

'Oh I don't really think so, Alice . . .' he started. 'I don't think that's the sort of thing I would wish to get involved in at all.'

'Well I do, Andrew,' she said. 'You've always claimed that I don't need an agent, that you could take care of everything, well now I need you to take care of this.'

He gave in without grace.

'Very well, Alice,' he said coldly.

There was a stiff smile on his face when he strolled, with too much nonchalance, into her hotel room an hour or so later. He kissed her too warmly with a fatherly aspect and she saw immediately that he and Rita had agreed a strategy.

He took the contract which Jim Crane held out to him with thin disgusted fingers.

'I'd like to see my client alone for a moment,' he said frostily.

Sitting opposite her he linked his fingers in his lap thoughtfully.

'Alice,' he began. The voice was of one loving but

166

deeply concerned, the voice of one older and wiser. It was a voice she recognized as belonging to Rita.

'I'm not trying to dissuade you,' he said patiently, and then went on to attempt to do exactly that.

'Think of your literary reputation, Alice,' he said.

She said, 'I am, Andrew. Believe me, I am.'

He got up from his chair then; walked to the window. His hands were in his pockets. He appeared deep in thought. For a moment he stared out, then he turned and said, 'It's the money, isn't it, Alice?'

She wanted to laugh, to throw back her head and howl. Instead she said, without a shadow of a smile, 'That's very perceptive of you, Andrew.'

He took a deep breath as if he had made a decision.

'Look, Alice,' he said, 'I know the sort of advances which we offer are not, well, to be frank, not as handsome as some of our authors, you included, would like. And to be fair, they're not as handsome as we would like either. But as I've said before, these are difficult times. And frankly, Alice . . . given your past sales . . . well . . . to put it bluntly . . . it's an act of faith on our part even to agree to publish your new novel.'

At this point Andrew had raised his hand as if anticipating an objection. It was unnecessary. He was wounding her with every word but despite this she had intended to say nothing.

'Not that all this makes any difference,' he said. 'You know that we are deeply committed to your work, as indeed we are to the work of all our authors, regardless of its commercial success.'

He began to pace up and down then, staring at the carpet.

'However, Alice, I'm obviously concerned about

your situation, as any publisher would be. It's not easy financially, I know, for any writer who is not in the mainstream. Anyway' – he raised a tired hand across his brow – 'to get to the point, I think, even with our own financial difficulties, I think we could manage a slightly larger advance for your next book.'

He sat down and smiled at her in the manner of one who considers himself generous and expects any moment to have to raise a magnanimous hand to ward off effusive thanks. Her response, therefore, offended him.

'How much, Andrew?' she asked abruptly.

'Oh, I don't know.' He flapped a hand in the air in irritation. 'Obviously we'd have to discuss it.'

'But give me a clue,' she persisted.

'Oh . . .' he said. He grimaced. He whistled through his teeth. He reminded her suddenly, in all of these things, of the builder.

'Give me an estimate,' she prompted ironically.

'Well . . .' he said. 'Obviously I wouldn't want to commit myself until I've talked it over with the board, but I think we could up it to five thousand. In two stages as usual, of course,' he finished hastily.

She put both hands over her face. She began to laugh.

He looked disconcerted at first, then distinctly piqued. But it was her turn to be patient now and she shook her head before him.

'Andrew,' she said, 'you're offering me five thousand pounds in two stages with a year in between. They're offering me thirty thousand, in my hand, here, now.'

She stretched out her hand palm upwards from the arm of her chair, making a grasping movement in the air. It was at this his fragile hold on civility snapped.

'Really, Alice,' he burst out in exasperation. 'This is so disgusting. So entirely vulgar. You simply can't do this . . . thing . . . for money.'

'Indeed I can, Andrew, and indeed I shall.'

She faced him, coldness concealing her fury.

'It's my belief, Andrew,' she said, 'that money exerts a peculiarly persuasive influence that it does not do to underestimate.'

Her eyes bored into his. She saw his gaze fall before her.

'It's my belief, Andrew,' she said, 'you simply don't know what you can do for money till you've been offered the chance.'

2

REACHING FOR THE salt as he talks in a desultory fashion to Alice Potter, he ventures another low quick look at Octavia.

Her head is bent over her food. One side of her beautiful immobile face is turned coolly to Andrew McCartan as she answers him monosyllabically, not troubling to hide her boredom.

As he lifts the salt, Octavia reaches for the pepper. Their hands collide. She looks up, raises a thin sardonic eyebrow. The smile that she smiles is dry and cool and amused and her eyes are a clear, deep, unwavering blue.

To his irritation, a long slow blush rises up from his neck, suffusing his face.

'The editor's blue-eyed girl.'

It was what Bullerman had called her. He snorts, silently, staring down at his steak.

When he had told Bullerman, with a certain embarrassed pride, that Alice Potter insisted that he, Crane, do the interview, Bullerman had started to chuckle.

'Oh dear, oh dear, Crane,' he said, 'and her supposed to be a dyke too. Well there, you never can tell.'

He spoke slowly, with obvious enjoyment, his voice rich with the satisfaction of someone else's misfortune.

'You see the thing is, Crane,' he said, 'there's something I think you should know about Octavia. She's a good operator. Professionally speaking – and personally as well, so I've heard – she doesn't take

170

any prisoners. She's also what you might call being groomed for stardom. So I think I'll just leave it to you to break the bad news to her that Alice Potter will only talk to you. Or what you could do, Crane – and frankly, I think I'd recommend this for all our sakes – is you could go back to our Miss Potter and have another word with her, tell her, in short, that we're calling the shots, that we decide who does the interview and if she wants the cash then she does the interview with Octavia or she doesn't do it at all.'

' "Octavia"?' he said angrily to Bullerman. 'What sort of a bloody name is that anyway?'

'It's features, man,' said Bullerman. Suddenly the wicked delight had all fallen away and the voice, down the line, was very bitter.

'Times change, Crane,' he said. 'Or hadn't you noticed? It's all fancy degrees in features now, with fancy names to go with them. Like Octavia. Daddy's something big in the City. Very influential too, so I understand, in the corridors of power. Has the ear apparently of the Prime Minister. Another reason why she's the editor's blue-eyed girl. All things considered, best not to disappoint our friend Octavia I'd say, Crane.'

It was then that the knock had come. He shouted, 'Come in,' and there she was, standing in the doorway before him. He stared at her, mesmerized. For one brief moment he thought he must be hallucinating.

'Octavia Eagleton,' she said, thrusting out a hand and advancing across the room towards him with a dazzling smile showing the small white pointed teeth he remembered so clearly. 'I called you from the lobby but your phone was engaged so I just came on up. It was an easy journey. I got here quicker than I thought.'

171

Lowering the phone to the cradle, forgetting to say goodbye to Bullerman, he stammered his introductions. He moved towards her, his hand outstretched too, but in his confusion tripped on a small ruck in the carpet and almost went sprawling in front of her.

Going through the formalities, settling her down, ordering her coffee, he felt like a man trying to drag himself out of a dream.

'There's just one small problem, Octavia,' he told her, pouring from the silver jug.

He was determined, more than ever now, to do the interview with Alice Potter. He liked Alice Potter. Hadn't he been saying as much to Malone? Now, more than ever, he did not think she should have to face Octavia Eagleton.

'It's crazy of course,' he told her, off-handedly, lifting his cup to his lips, 'but she's quite adamant. She feels she's got to know me, you know how it is. The problem is, frankly, we can't blag her like we could the average punter. I mean she's not our usual socio-economic class, if you understand me, and she's not going to be talked into anything she doesn't want to do. And the thing is, we don't really have time to argue anyway. So I think, if you agree, we should play ball with her. I suggest I do the interview then you and I can write it up together afterwards. You can file it and no one will ever know the difference.'

'And Alice Potter?'

She looked at him. A smile played about her lips. It was there the whole time, he noticed, that cold smile, as if she found the world permanently amusing.

'Well . . . by tomorrow it's too late. And I don't figure that she's really going to bother once it appears

172

in the paper and she's on the way to getting the cheque in her hot little hand.'

What was he betting on with Octavia Eagleton? A certain languid quality? Yes, that was it, that certain absolute indifference to the rest of the world he had seen in her eyes that night.

Sitting opposite her in his room, she had stared at him, pursing her lips. Then she had lifted a packet of cigarettes from her handbag, those long thin black cigarettes fashionable at the moment with a certain sort of woman. She pulled one out with her very white red-tipped fingers and flicked a heavy gold lighter at its end.

Looking at her, the eyes cast down over the lighter, he had marvelled again at the extraordinary perfection of her, at the tone of the skin and the perfect smooth lips, at the sheen of the long golden hair held back now with a black velvet band, at the long legs, folded one over the other in their dark shining tights.

Raising her head, she stared at him through the smoke, her tongue pushing out her cheek as she considered him. Her eyes were the same astonishing clear blue as he remembered, unashamed, unwavering and empty of all expression.

The small chill smile widened a fraction. Her shoulders twitched in an elegant shrug.

'No problem,' she said.

She stretched her arms up in the air luxuriously and yawned.

'As a matter of fact,' she said, 'I had a fairly rough night last night. I could do with a bit of a kip.'

'Help yourself,' he had told her, with a jerk of the head at the bed.

He walked out lost in the contemplation of what precisely a rough night might mean to Octavia.

Reaching for more vegetables, careful not to catch her eye, he thinks that if their meeting was a battle of wits, then unquestionably it was she who had won it.

He was the one who had fumbled and flushed, overcome by the memory, while not the tiniest flicker had so far disturbed her composure.

Staring down now, at his steak, he tries again to reason it out.

She must recognize him. She must do. She looked directly at him that night as he stood in the shadows. She must have seen him for she smiled at him, that awful smile, the smile that dripped blood. It was for him, like a puppet-master, she had spun the chair round, revealing for him his editor, *post flagrante*.

Yes, he was sure that she knew. He was sure that she was playing with him now, just the way she played with the editor, the way she probably played with everyone.

She was beautiful, so beautiful. She was beautiful and clever and fearless but more important than all of these things she was entirely indifferent. A formidable combination. She would go far.

'Look in their eyes,' Sally had said. 'There's nothing there.'

The editor's blue-eyed girl.

A chuckle rises up inside him. He smiles a smile of his own.

God help him, he thinks now with relish.

SHE GOT A postcard from Madeline. It said, 'Sorry, Alice, I needed the money.'

It said, 'I just told them what they wanted to hear, Alice.'

She did not know why Gerald took the paper for he railed against it regularly each Sunday. 'Disgraceful,' he would say. 'The way they intrude on people's lives.'

This particular Sunday morning though, he tapped with it nervously upon the kitchen door.

'I think you should see this, Alice,' he said.

The Honourable Madeline Tarrant lay across the centre pages, trussed up in black leather. Boots with very high heels encased her legs to her thighs, while her breasts trembled gently over her tightly laced belly. Her hair was long, matt black, lying in points and darts about her face. Her eyes slanted out to her temples and her lips were bee-stung with blood. In one hand, its lash delicately fingered by the other, lay a long, thin, pearl-handled whip.

She looked beautiful, like a perverted principal boy, all things to all men and all women too, chaste and at the same time outrageously sexual, androgynous but absolutely female.

'The girl's a whore,' Gerald said, outraged, peering over her shoulder.

'No,' she said. 'She's a dominatrix. It's different.'

'Well anyway,' he said, 'I don't know how she can

do it. I mean her father's a fourth cousin of the Queen.'

Falls from grace by the aristocracy affected him deeply.

For a few moments Gerald paced the kitchen floor deep in thought. Then he cleared his throat and raised his chin in the manner of a man about to make a speech of some importance.

'Alice,' he said, 'the fact is . . . these things they're saying about you . . . I don't know . . . I don't care . . . It's your business . . . all of it. What I mean to say is it makes no difference to me . . . to us . . . next door.'

He said it all so stiffly, looking out deliberately through the kitchen window, as if to spare her pain or embarrassment. She had got up from her chair, deeply moved, and hugged his back gently.

'Thank you, Gerald,' she said.

He turned, putting his heavy awkward arms about her in a reciprocal embrace. He cleared his throat again, overcome with the emotion of the moment.

'Well . . . damn it all, Alice,' he said after a moment in a bluff new voice, 'you are our neighbour, Alice.'

In the interview, which took up the two pages, Madeline said it had been a passionate affair. Yes, she said, Bernard O'Donaghue had been mad for her. He would tear off her clothes the minute she came through the door. They had sex everywhere: in the bath, on the kitchen table, once on the hall floor. He was insatiable. Six times a night. Seven sometimes. He liked her to dress up for him, black underwear, suspenders. Sometimes he liked to spank her. Once a girlfriend came round and they smoked drugs and all ended up in bed together.

176

Madeline said she'd been heartbroken when it ended. She'd come here, to New York, to get over it. She'd been out of work and then a girlfriend had told her about this job.

It wasn't a brothel, she said, it was a house of correction. Her clients were the best names in town, lawyers and bankers and real-estate men. Being English, they thought her a cut above the rest, and when she beat them they could call her 'm'lady'.

No, she said, there was no sex with the clients and anyway most of them were married and she didn't go to bed with married men. It was true, of course, that Bernard O'Donaghue was married, but then he had told her his marriage was over.

He hadn't been famous when they'd started going to bed. Just an out-of-work actor. She'd been a student at the time, lodging with him and his wife. That was the problem, she said. His wife. Alice Potter. The women's lib writer.

She'd come home one day, caught the pair of them in bed and thrown them out. She was jealous, he told her afterwards. Not jealous of him, jealous of *her*.

He said he wasn't surprised. He thought it had been happening for some time. He knew she was turning into a lesbian. It was the way she looked, the way she dressed. He blamed the meetings, all those man-hating books she'd been reading.

It was funny really, he said. You'd never have thought it would happen to Alice. Bearing in mind what she was. Considering how it was he had met her.

It had been strange recalling it all for Jim Crane.

177

It had been so long since she thought of it, that strange life, that half-life holding on by its fingertips to respectability.

She'd spent six months getting to Hong Kong. She went the way everyone went then, the sixties generation in pursuit of something, they didn't know precisely what, only that it had to be different from home.

'Iran, Afghanistan, Pakistan,' she'd said to her grandmother, holding the names up for her like jewels to the light. After that there was India and Thailand and Malaysia, Indonesia and the Philippines, no longer clear in her memory, just colours now, hot colours, deep green, deep blue, deep orange, deep dirt brown.

When she flew into Hong Kong it sparkled beneath the plane and burnt a deep, bleached white. She was used to the heat but this heat was different, rich and heavy and still, as if even the air itself had been squeezed out by the fight for life and space. When she stepped off the plane she smelt money and gasoline and food and hope, the heady perfume of mankind in pursuit of dreams and limitless possibilities.

She met Céline the first morning at a noodle stall when she already knew she would have to stay.

Céline introduced her to Patrick who looked her up and down, a doubtful sad smile on his face.

He photographed her though, put her picture in the agency's books, and surprisingly she did well, mainly thanks to Céline.

'Let them talk, Alice,' she said, the first night, and so she did.

She, Alice, found to her surprise that it was talk that they wanted, most of them – fathers, grandfathers sometimes. They wanted to talk about their houses and their boats and their families as if no one had asked about them for a very long time, as if no one had thought to say how well they had done to get them.

In return they wanted to ask her what a nice girl like her was doing in a job like this, because that was the way they wanted it to be, that was the vision they had of what was happening. They wanted to tell her how much she reminded them of their daughters. They wanted to steal chaste kisses, ache a little for a lost opportunity, part with a little sorrow and an over-generous tip to face a new and blamefree day.

She avoided the young men. They were belligerent in the main, she found, disappointed that the world's most exotic city had somehow so let them down that they were reduced, on the evening of their first night, to calling an escort agency.

They wanted romance; she saw that. They wanted life to provide a girl, not a catalogue. They wanted a simple twist of fate, someone small and exquisite, irredeemably oriental, to fall over their case at the airport. They wanted to stretch a hand to her, to lift her to her feet, to see her eyes turn upwards, almond eyes, dark as chocolate, warm and eternally grateful. And when she, Alice Potter, turned up at their hotel, well, it was she who had to bear the responsibility for life's abysmal shortcomings.

Yes, mainly they wanted to talk. Occasionally though, it was something more.

She remembered still, very clearly, the first time, the movement of the pale perfect ovals of his finger-nails against the dark suit.

Pulling back the lapels, he had plucked into the breast pocket and taken from his wallet a number of notes, notes of a large denomination, tucking them gently beneath her plate.

'Naturally I should expect you,' he said, 'to require some compensation.'

'It's my belief,' she had told Andrew, 'you simply don't know what you can do for money till you've been offered the chance,' and this she knew, from her own experience, to be true.

It was not just that it was a great deal of money lying beneath her plate. No, it was more than that. It was like the money that Jim Crane was offering her now. It was a great deal of money *for doing so little*. It was so astonishingly and pleasantly unearned. It was like a gift. It could be hers. It *was* hers already, by virtue of where it lay, beneath *her* plate, and she could lift it up, quite legitimately, and no one would stop her, and she could hold it crisply in her hand, and in the morning take it to the bank and push it under the glass screen in return for a slip of paper which would prove, for ever, that it belonged indisputably to her.

It helped that she liked him, of course. It was her one rule, if rules she had. He was silver-haired and plump and small and scurried on small expensively shod feet. He was rich too and successful, and better than all of these things, gently and engagingly courteous.

'I should be grateful,' he said, in his precise accented English, 'if you would think about it, over dinner.'

And so she did, feeling the silverware weighty in her mouth. She thought about it and, having decided what she would do, found it easier than she had dreamed, when the moment came, to kiss him softly, to help him take off his clothes, to lie down next to him and hold him and encourage him, and whisper, 'Yes, yes. That's good,' and afterwards to let him fall asleep in her arms. It was easier all round, she found, with the money in her bag.

The next morning, standing in the queue at the bank, it came to her that the world believed there was a line, some magic boundary or irrevocable divider over which you must pass. But there was no such line. Life, she thought, was a disappointment like that. It was like the equator. The sky stretched overhead in a seamless blue as you sailed over, the sea glittered beneath and remained unbroken and so the schoolgirl image of that thin black line girdling the earth dissolved and was gone for ever and you saw the truth. That the line was only there on the map.

She stayed in Hong Kong five years in the end. She travelled. Wrote her first novel, sunk down in the lotus-eater life that was the essence of the place. When she looked now at pictures of herself at the time she felt a peculiar sense of disconnection, as if the person were someone else. The person in the picture was thin and very brown with that practised appearance of someone whose money came from looking good.

The letter telling her of her grandmother's death arrived on her thirty-second birthday. After she had wept, she knew it was time to go home or be caught there for ever.

It was the last night she was working for the agency.

Céline said, 'Tonight is special. We shall do well tonight, Alice.'

'Darlings,' said Patrick, not to them but to the furs, running a heavily ringed finger along the rack.

Patrick loved the winter, the Hong Kong winter, blowing straight in from the steppes, sharp and chill but so short that sometimes it did not arrive at all so that Patrick, shaking his head sadly, had to send his beloved furs away, back into storage.

Each night Patrick would pat his jacket pocket and take out the key very slowly. He would pad to the cupboard in the corner on soft feet like a mandarin, to place the key in the lock where he would turn it carefully and throw wide the doors.

'My girls,' he would say, hands flung high in the air, 'are the best dressed in town.

'My girls,' he would say, turning with a flourish, 'can go anywhere.'

Patrick's furs were old-fashioned, minks and sables saved from duchesses and dowager aunts. Despite this he placed them with great tenderness around his girls' shoulders.

'You look lovely, my dears,' he would say, to them or to their furs, they were never sure which.

While they were out he paced the floor, like a worried parent, waiting for the furs to come home. He kept a small black register open upon his desk in which he ticked them off, one by one, as they returned, taking them from their necks, murmuring endearments, hanging them lovingly back in the cupboard.

He distrusted them, her and Céline, because sometimes they would disobey his instructions and take their furs home with them. He suspected them of tossing his beauties upon the bedroom floor, of trailing them across brimming ashtrays, of upsetting upon them glasses of brandy and boxes of face-powder, all of which of course they did. And sometimes a lot more.

One night Céline threw her mink on the floor of the hotel toilet and danced a wild fandango on it.

'Hey, Patrick,' she said. 'See I stamp on your stupid old stole.'

Another time, going home in a sampan in the early morning, with the lights winking on the Peak and the harbour blood-red from the neon, the boat full of Minotaurs gazing out over the water, full of too-long legs and tell-tale hands and dreams of sex-change operations, Céline, half-asleep, lurching against her, let her stole fall so that it slipped silently over the side, its end still caught at her back, and spread out on the surface of the water following them, a shining slick of sable.

'We shall do well tonight,' Céline had said.

The address was an expensive one on top of the Peak. An amah let them in, padding before them like Patrick on very small feet.

Emerging from the corridor, they came out on to a gallery with a large room beneath them. Glass doors led out on to a balcony and beyond that to the glittering Hong Kong night.

There were two men in the room.

One, crumpled and boyish with greasy hair and bad skin, came forward, rubbing his hands unctuously. 'Come in, girls,' he said.

The other did nothing, just stared at them silently, his glance sliding languidly between them.

He was very fair and very tall and very thin, a few

years older, she thought, than herself. He was dressed in a cream suit and was altogether so colourless that he seemed to disappear into the pale walls and sofas and light polished floorboards like a wraith or a ghost or a Victorian *gwailo*, the sort of Englishman for whom they might have first coined the phrase which literally translated became 'foreign devil'.

'To dinner,' he said, ignoring the introductions.

Without moving he stubbed his cigarette out in an ashtray on a bamboo table, lifting from its top a panama hat, a pair of white gloves and a silver-topped cane.

Placing the cane beneath an arm, he put the hat upon his head carefully as an old man might do, pulled on the gloves and, grasping the cane in front of him, stared fixedly at the pair of them.

'To dinner then,' he said again, this time with asperity.

'Jesus Christ,' she said softly to Céline.

Over dinner Céline played the whore, touching his hand across the table.

Lifting the cane from the table, he placed the tip beneath her chin, tilting her head so that the rich cap of heavy Oriental hair swung back like a curtain.

'Look,' he said. 'Skin like silk. Not a blotch. Not a blemish.

'Perfection,' he said softly, then, still staring at Céline. 'Let's dance, Alice Potter.'

'Let them talk, Alice,' Céline had told her. And so she did.

'I can get anything I want in this town,' he said, a cold hand at her back as they danced.

'I can get a ten-dollar blow job from a bar girl so delicate and so exquisite she makes the average Englishwoman look like a carthorse.'

Above their heads as they swayed stiffly, a glittering ball shot shards of colour down on to their faces.

'Englishwomen,' he said, 'are so dreadfully boring in bed. Prudes, of course, but the worst sort of whores as well. They'll do what they have to but only if the price is right – dinner say, or some bauble that they want, or a houseful of babies.'

As he spoke the last word his lip lifted in disgust. His nose wrinkled, as though he smelt one of them somewhere in the room.

'And then there're American women,' he said. 'Now American women are castrating bitches. Give them an orgasm like a good little boy or they'll string you up by your balls from the bed-head. It's all this women's liberation nonsense of course.'

His eyes bored into hers. He said, 'I hope you won't have anything to do with that, Alice Potter.'

'Let them talk,' Céline had said. And she did. She let him talk, his jaw working with the staccato phrases, his palm growing damp against hers.

'The system,' he said, 'has served us well. Since the caves. It's finely balanced. It fits together. Men and women. And now we're going to let this *feminism* overturn it.'

His voice had grown heavy with sarcasm; didactic, academic. But then, as if aware that he had exposed himself with his anger, he gave a light laugh.

He said, 'You should use your time here wisely, Alice Potter. It's an ancient tradition. It understands all about pleasure.'

He told her then things that he had done, things he still hoped to do. He murmured them to her like endearments, savouring the words as he said them.

Mocking her, he said, 'There's a lot you could learn.'

185

She stared him full in the face. She smiled.

'Perhaps,' she said. 'But on the other hand I don't see it as a major step forward, learning to smoke a fag in my fanny.'

It was extraordinary. She remembered it still. His face had contorted in rage. He dropped her hand from his. Pulled away from her, his eyes quite black with fury.

'You stupid bitch,' he said. 'You stupid fucking tight-assed English bitch.'

He spat the words at her. Others too. Insults. Obscenities. Around them, several couples turned nervously. Noticing the movement, he recovered himself but still she could see he was trembling.

Around them the music was drawing to a close.

'I must go,' he said, forcing another laugh. 'You must excuse me.

'My colleague,' he said, 'will look after you.

'Thank you for the dance,' he said. 'Such a pleasure.

'Enjoy,' he said, clicking his heels together in a mocking bow, your petty revolution.

'As for me,' he said with malevolent smile. 'The rest of the planet awaits me.'

Standing still in the middle of the floor, she saw him speak to the other man, who got up and began to walk across the dance floor towards her.

Leaning over Céline he began fastidiously buttoning the white jacket, at the same time whispering in her ear, whereupon she rose, picking up her bag and her stole.

Placing his hat carefully on his head as before, he gathered up his gloves, lifting last of all the silver-topped cane.

From the edge of the floor Céline raised an eyebrow

and waved. In curt farewell, he merely raised his cane.

'Don't even think it,' she said as the other man came towards her, crumpled and boyish, on to the dance floor.

Side-stepping his outstretched arms, she strode to the table where she snatched up her bag to leave.

She was halfway to the door when she felt a light touch on her shoulder.

'Excuse me,' said a voice, 'but I think you left this.'

It was her own twist of fate.

It was her fur.

The man holding it out was Bernard O'Donaghue.

4

THEY HAD WORKED for two hours before lunch, he and Alice Potter.

They sat opposite each other in her room, he with his notebook on his lap, Octavia's tape-machine hissing gently and clicking on the coffee table between them.

Walking back up the stairs now to start work again, she says to him, Alice Potter, 'They won't be able to sack you now, will they? I mean you've got the interview they wanted.'

'Oh they'll find something else,' he says, turning to smile at her.

'But what will you do,' she persists, 'if they do eventually sack you?'

'God knows,' he says. 'Go begging to the local paper. Send out press releases for the Gas Board.'

'But surely,' she says, 'you could work for someone else. I mean what about the *Guardian*.'

It makes him laugh, heartily, throwing his head back. He tries to explain.

'Look, if I put on sackcloth and ashes and stood on the *Guardian*'s steps shouting "I recant", they wouldn't have me, although as a matter of fact I could beat the ass off any of their men on a decent news story. No, I'm a nasty tabloid man. I've got the mark of the beast on me. Anyway, the truth is, I wouldn't want to work for the *Guardian*.'

'What would you like to do then?'

'You mean if you could wave a magic wand?'

'Yes.'

'Well, actually, I'd like to be a chef.'

When he looked at his life, when he tried to search out something, one thing, that gave him pure, open-hearted pleasure, he found that it was cooking. It was the reason he'd had the idea for the pub with Malone.

He loved the whole process, not just the cooking itself, not just the rolling-up of the sleeves, the measuring, the stirring, the juggling, the watching and waiting; no, what came before as well, the settling down with the cup of coffee at the window, the making out of the list, the wandering and pondering up the aisles of the supermarket, the packing away of everything into the cupboards when he got home – rare pastas, unusual spices, anchovies, artichoke hearts. He hated empty cupboards just like he hated bad food.

There was a lot of bad food around these days – hotel chains, motorway services, sometimes even the best restaurants. That place where he had taken Malone, for instance. Eighty pounds for two and the vegetables were overcooked.

The worst food, however, that he had ever tasted in his life, possibly, he thought, the worst food in the whole world, was his mother's mince and dumplings.

He was thirteen years old when she'd gone away for a few days to look after an old aunt and had left it for them, for him and his father and Gabrielle.

It sat on the top of the stove, a grey mass in a Pyrex dish.

Gabrielle stuck a spoon in. 'Yuk,' she said, sticking her tongue out and putting a hand to her throat.

His sister was no admirer of their mother's cooking.

To this day he didn't know how he had the courage to do what he did, but he picked up the mass and poured it into the bin. Then he fetched down the cookery books his mother never used and searched out a shepherd's pie.

When he served it proudly at the table Gabrielle rolled her eyes and made smacking noises with her lips. 'Jimmy made this,' she said challengingly to their father.

By the end of the week he had managed a spaghetti bolognaise and a steak and kidney pie with passable pastry.

For her return he baked a victoria sponge, but when he set it down on the table she stared at it like a bomb about to go off.

'What's this,' she said in a very cold voice.

What came to him then was wisdom beyond his years.

He said, 'I got Shirley next door to help me make it, as a surprise. Well actually, I didn't do very much. Shirley did most of it.'

He looked away but not before he saw Gabrielle's eyes go wide with disgust. But his mother was all smiles. She patted his hand. She said she'd make a good little baker one day, that Shirley.

Several months later, though, his school offered boys for the first time the chance to do domestic science instead of woodwork and he came running home full of it to ask his parents.

His father said, 'Sit down, son,' and took out his pipe.

Thirty years on, he would still instinctively slink deeper behind his paper at the sound of his father filling his pipe.

Thirty years on, the sound of the fingernail scraping across the plastic lining of the pouch, the sound of the poking and the pummelling, still caused a small depressing sinking of his soul.

His father lit the pipe up slowly, puffed it for a moment, stared out into the middle distance in silence. In front of him his son chewed his lip and wanted to shiver.

Eventually his father took the pipe from his mouth and, fixing his eyes on him, pointed the stem in his direction.

His voice was very kind and very friendly as if he were trying very hard to be fatherly.

He smiled at him. He said, 'Best keep up the woodwork, son.' His father was good at woodwork.

'Cooking . . .' said his father ponderously. 'Cooking, you see, son's for women.'

So he did. He kept up the woodwork. He kept it up for three more years, till the day he left school. In that time all he managed was a pair of bookends and a table with a rickety leg that in the end his father had to finish.

To this day he could not put up a shelf.

Gabrielle had spoken out for him though.

'Chefs are men,' she said, fifteen years old and looking at her father with a new and peculiar scorn.

Gabrielle, two years older than him. Gabrielle his sister, his friend. God, how he missed Gabrielle still.

His first memories were not of his mother but of Gabrielle lugging him around, his arms around her neck. Life was so much easier with Gabrielle.

He thought the reason that he liked women was

because of Gabrielle. If she were alive now she'd be forty-five. He wished she was here. It seemed to him now that he needed her more than ever.

From the early days, Gabrielle had eased his way with women.

'Who do you fancy then, Jimmy?' she would say.

Helen Peters, who had red-brown hair that fell in a perfect bob to her chin and wore a John Lennon cap and a black PVC pinafore and who was the woman every man in the third form wanted to be seen with, only went to the pictures with him out of respect for Gabrielle.

'Bloody 'ell, Jimmy, just go ahead and ask her,' Gabrielle said. He was impressed at the time with the way Gabrielle was learning to swear.

When he wouldn't, couldn't, ask Helen Peters out, Gabrielle did it for him.

'Hey, our Helen, I want to talk to you. Our Jimmy wants to take you to see the Beatles film.'

It would have taken a brave woman, he saw afterwards, to say 'no' to Gabrielle.

It didn't do him much good, of course.

Helen Peters let him walk her to her gate, even proffered her cheek for a goodnight kiss, but that was the end of it as far as she was concerned.

She drew back from him under the streetlight outside her house and gave him a cool, unashamedly critical stare. Tempering it with a kindly smile she spoke the words that he thought should be chiselled on his tombstone.

'You're not very good-lookin', Jimmy Crane,' she said in rich worldly-wise scouse, 'but you're a nice person.'

He didn't dare tell Gabrielle. He was frightened of what she might do.

'She's borin',' he said non-committally by way of excuse, his young heart breaking, when Gabrielle enquired.

It was Gabrielle who had explained about sex. It was extraordinary how entirely without embarrassment she had been. They pored over the book she got, God knows from where, in her bedroom together.

'It looks awfully *difficult*,' he had said nervously in hushed tones.

'It'll be all right,' she said, grandly, with an air of experience. 'You'll like it when the time comes. It'll be easy. When it's with someone you love.'

He still wanted to talk to her about that.

Gabrielle. Gabrielle. Crazy French name his mother had seen in the credits of a Sunday afternoon 'B' movie. Gabrielle.

Yes, everyone was in love with Gabrielle. The fifth to a man. Fackers, the most beastly of prefects. Even Holmsey the history teacher who was as old as their father.

He could still see Gabrielle now, Gabrielle at the school fête, waist pressed against the barrier of the hoopla stall, skin like honey and hair drawn up in a pony tail, leaning forward, all innocent concentration, to throw the hoop, unaware the world around her watched with rapture the teasing antics of her drawstring blouse.

'Jimmy, Jimmy, turn down the television.'

The last words from his beloved Gabrielle. Her last words, all the honey gone from her face, bright eyes dull, the voice, which used to run up and down in the air like rippling water, petulant now and fretful.

'You're so noisy, Jimmy.'

And all this so short a time later.

He wanted to weep. He wanted to scream. He wanted to say, 'It's not me, Gabrielle. It's not me making the noise.'

He wanted to get up from the bed and push his head through the curtains and shout at them, talking and smiling by the beds. He wanted to tell them to shut up. He wanted to tell them Gabrielle wanted to sleep. He wanted to tell them to be quiet because Gabrielle was dying.

He wanted to tell them all of these things but he was frightened. He was frightened because when he got up there and stood with his head through the curtains, he wanted the bellow to come out deep and manly, like it did sometimes, each time to his own amazement, when he wasn't expecting it. But he was afraid it would not, that at this moment when he most needed it, this depth and this manliness, what would come out would be the other voice, the squeak, the croak.

He was afraid that at this time when Gabrielle most needed him, all that would come out would be a whistle, a whisper, thin as air.

He always thought of Gabrielle when his mother cooked Sunday lunch. He would see her face, the tongue out, the hand at her throat, would hear somewhere in his ear a faint 'Yuk'.

He hated his mother's Sunday lunch. The dreadful smell of charring beef, the belligerent crashing of saucepans, her absolute insistence that he and his father play the chauvinists and go down to the pub for a drink while she stayed at home and cooked the dinner.

When he used to visit them he would beg, positively beg, to be allowed to cook it.

'No no,' she would say, her eyes cloudy with the reassurance of martyrdom, 'you work hard all week. You need a rest on Sundays.'

Only when he and Janet started living together did she consent to forgo her duties. If he had to date, he thought, the planting of the first seeds of the disintegration of his and Janet's relationship, it would probably be that first fatal Sunday.

'Where's Janet?' his mother said, accusingly, as he hurried from the hall to the kitchen.

'She's upstairs, Mum,' he said. 'Studying.'

He tried to tell her about Janet's course but her face had gone flat and hostile. In the kitchen she began lifting pan lids and pulled on an apron ostentatiously.

'I'll give you a hand,' she said, her lips pursed in disapproval.

'There's no need,' he said, sorry to hear the irritation in his voice. 'I like cooking. Janet doesn't. That's the way that we work.'

When Janet came into the kitchen and made a joke about her and his dad going to the pub, his mother's face froze in horror. He saw her look away as though Janet had said something obscene.

Later his mother tried forcefully to help him clear away and wash up.

'It'll give you a break, dear,' she said.

'I don't like to see a man in the kitchen,' she said, shaking the apron out challengingly at Janet.

'Really? Oh, it doesn't bother me,' said Janet.

5

'NOW WHERE WERE we . . .' says Jim Crane.

He is fussing with the tape-machine on the table between them, setting it straight, adjusting his pens and his notebook. It amuses her, this certain preciseness about him.

'In Hong Kong,' she prompts. 'My simple twist of fate.'

'Ah yes,' he says. 'The night you met Bernard. I suppose we could say it was love at first sight?'

She ponders, considering the notion.

'I suppose we could,' she says, 'if we had the least idea what it meant.'

Bernard had called her up, three weeks ago now, the day after the interview with Madeline had appeared in the paper. It was the first time she had heard from him in the four years since he left.

'Alice,' he said.

To her astonishment he pronounced her name in a warm reverberating rush of affection.

'How *are* you, Alice?' he said.

It occurred to her that she was speaking to Father Dwyer.

He said, 'Alice, I'm in Edinburgh launching an anti-drugs campaign . . .'

She said, 'Oh, does that mean I can throw out your bubble-pipe, Bernard?'

His laugh was laced through with irritation. 'Same old Alice,' he said.

She had not been surprised when Bernard became the country's number one thinking woman's crumpet. Horrified, yes. But not in the least surprised.

She read somewhere that eighteen million people watched Bernard twice a week. She tried to imagine it, eighteen million television sets, in eighteen million corners, all with Bernard on the screen. It was like being a child again, trying to imagine the Milky Way. She gave it up in the end.

She had caught his début quite by accident. It was some two years after he had left and she was switching channels in search of the news.

As she sank down on the sofa in shock, the phone went. She picked it up, her eyes still on the screen. It was Gerald.

'I say, Alice,' he said, 'you'll never guess . . .'

'I would,' she said, 'I'm looking at him now.'

'Well . . . um . . . I'm sorry to say this but really he's awfully good,' said Gerald.

And of course he was.

After ten minutes of watching him, though, she rose to her feet, walked to the set and switched it off sharply. She had seen all she would ever want to see of Father Dwyer.

What she saw on the screen jarred her heart with sadness and longing, for what she saw there was a monster, a Frankenstein created by the wonder of television, the beautiful shell which she knew to be Bernard infused with the personality of the unselfish, idealistic, perspicacious parish priest.

Once, infuriated with his selfishness, she had consulted the thesaurus to compile a list of associated insults to hurl at him. She had been astonished at how many there were and how they all fitted Bernard. In conjunction with his astonishing selfishness, Bernard was self-indulgent, self-admiring, self-obsessed and utterly and completely self-absorbed. Through the medium of Father Dwyer, however, he was devoid of all self-interest, a messiah of a man, a man devoted to the needs of others, a man thoughtful, sagacious and utterly self-sacrificing, a man, in short, conspicuously the reverse of everything he was in real life.

She saw afterwards that there was something remarkable about Bernard's self-centredness. It was so immense, so wholly unflagging as to be almost noble, as almost to achieve tragic status. He was the linchpin of a small and private world that revolved about him, that left all other worlds entirely irrelevant, a world of one where nothing of note ever happened that did not happen in direct relation to Bernard O'Donaghue.

He was also, as was to be expected, astonishingly vain.

In the first flush of her love she had found his vanity oddly endearing. It amused her how he always stopped when passing a mirror to adjust something about his person.

He was fanatical about his appearance, capable of flying into a tantrum if his hair were not cut to his own satisfaction or striding from the house, as he did once, on discovering a shirt he wished to wear was still in the wash.

The truth however was that Bernard O'Donaghue had much to be vain about.

Bernard was beautiful. When that had been stated – and this too she saw afterwards – nothing more needed to be said.

Yes, Bernard was beautiful. Handsome wouldn't do, or good-looking. They were cheap cut-price terms for something that deserved only the finest, hand-crafted accolades.

Turning round to face him, that first time in Hong Kong, her heart had quite literally stopped. A weakness attacked the back of her legs like cramp so that she felt a sudden need to sit down.

Seeing around his lips the hint of a small smile that said he was used to having this effect upon women, she had snatched the fur from his hand.

'Thank you,' she had said stiffly.

But before she could turn on her heel again, the dark brown eyes with their astonishing black pupils had clouded humbly, the full lower lip to which she later thought she could have written a sonnet trembled and Bernard O'Donaghue, using the tools of his trade, became before her eyes a lonely traveller in need of a friend.

'Look,' he said, hands upwards in the air in a clever intimation of early surrender, 'I'm here all alone in Hong Kong. I don't know a soul. Please let me buy you a drink.'

Bernard O'Donaghue, she came to learn, could lift his fine, slim, aquiline nose in the air and smell a woman with a predilection for his kind of romance half a mile off. He was selfish and vain and, in many ways, completely vacuous, but when it came to the psychology of such women, he, Bernard O'Donaghue, had nothing to learn. And she, of course, was such a woman.

'The trouble with your mother,' her grandmother had said to her, staring sadly into space the day she left for her travels, 'was that she was an awful romantic.

'Don't ever be a romantic, Alice.'

By then of course, she saw now, it was already too late.

Bernard had arrived in Hong Kong from Australia. He was twenty-six, six years younger than her. He'd gone there after a couple of thin years in London following drama school. In Australia he'd ended up doing the variety of exotic labouring jobs in the outback for which the continent is famous, sheep-shearing and the like, and now, like her, was on his way home. Two weeks after they met, they sat side by side on the plane back to England together.

For three years or so, and this she could still not deny, she had been absurdly happy.

Such was the combined effect of his beauty and his charm, it took that long before the first flickers of doubt occurred, before she took the first ferreting little pokes of her stick into the bushes of Bernard's soul to see what might lie beyond.

The answer, of course, as she should have known, was nothing.

She remembered that first occasion. She came into the lounge one evening and found Bernard sitting, as usual, in front of the television flicking from channel to channel, searching for plays and films and soap operas, so that he might shout to her, wherever she was in the house, to come quickly and see this man or that, whom he had worked with or whom he knew, who, either way, was a mightily inferior actor to himself.

That night, watching the picture snap backwards and forwards, she felt a small, hardly discernible sickness in the pit of her stomach.

'Bernard,' she said, conscious that the words were momentous, 'we don't seem to talk much, do we?'

Bernard though was totally unoffended.

'Talk?' he said, taking a long toke from his joint in bemusement. 'What about?'

'Oh, I don't know,' she said, laughing lightly. 'Books. Plays. You know the sort of thing. I mean you're an actor and I'm a writer. We ought to be able to come up with something.'

'OK,' said Bernard obligingly. As long as something did not inconvenience him, Bernard always did his best to be obliging. 'What would you like to talk about?'

'Oh, I don't know,' she said, dragging a hand through her hair, aware with sinking heart, of the leaden impossibility of the conversation.

'Come on, come on,' he said, 'you're the one making an issue out of it.'

She pinched the bridge of her nose regretting what she had done.

'OK,' she said, with a sigh. 'Shakespeare's women.'

'Ah ... now ... right ...' said Bernard, swinging his legs off the sofa and sitting up facing her. 'Now, did I ever tell you about the time I played Orlando ...'

There were many joints, as there were many bottles of champagne. Champagne she found was Bernard's favourite drink. He had ordered it that first night.

'Champagne,' he said grandly, clicking his fingers in the air, 'to celebrate our meeting.'

When the bill arrived later, though, he found to his horror he had left his traveller's cheques back at the hotel.

'Don't worry,' she said, opening her bag.

At the beginning she said it many times, 'Don't worry,' as many times as she opened her bag. Eventually, though, she stopped saying it. Eventually she just drew out her purse or her cheque book or her credit card, for the words, she found, were entirely superfluous.

Bernard, she found, never worried about anything. And that, she found, was where she came in. She did the worrying. That was her job. She worried about how she was going to pay the rates and the gas and the electricity bills, and, in particular, about what she was going to do about the steady depletion of her savings.

For Bernard's acting career did not fare any better returning to his homeland than it had before he left. In common with ninety per cent of the acting profession, he was almost consistently out of work.

The season with the repertory company that had brought them north had come to an end when the first faint chill wind of the recession blew through the city hall.

After that there was the lead in a fifty-second advert for the local suite centre but not a lot more.

Did she mind supporting Bernard? No, she did not, not because she was convinced he was a fine actor – although indeed she told herself continually he was – but for another more subtle reason.

She did not mind, nay indeed she felt privileged to have the chance to pay the bills for Bernard because of what it said about herself, about the way it demonstrated, so clearly, how much more liberated she was than the rest, how it showed that she belonged to a new age, an age that had abandoned the old sex roles, an age when men were men and women were liberated enough to pay for them to be that way.

In short, she saw afterwards, she was hoisted, neatly and perfectly, on her own feminist petard; her liberation the leg irons which she shackled on, with a proud smile, in support of Bernard.

Walking past the new estates where women pegged out their washing and waved their men off to work, she would smile smugly and hasten home with happiness in her heart, secure in the knowledge that she was different, that she did not subscribe to this conventional, semi-detached existence; hasten home to gather her own washing together to take to the laundrette, moving around the bedroom on silent feet so as not to disturb the still sleeping Bernard.

In the laundrette, watching her underwear and Bernard's interweaving in the water, she would tell herself that she had never wanted a John Wayne.

And only occasionally, very occasionally, perhaps after one drink too many, or one extra joint, she would ask herself, trying out the thought, no more, whether a gingham dress and frilly apron would be such a high price to pay to have somebody else take care of the bills.

And so she and Bernard drank lots of champagne, and smoked a great deal of marijuana, and went out for expensive meals when they were depressed, and once – when the rain was sheeting down outside the window like grey gauze, and Bernard said, 'God I hate this place, Alice' – even jumped on a plane to Jamaica, and in this manner a further year passed away.

She continued to pay the bills. Bernard continued to be unembarrassed.

Her grandmother's legacy had been substantial. After the house had been bought there was still a pleasing amount left over which sat comfortingly in the bank, and to which she added the scraps she earned from her writing. Her first novel had now been published and she was working on her second.

Occasionally, unfolding a bank statement, she would be surprised, and even more occasionally alarmed, at the rate at which her savings were dwindling.

For several weeks then she would instigate economies, insist on wine instead of champagne, cook dishes from *The Pauper's Cookbook*.

Bernard treated the economies with fond amusement, agreeing to them as if to a game, and before long they would slip back into their old ways.

Then one day she got a stiff letter from her bank manager informing her that not only were her savings quite gone but she was now, in fact, overdrawn.

Which probably wouldn't have mattered that much to her, for at heart she cared about money little more than Bernard.

Except that close on the heels of the disclosure of the demise of her savings came the discovery that the man whose bills she had been paying had been habitually unfaithful.

6

'I SUPPOSE WE could say,' he had asked her, 'it was love at first sight?'

'I suppose we could,' she had said thoughtfully, 'if we had the least idea what it meant.'

He ponders the words now, waiting for room service to order some more coffee and cigarettes for her, the phone to his ear. Behind the bathroom door he hears the toilet flush, the sound of water turned on very fast.

She was right of course. It was true. The older you got, the less you understood what words like 'love' and 'in love' were supposed to mean.

Was 'love', for instance, the painful indignity he suffered with Sally? Was 'love' dragging a fingernail across a table-top? Was 'love' that leaden feeling in the belly? And did being 'in love' fade to 'tell the truth for once in your miserable life, Crane, say you don't fancy me'?

Had he ever been 'in love' with Janet?

When he hunted for signs of passion in their relationship, his and Janet's, he could find none. They met at a party, spent the evening together, found they had enough in common to meet again.

He had thought, in the early days, that they were alike, that they were the same sort of people, unadventurous, dull some might say, middle of the road, the soft left that Thatcherism exposed as apolitical.

After a year they were spending every weekend together, at his place or hers. When Janet decided to do a degree, it seemed logical that she should sell her place to save expenses and move in with him.

At first it had been fun. Lots of shopping and redecorating. Yes, that was it. Fun.

Janet liked gardening. He remembered one Sunday making lunch, staring out through the kitchen window. It was a hot day. She was standing in the vegetable patch in T-shirt and dungarees, her legs wide apart. She unbent. Wiped a hand in its gardening glove across her forehead. Catching his eye, she raised her small fork in the air. For one moment, just for one moment, he thought, OK. So this is it. This is happiness. It's not what you think because you don't know what you thought. But that's OK. This is it.

It was hard to put a mark down now, hard to decide exactly when things had begun to go wrong. In her second year of college, though, they had begun to spar, lightly at first.

'Trot,' he would laugh at her affectionately.

'Closet Thatcherite,' she would throw back in mock anger.

And then one day it had boiled over at Sunday lunch.

She hated having his parents to lunch. She did not care for her parents and did not understand his son's sense of duty, indeed she despised it.

He tried to explain. 'It's hard for them. It's only me now.' But still she banged the mats down belligerently upon the table-top.

He had come to dread the Sunday lunches because of her attitude. He knew he would spend them fielding provocations from both sides. He knew he would spend them soothing and smoothing over and drinking too much in the process.

He knew what was coming this Sunday when his father began to talk about a story in the local paper, an old woman robbed and terrorized by teenagers.

Trying to protect him, he butted in with the football scores but his father would not be deflected. The trouble was, he said, people didn't look after each other any more, there was no sense of community since they swept away all the old streets.

At the end of the table, Janet's lips drew into a grimace. He knew exactly what would be her tone. Offhand. Cutting. And so it was.

Yes, she was sure they were all *bursting* to have their old outside toilets back.

He knew, too, the exact nature of the hurt look that would appear on his father's face, and of course it did and he sighed for the sheer sad predictability of it.

His father said, No, Janet, no. You don't understand.

His father wanted to like Janet, he knew that. He had seen him lay a hand around his mother's shoulders when she wept about Janet moving in.

'Don't upset yourself, pet,' he said. 'They're not like us. Times change. They don't have to get married these days.'

Now Janet made his father feel like a fool and he, Crane, felt the anger rise inside him.

His father concentrated on his food. He held his knife carefully like a pen. He said, Well, reaching for the mustard, at least there was some decency around them old streets, some respect for age. Things were better in some ways, no matter how you looked at it.

She became even colder then, goading him. Oh yes, she said. Better then. That would be before the

National Health Service, would it? Before they got the yard unionized. When you never knew where your next day's work was coming from?

His father tried to stick to his guns. Of course, he said, some things were better. But other things had gone. Like what? she said. Like values, he said. Oh, values, she said, like Victorian values, you mean? Like children up chimneys, you mean, she said triumphantly. And down the mines.

His father was beaten. He shook his head very slowly at the mystery of it all, at the age-old working man's mystery of how something could be there so clearly in the mind yet somehow fail to make it out of the mouth.

If she had left it there perhaps everything would have been all right but she did not.

God, she said, a last scathing little shot, this things-ain't-what-they-used-to-be stuff is such crap.

His mother's head shot back a little with the word. He jumped to his feet. More meat anyone? he said, and he grabbed the carving knife and fork and at the same time looked at Janet, eyes pleading. Don't hurt them, they said. They're old. We know what they are. We could be like that one day. Don't hurt them. But Janet didn't stop.

Well, she said, I suppose this is the sort of rubbish that's going to win her another election.

And then, of course, his father rose.

Well maybe she's what we need, he said.

Oh my God, she said, throwing down the napkin. There speaks the life-long Labour man.

And then the knife came up, the knife like a pen, pointed at Janet. Why not? he said. Why not? It's not the Labour Party I joined.

Right, said Janet, that's it, flinging down her napkin, striding to the door, I have an essay to write.

Her eyes caught his as she went out.

These are *your* parents, they said.

Left behind, his father had wanted to apologize.

'I'll go upstairs, son, say I'm sorry.'

His humility caused a great wedge of anger inside him. Against her, Janet, but against his father as well.

He said, 'No, Dad,' sharply, and then, 'It's OK,' softer this time.

He said, 'She's working very hard, you know. This degree means a lot to her.'

'Aye, son. We understand,' said his father.

Then his father tried to explain again.

He said, 'I know we seem like old fools. It's just that you think you fought for something. You don't know what. You only know it seems to be slipping away.'

He laid a hand on his arm.

'It's OK, Dad,' he said.

Later he tried to talk to her about it. He sat on the bed, behind her back, his hands clasped between his knees. He said, 'They're old, Janet, for God's sake,' but she would not look up from her essay.

She turned a page and when she spoke her voice was coldly amused.

'Too old to vote if you ask me,' she said. 'When I see people like your parents it makes me think there should be an upper age limit for voting as well as a younger one.'

He exploded on the bed. 'Oh God that's so fucking superior. You really do think you're better than the rest of us, don't you?'

He began to pace up and down the bedroom.

'Actually,' he said, 'I happen to think there's something in what the old man says.'

She refused to lift her head, continued to make ostentatious marks upon the notepad.

'I'm sure you do,' she said.

'What's that supposed to mean?' he said.

'Well . . .' she said.

'Well what?' he said.

'Well,' she said, 'given the rag that you work for.'

'Oh,' he said. 'You mean the rag whose salary pays the mortgage and the rates and the rest of the bills so that you can play the trendy Marxist at university.'

At last she turned.

'That's despicable,' she said.

And, of course, it was.

The fall-out from the row had lasted a fortnight.

They moved around each other without speaking and the atmosphere in the house was like ice. Then they went to a party and came home very drunk and made love.

It was an odd, awkward, unsatisfactory coupling.

A car beam cresting the top of the hill caught her face as it lay sideways on the pillow. It had a flat, very faraway expression on it and something else, something around the lips. Distaste was it? Scorn?

'Janet?' he said uncertainly.

She turned to face him, her eyes empty. Then she pulled her head down to him and thrust herself on to him and shortly afterwards he climaxed unhappily.

The following month Janet missed her period. A few weeks later she found out that she was pregnant.

7

'AS A MATTER of interest,' says Jim Crane, 'have you heard from Bernard since all this started?'

'Yes, he called me up. It was about three weeks ago. He was in Edinburgh. He wanted to stop by and see me but when he heard I had half the world's press on my doorstep he changed his mind.'

She laughs.

'He was frightfully suspicious. He said in his best actor's voice, "I trust you're not going to speak to them, Alice?".'

What Bernard had wanted, of course, was to talk about a divorce.

'Now don't worry, Alice,' he had told her, 'you don't have to do anything, Alice. My lawyers will take care of everything, Alice.' He spoke very fast, something she remembered afterwards he had always done when he wanted to avoid a discussion.

She said, 'I'm not sure, Bernard.' It was wicked of her but she couldn't resist it.

There was a small silence. When he spoke his voice was very cold. He said, 'What do you mean, Alice?'

She said, 'Well, I think I might have to contest it. I mean, I think, bearing everything in mind, Bernard, I mean when you think that I supported you as a penniless actor, through thick and thin – even, as I recall, through infidelity – well, I think I should go for alimony.'

*

When her savings ran out she sat down and did what half the country was doing at the time, she sat down and filled out a form for a bank loan alleging home improvements.

Putting the cheque into her account she decided to celebrate and went shopping for Bernard's birthday. She bought some champagne and some cigars and what appeared to her a discreetly sophisticated silk tie. And then because he claimed the reason he was out of work was that he was missing telephone calls, she splashed out and bought him an answer machine.

As if to underline the strength of his argument, the first message on the machine was from his agent. The next was from Bernard saying the audition had gone well but he would have to stay in London an extra night. The third time the red light was flashing it was a rich throaty theatrical voice belonging to someone called Frieda.

Frieda thanked Bernard for the splendid evening, recalling for him, quite explicitly, some of its more erotic highlights. She said she hoped they would see each other again soon and finished with, 'Oh, by the way, you left that appalling tie in my flat.'

She played the message several times, the words causing small barbs of pain in her heart. Leaving it on the tape, with a note on the hall table to direct Bernard to it, she went to the cinema and to punish herself for her own unhappiness chose an obscure Polish film with sub-titles.

He was standing before the fire when she came in. She caught him moving into position a little too slowly, a little too late. The effect though, when he achieved it, she had to admit was quite devastating. He stared at her as she stood in the doorway via the mirror above the mantelpiece. He was smoking, lowering and raising the cigarette slowly. The wall lights lit up the pale gold of his skin, the gleaming brown hair that rose high off his forehead and the soft full pout of his lips.

'Alice,' he said, eyes burning, holding out his hands either side of him in a gesture of despair.

He said, 'I'm an actor, Alice. Sex doesn't mean to me what it means to other people. It just doesn't affect us, Alice.'

He said, 'We don't have to live like the rest of the world, Alice.'

It was crazy. Of course it was crazy. But she fell for it. It was the last line that did it. That wicked insidious suggestion that somehow she was more advanced than the rest of womankind. In that moment Bernard's unfaithfulness ceased to be an outrage and became instead part of their general scheme of things. In the same way that supporting him had become the necessary proof of her own emancipation, so too did an adult acceptance of his infidelity. This too, she saw, was part of living.

Later, in bed, her head under his chin, he said, 'I think we should get married, Alice.'

He said, 'It'll put your mind at rest. You'll know that none of this other stuff matters.'

And so, three days later, they were man and wife.

He made it seem like an adventure. That, too, was part of his art.

'Let's do it secretly, Alice,' he said.

And so they used register office staff as witnesses and disdained the formality of rings although Bernard bought a new suit for the occasion. He also booked their wedding breakfast in the town's most expensive restaurant. She paid for both with her Barclaycard.

As they tottered tipsily out of the taxi, Gerald, home early from the shop, peeped curiously out from behind a deep blue election poster in his front window. He gave them a cheery wave, and in doing so precipitated their first post-marital row.

'Fascist bastard,' said Bernard.

It had occurred to her before that Bernard's cavalier use of language was one of the more obvious manifestations of his vacuity. Now, muzzy with the beginnings of a hangover and still smarting from the size of the bill, the word dragged across her brain like a nail on tin.

'God,' she said in irritation, her key in the lock. 'I wish you wouldn't call him that. I mean if you're going to waste "fascist" on Gerald, what exactly have you got left for Hitler?'

Bernard, similarly over-blown with champagne, reacted in a predictable manner.

'Oh for God's sake, Alice, why do you have to be so pedantic? OK, Thatcherite. Bloody Thatcherite. Will that do?'

'No it won't, as a matter of fact. He can't stand the woman. He's a Heath man. Always has been.'

And so, seven hours after the marriage ceremony, there they were, screeching at each other in the hall.

Bernard flounced into the lounge to play with the television and she flew up the stairs, banging the bedroom door.

Lying on the bed, she saw that life did not play games when it wished to teach lessons. It had reminded her with awful alacrity of what she had been attempting for three days to forget, that the man she had wilfully and deliberately chosen for her husband, for no better reason than his physical attraction, was entirely without content, an empty vessel, a blank sheet of paper, hollow in the extreme.

'Wrong', she thought, was a solid, unambiguous, old-fashioned word. It stood fair and square and would not be gainsaid. It was wrong of her to have married Bernard.

She was thinking these things when Bernard grew bored in the lounge and, growing bored, fished a bottle of champagne from the fridge and came upstairs to make up.

He did it well. He had an aptitude for such things. One of the fundamental reasons for his success, she saw, was an absolute refusal in such circumstances to be rebuffed.

'I'm sorry, darling,' he said, drawing a finger lightly in a circle about her face.

Another, she saw, was that he had that talent, rare in a man, of using the world 'darling' with complete conviction.

And so she fell asleep in his arms, and for several months things went on as before, until one day, for so she saw it in her gratitude later, the Gods decided that enough was enough, and in their wisdom stretched out a divine finger, causing the first tiny fissure, the first small but significant shift to occur in their life together at Tanglewood.

She recalled still, very clearly, the morning when she knew that things could not go on as before.

She woke as usual with the pain and the thickness in her head and the sick feeling of waste and remorse in her soul. Beside her Bernard was a shape beneath the bedclothes. Around the bed, like offerings, or

215

droppings in a horseshoe, were the discarded clothes and the glasses and the champagne bottles and the ashtrays with the dumps of the joints.

Suddenly, as she stared, the sun came out on the other side of the curtains and made their pink linings glow, and then it began trickling through the gap, across the carpet and up over the coverlet.

And so she sat up and leant her head back against the wall, and closed her eyes, and felt the warmth rise up over her breasts and her neck and her face, and she said to herself, Busy old fool, unruly Sun, and when she heard the words echoing around in her head, she felt a catch in her throat so that she began to repeat them, over and over in her mind, and she felt Donne in her soul, smooth and golden like honey, and she felt him warm on her skin, as warm as the rays of the sun that were flooding now all over the bedclothes in front of her.

And she got up and slipped on her kimono and went to her study and wrote it all down, everything that she had seen, and having done so felt for the first time for many months the intense yearning that precedes good work, and so at long last, took up seriously her second novel.

She had been at it some three hours when Bernard surfaced.

He came in scratching his head in confusion.

'Alice,' he said, bending over her shoulder.

Poor Bernard. It was the first time in the four years that they had been together that she had forgotten to bring him his tea.

He came round to the side of the chair, got down on his haunches and put his arms around her waist. He laid his head, his beautiful head, in her lap, his eyes closed, yawning.

Stroking his lovely forehead, she was struck by a deep sense of melancholy at the absolute isolated perfection of the moment.

She wondered, one last time, whether it might not be possible to push aside all other considerations in the pursuit of this perfection, whether indeed it might not be possible to sell her soul to the devil in return for life, however pitiful, with Bernard.

With one last stroke she said briskly, 'Bernard, I've been thinking about everything, about our finances, and I think we should take in a lodger.'

8

'I T ALL SOUNDS crazy, doesn't it?' says Alice Potter.

Before him, she shakes her head, twists her fingers in her lap.

'I can't believe now that I married Bernard. It seems impossible that I could have done it. The thing is, I guess, all my life I'd built marriage up into something huge, something I was frightened to do. It had always seemed something that other people did, not me. Then, all of a sudden, there was this man saying, "No, it's not big at all. It's this easy. It's this unimportant." And so I thought, Well maybe he's right. Maybe this is all it is. Maybe it's the world's best-kept secret, that getting married is really this ordinary.

'Do you know what I mean?' she says.

Yes. He knows what she means. He knows what she means very well. Because it had been much the same for him.

It was a shock to both of them when Janet discovered she was pregnant. He saw now that they were both aghast, that both of them turned their heads away when they talked about it so that the other should not see their horror.

It was an accident of course. One of those absurd accidents. Janet was on the pill. A month earlier, though, she had slipped and fallen badly on the college steps and put her neck out. In a million-to-one chance, the painkillers she had been given had somehow affected the pill.

It seemed appalling bad luck, and both of them knew it. Yet neither, for some reason, had the courage to turn round and say, 'This is not what we want.' He saw afterwards that that was because whoever said it was also saying the relationship was over.

Then, a month or so into her pregnancy, he had found himself changing, thinking, Well? Why not? A wife and children. At last, thinking that this was the way, according to the world, things were supposed to be.

Their marriage, of course, he saw afterwards, was nothing more than a Band-Aid, a flimsy piece of sticking plaster with the impossible job of holding their lives together. Probably, he thought, it happened often these days. The marriage that was already over on the day that it was celebrated. A new and potent symbol of a disappointed century.

It astonished him, now, that he could find so little to say about it. They both knew it was a mistake. A strange embarrassment engulfed the pair of them as they went about organizing it. He was over-polite to her. She smiled too much back at him.

The woman registrar, who was grey-haired and kind, explained to them that they could inject into the basic wedding ceremony such things as they felt would make it special for them, such things as would give it extra meaning.

Sitting before her desk, they looked at each other nervously. They umed and ahed and in the end they could find nothing.

And so the ceremony was as austere and as heartless

as the post-modern architecture of the civic centre where they married; where, too, he thinks wryly, Alice Potter and Bernard O'Donaghue were wed; where all such as themselves pledged their lives so lightly together, sixties children, hurled into the great blue yonder by the slipstream of their own history, buffeted by the curious cross-winds that beset their pilled, perennially young, post-war generation.

A chill wind blew about the graceless concrete columns making them shiver as they posed for photographs by the dry, litter-filled lily pond.

They were a small group, a few of her friends, on his side just his parents and, of course, Malone.

Malone was his best man. He had bought a new suit and coat and yet still managed to look old-fashioned. He gave them a set of fine cut-glass tumblers as a wedding present. He, Crane, knew they must have cost a great deal of money. He was very moved by them. Janet, though, tried unsuccessfully to smother a grimace.

'Very nice,' she said.

At the small reception at the house after the ceremony, her friends were over-polite to his parents, his parents were awkward with her friends. In the middle Malone bustled, replenishing plates too enthusiastically, refilling too quickly too many glasses.

The bride and the groom, as so often happens, had both drunk too much. When everyone had left, they ended up quarrelling. About Malone.

'I can't help it,' she said. 'I just find him hard-going, that's all.'

The next morning he woke to a pounding in his head and the sound of Janet being sick in the bathroom.

Opening his eyes by chance, he caught her staring at him from the doorway as she returned to bed.

He closed his eyes sharply with the pain of what he saw. For both their sakes he pretended to sleep.

There was anger in her eyes and bitterness, but worse than both of these things, the most terrible resentment.

9

'I REALLY SHOULDN'T have joked about the alimony to Bernard,' she says to Jim Crane. 'I'd forgotten he has no sense of humour. He got frightfully pompous with me. "Well if you make difficulty over the divorce, Alice, I shall simply put in a counter-claim for unreasonable behaviour, and think how that will sound in court."'

'Unreasonable behaviour?' He looks at her, his pen poised over his notebook, smiling questioningly.

'Yes, I remember it was what he shouted at me the day he left. Extraordinary really. I'd just seen him leaving Madeline's bedroom in the buff and he's yelling at me about my behaviour. Something to do with the clothes I wore, as I recall, and the books I read – oh yes, and my dreadful new haircut.'

Beneath the photograph of Madeline stretched across the centre pages there were two more pictures. One was a snap of the pair of them, Madeline and Bernard, fuzzy, caught at a party with many other people around. They looked very handsome and very chic in a penurious, attractively down-at-heel fashion. There was a pucker of irritation though between Bernard's eyebrows which she could have told Madeline could only spell trouble. It said that here was not quite where, given everything he was, he thought that he should be.

The other picture, very small, scarcely more than

passport-photograph size, was of her, Alice. She recognized it as one of the ones Madeline had taken, the time they went to Greenham.

She remembered it as a strange sweet occasion, an occasion full of warmth and talk and images, at the height of their friendship. They had arrived there the night before for the vigil. It was very cold and very clear with very many stars.

They huddled in their sleeping bags, she and Madeline, against the airbase's perimeter fence.

'Look,' said Madeline.

She, Alice, had taken off her boots and laid them beneath a weedy sapling planted on a small mound.

Madeline pointed at them, smiling in the glow of her cigarette. 'It's like *Waiting for Godot,*' she said.

'Do you think there's anybody out there,' she said, tilting her head back and staring up at the stars.

'No, I don't think so,' she, Alice, had answered, tapping her cigarette on the ground. 'I think it's only us. That's the miracle of it. That's why I'm here.'

The next day, standing looking through the wire in the sun, she heard, 'Alice, over here, Alice.' She turned, laughing, and there was a click, and she was caught for posterity in the boots and an old donkey jacket and her hair half an inch all over.

'Takes years off you,' Madeline had said, watching her shoulder-length hair fall on to the floor.

It was extraordinary. She had liked it. It was soft like the fur of an animal till you raised it with a finger, then it stood up like stalks of corn, freshly cut, gleaming orange gold in the sun.

Madeline had been with them for two years then and in that time she had come to defer to her in matters of style.

When Madeline had first appeared upon the doorstep in answer to the advert for a lodger, she, Alice, had thought her very beautiful, beautiful in that quite new way young women were beautiful, when they pleased themselves rather than others before the mirror.

Madeline's own hair then was caught up in tiny clumps with slides and bands and dyed many different colours. Beneath it her face was very smooth and white, with black lines surrounding her eyes. She wore boots, and a very long man's mackintosh with a small leather bag across it, which she took off and hung upon the kitchen chair like a member of some people's militia.

Taking a packet of cigarettes from the bag, she lit one up with small, very young fingers. With the match in the air, she said, 'I'm sorry, do you mind?' and instead of objecting, for at the time she, Alice, had given it up, she found herself answering 'No' and 'I used to myself', and reaching down from a high cupboard an old ashtray, which altogether was strange, for she had firmly stated in the advert 'No smokers, please'.

She offered her coffee but Madeline said, 'Tea please,' calmly, without embarrassment, as if she were used to getting precisely what she wanted. An hour later, there they were still, the pair of them, eighteen and thirty-six, sitting over their mugs of tea, arms in two deep Vs upon the table-top, she praying that this Madeline would stay.

'Makes you feel young,' Bernard said some time later, rubbing his hands, 'having someone like Madeline around the place.'

But Madeline did not make her feel young. No.

Madeline made her feel old. Madeline made her feel like an old old woman from an old old tribe with some old old tales to tell before she died.

What happened between them, between her and Madeline, was nothing complicated, she saw afterwards. Madeline was young, that was all. She was doing what the young always did. She was testing the waters. First she tested them with her, Alice, and afterwards she tested them with Bernard.

They spent many hours together, she and Madeline, talking about books and plays and films, for Madeline was studying English. They would sit in her study, one each end of the old sofa, their legs tucked up under them, the old gas fire hissing. They went out together too, to the cinema, the theatre and exhibitions.

'You're always together, you two,' Bernard said once, looking up from the television as she came in from a fund-raising concert for medical supplies for Nicaragua.

'You know,' he said, 'sometimes I think you fancy Madeline.'

Looking in his eyes she saw something greedy and hopeful and boyishly over-bold.

'Don't be ridiculous, Bernard,' she snapped.

It was not long after that that things began to change.

She had become used to Madeline thinking quite the same things as she thought, so that when she disagreed one day it came as a shock.

'No, I like him as a matter of fact,' Madeline said too casually about a famous writer whom she, Alice, had been castigating.

She turned her eyes up to Alice. They were very

clear, very unfrightened. She smiled, as if aware of the moment.

'Well,' she, Alice, had said, 'we have to agree to differ over that one.' She smiled back, but down her neck crawled a slow chill of disquiet.

Suddenly, it seemed, the differences of opinion grew more pronounced and more frequent. Suddenly Madeline was no longer free for the meetings, the workshops, the demonstrations.

'I thought this might interest you, Madeline,' she said, holding out to her a book she had recently finished reading.

Madeline looked up with an air of boredom from her *Cosmopolitan*.

'No,' she said, looking down again.

'Oh I'm sorry,' she had replied a little huffily, 'I thought you admired her stuff.'

'She's a lesbian,' said Madeline flatly.

'Well . . . yes . . . but I don't think that negates what she has to say.'

'Don't you?' said Madeline.

She laid the magazine down then with an air of decision, sighing, at the same time, with a world-weary air.

'If you want to know the truth, Alice, I'm getting a bit tired of all this rad. fem. stuff,' she said. 'All this banging on about what you've been through and what brutes men are. I mean sometimes it feels like some sort of permanent Remembrance Sunday, always stripping your sleeves and showing your scars and wittering on about the wounds you got on Crispin's day.'

A mocking smile appeared on Madeline's face.

'"We few, we happy few,"' she said. 'I'm sure you've all had a frightfully terrible time' – her lips twisting over the words – 'and I'm sure we've benefited. But frankly we can't go on being grateful for ever. Times change, Alice. We haven't got your hang-ups and we don't need your angst. As far as I'm concerned, old-fashioned feminists like you are just as much dinosaurs as the male chauvinists you're always shouting about, and frankly you'll become extinct in the same way.'

Rising from her seat, she picked up the magazine and walked past her across the room. In the doorway she turned. Her look was cold and superior.

'The thing is, Alice,' she said, 'some of us have decided we just happen to like fucking men.'

Several weeks later she, Alice, was lying on the study sofa reading when Bernard came in.

Leaning over her, he nuzzled her neck in an erotic fashion. Without lifting her eyes from the book, she slipped an arm gently round him and locked him into her. Lifting a hand, he grasped the book's top petulantly and pulled it out of her grasp and, closing it up, flung it on to the floor where it skidded on the polished floorboards, turning full circle, till it came to rest, its title staring provocatively up at them.

'Alice?' he whispered in her ear.

He had slid both arms around her and was pushing her gently down on the sofa, when she laughed and softly ruffled his hair. Two years had passed since they were married and this was the way she had come to treat him, like a child, petulant and charming. For so he was, and so she had learnt to soothe and smooth him, warding off the petty irritations and the small eruptions of rage that were the symptoms of their disintegrating relationship.

Somewhere in the back of her brain, she knew that things could not continue indefinitely. She knew that if she were honest, she would acknowledge that the time had come to sit down with him, to say, 'Bernard, it's just not working out.' But every time the moment arrived, her heart would take the old back flip at the sight of the pouting lip, at the feel of the thick sleek hair between her fingers. And so she would draw back, feeling a little ashamed and telling herself, 'I'll do it, yes. But not now. Not now. Tomorrow.'

And so, thinking all of these things, feeling the old familar sadness, she ruffled his hair and kissed him on the lips and said, 'I have to finish this book, for this workshop I'm chairing tomorrow. I'll see you later.'

He stared at her for a long moment, then he lifted himself back from her, pursing his lips. Sitting on the edge of the sofa, he reached towards the book.

'And what is this great work of literature you can't be parted from,' he said sarcastically.

His eyes narrowed at the title. Opening it up, he read out loud, pronouncing the words very carefully, '"Physically, the woman in intercourse is a space inhabited, a literal territory occupied literally."'

He looked round at Alice, his eyes very narrow.

'Tell me something,' he said. 'Do you believe that, Alice?'

She smiled at him. She tried to speak lightly. She took the book from his hands. 'It's an argument worthy of consideration,' she said.

He got up from the sofa then and walked to the door. Pulling it open, he turned to look back at her.

'Extraordinary,' he said coldly. 'And I could have sworn you rather enjoyed it, Alice.'

The next morning she woke with a deep sense of gloom. It was one of those grey mid-winter days which she knew would refuse to get light.

She had not slept well. She had lain awake, against her will, waiting for Bernard to come to bed.

She had stuck her head round the lounge door when she finished the book and said, smiling, 'I'm off to bed, Bernard.'

He said, 'Fine,' without removing his eyes from the screen. He was smoking a joint and she could see beside him an almost empty bottle.

She said, laughing, with mock allure, 'Are you coming?'

He said, 'No,' and, turning to look over the back of the sofa, he said, 'Not in the mood for occupation.'

She sighed. 'Bernard . . .' she began, but then she stopped. His face had the blurred look of someone who had drunk too much, smoked too many joints.

As they stared, he lifted an eyebrow questioningly.

She knew that she should go to him, that whatever he was, she owed him that. She knew she should walk over, and sit down on the sofa, and say to him, 'It's an academic argument, Bernard,' and pretend to discuss it, make believe they had something to say to each other. But all of a sudden she could not be bothered. And staring at him, staying firmly where she was, she knew that he saw she could not be bothered. And seeing that he saw it, she smiled sadly, dropped her eyes and closed the door.

The workshop was at the International Women's Day conference and the subject was female sexuality. Afterwards she saw that the ironies had come thick and fast that day.

The row seemed to erupt out of nowhere. Suddenly they were facing each other, the woman and herself, angrily across the circle.

'As far as I'm concerned,' the woman was saying

229

frostily, 'lesbianism is the only serious moral choice for a feminist.'

'Even,' she was saying coldly in reply, 'if she happens to be a heterosexual?'

'Sexuality,' said the woman with a thin smile, 'is merely a cultural construct.'

'And political lesbianism,' she answered with a smile that attempted to be thinner, 'would appear to further construct it.'

After that, entrenched in their positions, they hurled cold unhelpful insults at each other. 'Collaborating with the enemy' ... 'Appallingly authoritarian' ...

Shaking with rage, at herself as much as at the woman, she made excuses and left the conference early.

Letting herself quietly into the house, she was aware of a strange silence, ominous, brooding, waiting with bated breath.

Slipping off her shoes, which were pinching, she walked up the stairs in socked feet. Hearing the slam of a door she looked up the stairwell. It was Bernard going down to the bathroom.

They looked at each other for a long moment. Then he smiled, a smile both charming and unabashed, the smile of a naughty little boy who knew he was far too beautiful to be punished.

He raised his hands in the air, one either side, in his old gesture of surrender.

He was completely naked. It was Madeline's bedroom door he had come out of.

Poor Bernard.

In their bedroom, he tried to do what he always did.

230

He came up behind her, tried to put his arms about her, draw her back to him. But she moved out of his grasp.

She turned to face him. She felt neither sad nor happy, despairing nor triumphant. She felt nothing except the certainty that at last tomorrow had arrived.

'Alice . . .' he said, in his caressing voice, making a movement towards her.

'No,' she said.

'Look,' he said, 'it means nothing, you know that. I'll talk to Madeline. She'll realize she has to leave.'

She shook her head, appalled.

'How gallant you are, Bernard.'

His eyes were deep and brown and appealing. He made the helpless gesture again with his hands, which is when she realized how impossible it was to tell when he was acting, how, more importantly, it was entirely pointless to try. The man and the actor, she saw, were one. They always had been. Before her now, he was putting every last scrap of his talent to work on his life, trying desperately to shore up the status quo, trying to circumvent a conclusion of appalling inconvenience to himself.

'Alice . . .' he said a second time, softly, reproachfully.

'Time for you to go, Bernard,' she said firmly.

For a moment they stared at each other. Then, in an instant, the soft reproach on his face was gone and in its place was an expression of barely controlled anger.

'You're behaving totally unreasonably, Alice,' he said, tearing a bag from under the bed and striding to the chest of drawers.

'Hang on,' she said, 'you're the one who's been going to bed with Madeline.'

'I see. So that's it.' His voice was icy now, utterly

matter of fact. 'Well . . . I can't say I'm surprised . . . I've always suspected.'

'What . . .?' She had furrowed her brow. She had been genuinely confused.

'It's as I suspected. It's not me at all, is it,' he said, not looking at her, taking piles of shirts from a drawer. 'It's Madeline. You're jealous of me going to bed with Madeline because you want to go to bed with her yourself.'

'Oh for God's sake, Bernard.' She was so astounded she started to laugh.

'There's no need to try and deny it.'

'I'm not going to. It's all so ludicrous I'm not even going to deign to reply.'

'You're turning into a lesbian, Alice. The least you can do is accept it. I mean look at that haircut, for God's sake.'

He was pompous now. He folded clothes neatly, precisely into his case. The expression on his face was of a man tragically hard done by.

'As a matter of fact,' she said, trying to make a joke of it, 'this haircut is the height of fashion.'

'Well as far as I'm concerned,' he said, 'it makes you look like something out of a concentration camp. It's totally unfeminine. And as for those bloody boots you wear –'

'They're comfortable . . .'

'– and those man-hating books you read . . .'

At this point he had gone to the door bellowing Madeline's name.

'You've pushed me into her arms,' he said dramatically.

'Bernard, this is absurd . . .' she spluttered, dropping down on to the bed. She was outraged, less at him than at herself for succumbing to a faint, but nonetheless clearly identifiable sense of guilt.

Bernard, meanwhile, had picked up his hold-all in a firm, equally piqued grip.

'I'm sorry you can't love me, Alice,' he said, 'I don't blame you. I don't hate you for what you've done. I love you. I made you my wife. It's you who's throwing me out. Remember that.'

Sitting down a few minutes later over a cup of coffee with the empty house still resounding to his cry, she could not help but think it paradoxical that in the space of a few hours she had been accused of failing miserably to be a lesbian on the one hand and turning into one on the other.

That night, tossing and turning alone in the large bed, she dreamt about the woman with whom she had argued at the workshop.

They faced each other across the desk, both of them in uniform.

'I'm tired,' she, Alice, was saying. 'Tired of stripping my sleeve and showing my scars, tired of saying "These wounds I had on Crispin's day."'

'I'm sick of crawling in the dirt on my belly,' she was saying. 'All I want to do is to come in from the hills.'

Rising to her feet, the woman walked thoughtfully to the window. She stood there, tapping a finger against her tightly uniformed leg. Raising her head in determination, she turned and smiled, pronouncing the terms of Alice Potter's reconstruction.

She said, 'I'm sorry. Alice. It's for your own good, Alice.'

She had never forgotten the woman. She felt grateful to her in an odd sort of way. It was because of her, after all, that she had come home early.

To the woman's surprise, she always greeted her warmly when she bumped into her at meetings and conferences. She made a point of addressing her by name, receiving, each time, a frosty smile in reply.

She had never forgotten the woman's name. It was an unusual name, she always thought, an unsuitable name, a too-soft name for a woman as tough and inflexible as she.

'Verena,' she would say when she saw her. 'Nice to see you. How are you, Verena?'

10

'V ERENA.'

He stares at her, his pen still in his hand, says the name sharply.

'Forty-five, fifty? Grey hair? Very handsome? Large earrings?'

'You know her?'

'Not exactly. She was . . . is . . . a friend of my ex-wife's.'

She is looking at him curiously.

'It's a coincidence, isn't it,' he says, to cover his confusion.

'Not really. It's a small town. Your wife sounds like a radical woman and we radical women go all the same places.'

'Verena,' he says, shaking his head, one last time.

He had been out on a job with Malone, deep in the heart of the country. He called the office. Bullerman had given him the message.

He did not know what he was wishing for as he drove silently, a little too fast, along the country roads back towards town.

'Go straight to the hospital, old man,' Malone had said. 'I'll get a taxi back from there.' And so he did.

When he pushed open the door, she was sitting by the bed holding Janet's hand. They looked up sharply as he appeared, their eyes turned up to his, making him feel like an intruder.

Janet lay back on the pillows. Her face was very pale. When he bent to kiss her he saw that whatever it was that he had been wishing for, she had been wishing for it too. He saw relief in her eyes.

'This is Verena,' she said.

For several weeks, after she came out of hospital, they went through the motions of pretending that things were still intact. He took time off work; insisted on looking after her. It was with sadness that he saw how she chafed at their incarceration together.

When Verena did not visit or phone, he realized that she did both while he was out. He knew when she had called, because when he came back Janet had a subdued distant look but she was marginally kinder to him. Love works like that, he saw afterwards.

In this fashion the marriage tottered on for several more months and then suddenly, with astonishing quickness, it was all over. He was drunk of course. How else, though, could he have done it?

It was a Friday night. They had been watching the television silently together. They sat in separate worlds, she on the sofa with a glass of wine, he in his chair with a whisky.

He stared into his glass. He said, 'You were relieved, Janet, weren't you, when you lost the baby?'

'Weren't you?' she said.

'I don't know,' he said. And honestly he didn't.

There was silence then, both of them knowing that the time had come, that one or other of them had to say it. In the end it was Janet.

'Look, it's not working out,' she said.

He felt a need suddenly to obfuscate. As though it were his job, as though it were his part to play in the pattern of their parting.

'I'm not sure what you mean,' he said.

'Oh yes you are,' she said, betrayed.

'I've changed,' she said. 'We've both changed. We have nothing in common any more.'

He grew angry. He needed to argue.

'People do change,' he said. 'It doesn't mean they have to split up. They learn to live with the changes.'

'Not these changes,' she said.

She said, 'Look, I don't want anything. Just my things: the plants, the rugs, my books.'

'Wait,' he said, 'wait,' and it came out like a howl.

'There are things I need to know, Janet,' he said and as he said it her face closed with a snap like a trap.

'Where will you be going, Janet?' he asked.

She said, 'I haven't decided. I may get a flat or . . .'

'Or what?' he said.

'Or I may just stay with Verena for a while.'

There was a long silence. She stared down at the floor. Then she said, 'I'm sorry. It's nothing personal. I just can't get from you what I get from a woman, that's all.'

He laid his head back on the chair. He felt angry; wildly, unreasonably angry. He wanted to rail at someone, at some unspecified shadowy person whose job it was to have prepared him for this moment.

'Well, how could you?' he said, hating his voice which was very bitter.

He got up to refill his glass. Walking across the room he felt a need to lance the conversation, to drain it of its drama.

'How could you?' he said again, pleased with his voice now, which was clipped and amusing and superior.

He took the stopper from the decanter, a farewell present from colleagues when he had moved back here. He felt it cold in his hand. He poured the whisky into the tumbler, one of the tumblers Malone had given them. He took comfort from these things, from the feel of them, a cold masculine comfort. And something else. Courage.

'I understand,' he said. 'Of course you can't get from me what you get from Verena. How could you? Men and women are different, Janet. How could a woman get from a man what she gets from a woman friend? I mean I can't get from you certain things that I get from Malone.'

'Malone?' she said, looking up at him. Now she looked amused. Reflected in her eyes he could see the image of Malone, the clothes that always managed to look old-fashioned, the smallness of him, his awkward deferentiality in her presence. He felt a sudden rush of dislike for Janet.

'Of course,' he said, 'Malone. But perhaps that's not what you mean.'

'I'm sorry?' she said.

He said, 'Perhaps there's something else you can get from Verena that you can't get from me.'

He knew that things were becoming dangerous. He also knew he was unable to stop.

She became very cool, very scornful.

'There are, as a matter of fact. I won't go into details. I'm sure you've had lots of fun imagining them already.'

He was outraged.

'How dare you?' he said.

She rose and put her glass down on the table-top.

She said, 'There's no point in continuing this conversation. I'm going upstairs.'

He shouted at her, 'No,' and then, 'No!' again, harsher, louder.

'We haven't finished,' he said, putting a hand to his head.

Afterwards he wondered how a man could see a cliff, how he could see the blue above him and the long sweep of white beneath him and, yet further below, the deep aquamarine at the bottom. He wondered how a man could see all of these things and still make a dash for the edge.

'How long?' he said.

'How long what?' she said, turning.

'You know,' he shouted, 'you know,' and with the words he banged a fist down hard upon the arm of the chair.

'What does it matter?' she said.

'It matters,' he snapped.

'How long,' he said, 'have you been making love with me and hating it?'

'I didn't hate it,' she said. She wouldn't look at him.

'There was nothing *wrong* with it,' she said, 'if that's what you're worried about.'

The sarcasm in her voice tore into him. She sounded as though she were enjoying the words.

'The earth didn't move for me in the manner that your friend Hemingway liked to make out that it did. But then it never moved with any other men either and, like most women, I never expected it to. It's not a big deal. I just found out, in the end, it wasn't what I wanted.'

'You could have told me that, Janet.' His voice was cold and quiet with fury. 'You could have told me that it wasn't what you wanted. You could have told me what you did want. You could have had the decency to tell me where I was going wrong, told me how I might put it right. How I might please you.'

'Oh for God's sake!'

She shouted it at him. It astonished him. That she should find the suggestion that they might have talked this way so offensive.

'Tell me, Janet,' he said. 'Why are women so proud of the fact that they can fake it? Because they are proud of it, aren't they? I've heard them talk. Why would they rather fake it than tell a man what it is they want? Is it because they enjoy making fools of men? Tell me, is that it?'

He was very drunk of course, he could hear it in his voice, but the certain madness in him, he also knew, had nothing to do with the alcohol.

'Yes that's it, isn't it,' he told her, gloating. 'It's the power, isn't it?'

'Oh Christ,' she said. 'Don't talk to me about power.' Turning round, she spat the words at him.

'You want to talk about power. I'll tell you about power. Power is some bastard pounding away on top of you not giving a damn if you're having a good time.'

'Some bastard, some bastard?' he said. 'Hey. Come on, Janet. Let's name names here. That's me you're talking about up there.'

Oh how the hate had whirled about inside him. How the fingers of it clutched and unclutched at him as he stood there before her.

He ached all through. He wanted to moan, sob, lift his head in the air like a dog.

240

He wanted to spread his hands out, in the air, either side of him, in desperation.

He wanted to say, 'I'm not a fish, Janet. I can't scatter my sperm on the sea-bed.'

He wanted to say, 'I'm sorry sex has to be this way and that it doesn't suit you, but it's not my fault. I'm just a man, Janet. I didn't design the system. I just live by it, that's all.'

He wanted to say all of these things but he never got the chance because at that moment the phone rang and, when he picked it up, naturally enough, it was Verena.

Janet said, 'I'll take it upstairs,' and left the room without looking at him. When she did not come down again he went upstairs to find her. Pushing open the bedroom door, he found her packing.

'I might as well go tonight,' she said, and he did not argue.

The taxi was outside the gate when she came to say goodbye. She stood by his chair as he stared into the fire, very drunk and very angry.

Many obscenities, he thought afterwards, had passed between them, but what she said in parting was the worst.

When she said it, he looked up at her in disgust.

'There's no reason why we can't be friends,' she said.

11

'I COULDN'T KEEP it up any longer in the end, kidding him about the divorce,' she says, laughing across at Jim Crane. 'It was just painful. He was getting himself in a frightful state. Like I said, Bernard has no sense of humour. In the end I said, "Just kidding, Bernard. Of course I'll give you a divorce."'

Bernard had clicked his tongue like a parent when she said it.

'Oh *Alice*,' he said.

He had become conversational then, as if she were his best friend, his older sister.

'Of course we want to get married as soon as possible,' he said, 'with Zoë being pregnant. It's twins, you know.'

'Zoë?' she said. 'I thought her name was Mercy.'

'Really, Alice' – his voice was fond as he explained – '"Mercy" is the name of her character, Mercy Hellman, the neighbourhood lawyer. We had an affair, you know. In the series. I almost renounced the priesthood. That's why there's all the fuss.'

His voice said he could afford to be amused.

'Are you the *only* person in the country who doesn't watch the thing, Alice?'

She thought she might be from what she read.

'Is it true that you get two thousand fan letters a week, Bernard?'

'Yes, I'm afraid so. Absurd isn't it?' His sigh was entirely self-satisfied.

'Oh by the way, Bernard,' she said, as the conversation was drawing to a close, 'from what Madeline said in the paper, it appears you told her that nasty little story about me being a lesbian, presumably as part of your strategy to get her into bed.'

He began to bluster. 'Absolutely disgusting, Alice . . . You can't possibly think, Alice . . . I've instructed my solicitors to sue, Alice . . .' But then she started to laugh and he gave in.

'Well looking back, I suppose I might have said something . . .' he said.

Saying goodbye, he added affectionately, 'I never asked you, Alice. Is everything all right with you . . . with the old place and everything?'

'Not really,' she said. 'The roof's leaking and the pointing's gone and apparently my gable end is likely to come crashing down at any minute.'

There was a small silence. For one brief moment she thought he might offer her money. Then he said briskly, 'A second mortgage, Alice. That's what you need. To pay for the repair. I've got an awfully good chap I could introduce you to . . .'

She said, 'Thank you, Bernard.

'By the way, Bernard,' she said. 'They're offering me thirty thousand pounds to tell the story of our marriage.'

From the other end of the line there was a sigh.

He said, 'Be merciful, Alice.'

Madeline, standing on the doorstep, several coats over her arm and a bag in her hand, had turned coolly to her, the taxi throbbing and Bernard yelling from the gate.

'Don't think I don't know what you're doing, Alice,' she said. 'The broken-hearted wife bit may fool Bernard but it doesn't fool me.'

She gave her a deeply knowing smile.

'You've wanted this all along, haven't you, Alice?'

Leaning back against the closed door, she wondered if it were true. She wondered if it were possible that she had somehow played the pander to Bernard. She wondered it still.

Certainly, what Madeline said stopped the grief in her throat. It prevented her from indulging herself in what in other circumstances she might have done: gone to bed, for instance, turned her face to the wall, wept in a way which might have been expected of her.

In the kitchen, making a cup of coffee, she was disturbed by Gerald.

'Alice,' he said, a little nervously, poking his head around the back door, 'I've just seen Bernard and Madeline getting into a taxi together with a lot of luggage . . .'

'Yes,' she said.

'Oh,' said Gerald. 'Um . . . Are they . . .?'

'Yes,' she said pleasantly.

'Oh Alice,' said Gerald, enfolding her in his arms. 'I'm so sorry. Is there anything I can do, Alice?'

'Yes,' she said, extracting herself, walking to the stove and turning off the ring beneath the kettle with a decisive snap.

'You can drink a bottle of champagne with me, Gerald.'

And he did. Except that it was two bottles. Towards the end of the second bottle she became quite properly maudlin. So, eventually, she was able to do the things from which previously she had been prevented, going to bed, turning her face to the wall, weeping in the appropriate fashion. Falling asleep with the tears on her face, she awoke the next day feeling astonishingly refreshed and contented.

Bernard turned up later that day, clearly intent on trying again.

'This whole thing is ridiculous, Alice,' he said in his best really-this-thing-is-all-your-fault voice. 'It was a mild flirtation nothing more.'

'To you perhaps,' she said.

'Anyway,' she said. 'Yesterday you were accusing me of being in love with Madeline.'

'I was angry,' he said, 'I got carried away.' His voice became softer. 'I think we should try again, Alice.'

'I'm sorry, Bernard,' she said sadly. 'I would if I could. But I can't.'

A small dishonest chime sounded somewhere in her head, but then she looked up and saw Bernard's face. It was radiant, glowing with complacency, with self-satisfaction at this, his tragic inability to go through life without causing female suffering. Sitting on the sofa beside her, he took her hands tenderly in his.

'I'm so sorry, Alice,' he said. His eyes and voice trembled on the edge of tears. It was a fine performance and she could do no less than appreciate it.

'I don't blame you for being angry. But sex just doesn't mean to me what it means to you. I've tried to explain that. It's just the way I am.'

She sighed. 'I understand that,' she said gravely.

'You know,' he said, swallowing with emotion, dropping his head, 'I'll always think of you as my wife, Alice.'

And so he collected the rest of his belongings with a delicious air of grief. Only once did he almost forget himself. He called testily down the stairs, 'Where's my khaki shirt, Alice?' and when she called up at him, 'In the wash I think,' the smile on his face hovered momentarily but he recovered it in time, redoubling its rays, making it at the same time both magnanimous and melancholy.

'No problem, Alice,' he said.

At the door, he crushed her to his leather jacket, its pouches, flaps and buckles making small indentations on her cheek. He laid the side of his face tenderly on the top of her head in a long silent moment and then, releasing her, stared mournfully down into her eyes.

The sun, breaking out at that moment from the clouds, poured in through the stained-glass panels of the door. It lit up the skin of his face, danced on his hair and in his eyes. He looked astonishingly, stunningly beautiful.

'Don't say a word,' she begged, overcome with the sheer perfection of the moment.

Obeying her command, he merely raised her fingers to his lips and kissed their tips, lifted his bag and was gone.

Madeline also returned, some days later, for the rest of her things. She laid her key down on the kitchen table.

'We're getting a flat in London,' she said defiantly.

Turning from the sink, she saw that there was no triumph in Madeline's eyes, merely a desperate desire that what she said should be true. She looked suddenly very young.

'Of course,' she answered quietly.

It took her a week to work up the courage to tell Rita.

Rita, naturally, had never liked Bernard. She was still living and working in London at the time and had visited them only once.

'I'm sorry, Alice,' she had said then, kissing her farewell on the station platform. 'I can't imagine what you see in him, that's all.' And she, Alice, understood that. She knew that it was true, that what separated the pair of them, her and Rita, was imagination, an over-abundance of it on her part, an absolute lack of it on Rita's.

When she phoned Rita to tell her that Bernard had gone, Rita said exactly what she had expected her to say. She said, 'It's the best thing, you do know that, don't you, Alice?'

A deeply mutinous streak, buried deep inside her, surfaced at the sound of Rita's certainty.

'No I don't,' she said. 'As a matter of fact. I don't know that at all.'

She said, 'I'm sure it's the "right" thing to do, Rita, whatever "right" means. Bernard was vain, vacuous and entirely self-centred. Furthermore, he was unfaithful which is why I threw him out. One should always throw out people who are unfaithful, I know that. One should categorically not put up with it. It's demeaning and undignified.'

Her voice had risen. Rita said quickly, 'Dignity is important, Alice.'

At this, she, Alice, had been consumed suddenly by anger; consumed too, not for the first time in her life, with a desire to offend Rita.

She said coldly, 'Of course it is, Rita, of course it is. But unfortunately the thing about dignity is that it doesn't keep you warm at night. You can't make love to dignity.'

At the other end of the line there was complete silence. Just as suddenly as it had appeared, all her anger dropped away. She wished she were where Rita was so that she might walk up to her and put her arms around her and draw her towards her, this strange woman who was like her sister, who could lift weights and swim and run and cycle like a champion, and yet, for all of these things, was so very very frail.

'It's OK, Rita,' she said. 'Forgive me. You're right. It's better he's gone. I know that.'

'Well, I'm glad he's gone,' said Rita, satisfied. 'And I can't pretend otherwise. And now I can tell you what I've been wanting to tell you for the last ten minutes. I've applied for a job up there and I think I stand a good chance of getting it. Won't it be wonderful? We'll be together again.'

For a moment there was absolute silence as her best friend considered the implications of what she had heard. Then, laughing, she, Alice, gave in to her fate.

'You'll be able to keep an eye on me, Rita,' she said.

Three hundred miles to the south she knew a pair of lips were smiling a slightly superior smile, an eyebrow was raising itself and a pair of shoulders twitching in a small shrug. She knew this with certainty because of what she heard.

It was a sigh. A sigh coupled of course with a faintly amused, 'Oh Alice.'

'Will the marriage work, do you think? Bernard O'Donaghue and Zoë Fairley?'

Jim Crane's voice breaks in on her thoughts.

248

She stands looking out of the window at the winter gloom. A strong wind which has sprung up during the afternoon as they talked now whips the bare branches against a steel-grey sky and ruffles the water in small waves upon the river.

Gathering herself together, turning to him, she says, 'Oh yes. Almost certainly.'

'You seem very sure.'

'Yes. I suppose I am.'

'Why?'

'Why not? I mean it's all so perfect, isn't it? He's beautiful and soon he'll have a beautiful actress wife and two beautiful new babies. He's got a new part to play. Doting father. He'll be pictured in magazines with a twin on each arm and the country will fall even deeper in love with him than it is now, which of course will suit him down to the ground. They'll live in a lovely house with a lovely nanny to do all the nasty work and they'll go on being entirely beautiful. At last Bernard has arrived at the place he was always meant to be.'

'And will he be faithful, do you think?'

'On the record or off?'

'Off if you like.' She can see that he is curious.

She leans with her back against the window ledge, her arms crossed before her.

'Probably. Oh, he might have the odd fling for his ego. Although maybe not. All Bernard has ever really needed is the assurance that the female sex as a whole adores him, and two thousand fan letters a week I imagine helps with that little problem.'

'And no hard feelings?'

'Absolutely none. I wish them both all the luck in the world.'

She smiles at Jim Crane.

'You can tell your readers exactly what they want to hear about Bernard O'Donaghue. That he's beautiful and charming and now he's that most romantic of things, a reformed rake.

'You can also tell them,' she says, 'what they really want to know, those two thousand women who write to him every week. That he's simply wonderful in bed.'

12

WHEN SHE SAID it, that thing about him being good in bed, he had felt a sharp stab of disappointment. He had not expected it from her. Not from Alice Potter. It was what they all said, after all, the models, the masseuses, the page-three girls. The next thing she would be saying, he thought, was that he liked her in black suspenders, in high heels, that they had it away on the kitchen floor, in the hall, in the bath. The next thing would be all that seven-times-a-night stuff.

So he had rehearsed an encouraging smile, raised his head, opened his mouth to say, 'I was going to ask you about that, Alice,' but she was there before him.

'I don't mean all that seven-times-a-night stuff Madeline came out with,' she said. 'All that black-suspender, we-had-it-on-the-kitchen-floor, in-the-hall and in-the-bath stuff.'

'Oh, you don't?' he said brightening.

'All that garbage,' she said, 'that you print in your newspaper. Like some sort of sexual conspiracy, like some sort of propaganda put out by the state. Pretending that this is the way it is, the way everyone wants it, locking the world into the fifties, bonking and boobs, some strange perverted nursery ideal of sex.

'Imagine,' she said, 'if a Martian landed on a Sunday morning and the first thing he picked up was your paper. He'd have a completely false idea of what we're about.'

She turned away, stared back out through the window.

'It was the strangest thing,' she said. 'Out of bed, Bernard was vain and vacuous and selfish but in bed he was none of those things.'

She turned back to him, her hands splayed along the ledge either side of her.

'This is what they want to hear, isn't it,' she said. 'All his women fans. And as it happens it's the truth. Probably it was a part that he played like everything else, but it was a part that he played well. In bed he was everything a woman could want: gifted, unselfish, gentle, thoughtful, inventive. There was no regime with him, no goals. One part was as good as another. He did not separate things out. There was no adagio, andante and rondo allegro.'

And so she told him how they had made love, the where and the when and the how. She told him thoughtfully, her eyes very dreamy, giggling once, another time throwing her head back and laughing.

He felt himself growing warm as she talked. He reached up, loosening his tie. She was so far from the machine that the small red indicator had stopped flickering and so, not wishing to stop her as she reminisced, he took down all the words on his pad.

It seemed to him, as he watched, that his hand moved along of its own accord in his shorthand, his old-man's shorthand. He laughed a little to himself at the joke, his old-man's shorthand, yes, deep and flowing and smooth, not that modern stunted nonsense.

Along the page went the pen, sweeping and looping and sloping, in perfect time to her words, trembling and trailing with her, stroking and plunging till his hand was tight with the pain of it and he was flipping over the pages faster and faster in a fever.

His shirt was tight across his chest, the skin damp beneath his armpits. A drop of sweat dropped upon the page when suddenly she cried out, sharply, involuntarily, in tones of great sorrow.

'Oh, it was so *good*,' she said.

For a moment they stared at each other, silence all around them in the room. Before him a dull flush rose up from her neck and she turned back to the window in embarrassment.

'Ah yes,' she said. 'Bernard had a talent for all of that.'

He flipped the pad shut, turned off the machine, hands shaking. He collected it with his pad and his coat clumsily, dropping first one and then the other. He made excuses. He would phone the office. He would order coffee. He would give her a break.

Her door slammed hard behind him as he galloped down the corridor. In his room he turned on the taps in the bathroom wildly, plunging his face into the water.

Putting the lid of the toilet down he sank on to it, which is where he rests now, hearing it all again, his head back, a towel in his lap.

Somewhere above him on the wall, placed within easy reach of the shower, the phone rings.

Without opening his eyes, he reaches his hand up, grasps it and puts it to his ear.

'Is it good stuff, Crane?' says Bullerman.

He wipes a hand across his eyes, laughing.

'Oh yes,' he says. 'It's good stuff, Bullerman.'

Friday Evening . . .

1

ONLY OCTAVIA DIDN'T think so. Octavia didn't think it was good stuff at all.

She had tossed aside the rough draft of the stuff he had written out for her contemptuously.

'Jesus, is this what we're paying thirty thousand pounds for? I mean, is she still in love with this jerk or what?'

'I wouldn't know.'

He had answered her stiffly. In truth, it was a question which he had asked himself. The fact was that Octavia had a point. The more he went through the stuff, the more he saw that, despite everything, Alice Potter had managed to give the impression that there was something ultimately irresistible about the vain, self-centred, empty-headed Bernard O'Donaghue. Could it be that she was still in love with him? He assured himself it was merely a professional enquiry.

He knew she still carried pictures of him around. He had said to her, that first night at dinner, 'We shall need a photograph of the pair of you together.'

'No problem,' she said.

To his surprise, she opened her handbag, and feeling around inside, pulled out a small handful of snapshots.

'Take your pick,' she said. 'They're a bit old, I'm afraid. They were taken when Bernard and I first met in Hong Kong. They're the only pictures I have of us. We weren't really into that sort of thing.'

'Some people might think it's strange,' he said, flicking through the pictures, 'you've been apart for four years but you never bothered getting a divorce.'

She had stared into space thoughtfully.

'Yes, I suppose it is funny,' she said. 'There's no good reason why. I just sort of forgot about being married, that was all. And there wasn't anyone else so there wasn't any pressing need to get divorced.'

'And Bernard?' he asked.

'Oh, Bernard. Well I imagine Bernard figured it kept him out of trouble. He liked to play the field you know. He was very much the man about town and being married meant he couldn't get caught.'

'Until Zoë.'

'Yes, until Zoë, of course.'

And yet, he thought, if she were still in love with him, she hid it well, for there was no sign of jealousy or the least distress when she talked of Zoë Fairley.

Yes, the whole thing was peculiar. Against his will, therefore, he could see Octavia's point as she persisted.

'Look, the man is nothing better than a gigolo. A toyboy on the make. She pays his board and lodging for six years when he's a penniless actor, then he buggers off with the lodger. I mean she's supposed to be rubbishing him, for Christ's sake.'

'She doesn't want to rubbish him.'

'Well then we'll have to do it for her.' Her voice was calm, matter-of-fact. 'The editor wants him rubbished. He hates trendy priests.'

He exploded in irritation. 'He's not a trendy priest, for Christ's sake. He's just an actor playing a trendy priest.'

She looked at him with amusement through the smoke of one of the long thin cigarettes.

'It's not a distinction,' she said, 'our editor feels the need to make.'

She moved forward abruptly with an air of decision.

'Right,' she said, crushing the cigarette hard into the ashtray. 'Let's think now. What we need her to say . . .'

'No,' he said.

'No?' she said, looking up at him coolly, cocking her head on one side.

'Look,' he said, 'let's be sensible about this.'

He put his notebook down on the low table before them and rested his elbows on his knees.

'She's not your average C3 reader, neither is this guy McCartan. We try and screw them up and they're going to come down on us hard. McCartan is no fool. He insisted that I tape the interview, which I did of course on your machine. Now we can't start making things up. It's all there, on the tape.'

'Not necessarily.'

'Not necessarily?'

'The pause button was on by mistake. There was something wrong with the tape. The machine wasn't working properly. Take your pick. I've used them all.'

Once again it was her eyes that astonished him. They were so clear, so entirely free of any sign of misgiving.

'Look in their eyes,' Sally had said. 'There's nothing there.'

He sighed.

'You've used them all. Well I guess that comes as no surprise.'

He leant back in his chair and crossed his arms over his chest.

'Tell me,' he said, 'just for posterity. Between ourselves. To bring me up to date with the way things are, so to speak. Do you normally make it up?'

'Of course I make it up,' she said.

Again there was that clear-eyed stare, that look of amused superiority. She shrugged. 'I give them what they want,' she said. Her voice was impatient. She spoke as if to a child. 'When they get my stuff, they know they don't have to rewrite it or call up and ask for more. It's all there. I make sure of that.'

What was extraordinary, he saw afterwards, was the absolute lack of bravado in what she said. She did not brag. Her voice was entirely matter-of-fact. It told him that as far as she was concerned, she was merely stating the case; she was telling him that she had discovered the best way to go about the business and if he did not see it then the loss was his entirely. She was amorality, he saw, personified.

'So,' he said softly, 'this is what it has come to.'

'People don't say what you want them to say,' she said, as if by way of explanation.

'Of course they don't,' he said, smiling ironically. 'That's the thing about people.'

'So . . .?'

The unfinished sentence drew the pair of them in together. He knew that. He wanted more than anything else to argue, cogently and passionately, from the opposite corner; to be free to be against everything she stood for, but he knew that he was constrained by the bonds of his own collaboration. What was her position, he thought, but the logical extension of his own? And so he jerked and wriggled and inched like a prisoner tied to a chair.

'Yeah . . . but . . .' he started and then tailed off.

260

He got to his feet abruptly with the anger of it and walked to the window. It was dark now. Rain spattered heavily against it and trees lashed in the wind before the glare of the car-park floodlights.

'What happens?' he said abruptly.

'What do you mean?'

'Don't people complain?'

'Not if they're getting paid. Alice Potter won't either. Once the cheque drops on to her doormat, we won't hear another word from her. So what if the stuff that appears in the paper isn't what she said. You think she's going to give up her thirty thousand so she can complain? She's not stupid. She must know the score. She's sold herself to us body and soul. It's up to us what we do with her.'

'And what about people who aren't getting paid whom you turn over. Do they complain?'

'They don't matter.'

'*They don't matter.*'

He turned from the window and looked at her.

'I understand,' he said a second time, very softly.

'None of it matters to you, does it?' he said.

She looked at him very hard as if considering whether what he said was worth a reply. She reached forward and took another cigarette from the packet, her eyes still on him as she flicked the lighter at its end.

'Look,' she said, 'I don't know what life is like for a district man up here, but I sure as hell know what it's like in London. Ninety-five per cent of the stuff that I do down there is pure garbage, garbage stories about garbage people, minor showbiz, models, masseuses, people on the make, people using us as much as we're using them. So garbage is my business. I know all about garbage and I know how to operate in it, and let me tell you when you're dealing with garbage there's no need to feel hampered by abstract concepts like truth.'

'This is different.' He said it sharply, angrily.

'What's different? She's taking the money.'

Something dug down deep for no good reason into his soul.

'That doesn't make her garbage,' he said.

He shouted it out angrily. To his irritation, he could feel himself flushing before her curious gaze.

'Look,' he said, struggling to get his voice even again, 'I'm not saying bending the odd quote isn't OK. I mean we've all done that.'

' "Bending the odd quote" . . .'

She was laughing lightly as she repeated the phrase. He saw afterwards that she thought he was trying to ease himself out of his corner and into hers. She spoke the words as though they were in quotes, as if she were humouring him. She spoke them as if they were quaint and anachronistic, like 'going all the way' or 'having to get married', words that she had never had to use, belonging as they did to a previous genera-tion.

'Oh absolutely,' she said. 'Bending the odd quote.'

She all but winked at him. She spoke the phrase the second time more like a password, as if they spoke in code together.

'Well,' she said. 'I'd say thirty thousand pounds entitles us to do a bit of bending, wouldn't you? I'd say it entitles us to a certain poetic licence with Miss Potter's words, a certain . . . creativity.'

She was mocking him, still smiling. And so, for a moment, they stared at each other this way, and then, with an air of decision, he strode over to the table and lifted the machine and, opening it up, slipped out the tape which he dropped in his pocket.

'No,' he said.

'No?' she said, drawling, putting the cigarette to her lips very slowly.

'We use what she said, as she said it. I have the tape here and I'm keeping it. If she complains, I'll back her up.'

What was extraordinary, he thought afterwards, was that she couldn't be fazed. She didn't look shocked, or angry, merely continued to gaze at him with that unbroken stare. Again he felt the need to defend himself.

'As a matter of fact, they're good quotes,' he said. 'Quite good enough. She's saying what his fans want to hear, that he's been a naughty boy but now he's reformed and best of all, he's wonderful in bed.'

To his surprise, he found himself, suddenly, warming to his task.

'For God's sake,' he said, picking up his notebook again. 'We're always rubbishing people and all we get for it is writs. You know the current publishing sensation? A sycophantic magazine that has pages of mush on all your favourite stars. And it's making a fortune. But we won't learn. We just go on digging the dirt and getting writs for it. The fact is people don't want their heroes rubbished. They don't want their dreams ground in the mud.'

She said nothing, just stared at him, an elbow on the arm of her chair, her chin on her hand. Then she smiled at him, her superior smile.

'God,' she said, without rancour, 'you're so stupid. It doesn't matter what we send down, it'll get changed anyway if they don't like it. And then all we'll get is a bollocking from the editor.'

'No.'

'No?'

'No. Not in my case. In my case they won't bother with a bollocking. It'll just be the excuse they need for my last and final warning so they can get rid of me. I'm sure you know all about it. These things tend to be the talk of the office.'

'I'd heard something.' There was no sympathy. The look was amused, nothing more.

'And somehow,' he said, smiling back at her, his eyes staring directly into hers, 'I don't think you'll get a bollocking either. Not with your connections. I'd say you're one of the few people who could get this in the paper the way we want it . . . the way I want it. I mean, you're the editor's blue-eyed girl, right?'

He was taking a chance, of course. She could have been outraged. It could have all gone against him. But it didn't.

For a long moment she stared at him, then her smile broadened. She threw back her head and laughed, the first time he had seen her do it. Then she leant forward and picked up a pen.

'OK,' she said. 'Let's get on with it.'

They worked on it for several hours together. She was good. She was very good, and he knew he would remember with pleasure, for a long time, how it came out between them, smooth and clean, one good sentence on top of the other.

They were just finishing when there was a knock on the door and Gibb appeared.

'And where the fuck were you last night when you were needed?' he, Crane, asked him.

A foolish grin spread over Gibb's face. 'Sorry abaht that,' he said. 'Got into a little scene wiv the barmaid.'

Octavia, lifting her head, flicked a look over Gibb, which warmed his, Crane's, heart. She looked at him as though he were a very low form of life which had recently crawled out from beneath a stone.

'I'll phone this over then,' she said, ignoring his presence.

In the corridor, walking to Alice Potter's room, Gibb said, 'She's a bit of all right, ain't she, Octavia.'

He was intrigued at the way Gibb said her name, the way it twisted in his mouth, and bore no relation to its normal pronunciation.

Gibb said, 'Y'know, when I get back to London, I fink I might give it a go wiv Octavia.'

He, Crane, stopped dead in his tracks.

'What?' he said, not sure he had heard.

'Go for it wiv Octavia. Arsk 'er out. Whaddya fink? Fink I'm in wiv a chance there?'

He stood looking at Gibb. He felt a slow, sweet, satisfied smile spread over his face at the thought of Gibb attempting to chat up Octavia Eagleton.

'I don't think you've got enough time, Gibb,' he said gravely.

'Time. Whaddya mean time? 'Ow much time d'ya fink I'd need, like?'

He, Crane, sucked in a breath in the manner of a garage mechanic forced into an estimate.

'Ooooh . . . a couple of million years should do it,' he said.

*

Pushing open the bedroom door quietly now, he finds Octavia still on the phone. Her back is to him. She has not heard him enter. He smiles to himself when he hears what she is saying.

'She doesn't want to rubbish him, that's an end of it. We can't make her. Anyway, who cares? She's saying what all his fans want to hear. That he's a great lover and that once he was a naughty boy but now he's reformed and he'll be a wonderful father.'

Her voice is cold and bored and contemptuous and she stares at her fingernails as she talks. From where he stands in the doorway, he can hear a thin voice piping at the other end of the phone.

She blows out an irritated breath and breaks in on it impatiently.

'For Christ sake,' she says. 'We can't do that. Make it up and she'll sue. Jesus, we could paper the wall with writs we've got already. And it's all so bloody pointless. When are we going to learn? People don't want their heroes rubbished. I mean look at the magazine market. See who's making the money. Times are changing.'

At the door now, a floorboard gives beneath his foot. At the creak she turns. Her smile, at being discovered like this parroting his words, is entirely without shame or embarrassment.

He moves to the fridge and makes a drinking movement with his hand and she nods. As he opens the door and gets out the miniatures and the mixers, the piping continues.

'What's the matter with the sex stuff?' she says, her lips drawing back in exasperation.

Jamming the phone into her neck, she reaches up for her drink and at the same time for one of the

266

long black cigarettes which she lights up in a long unhurried movement. Removing it from her lips, she blows out a long, thin stream of smoke.

'Well,' she says, her voice low and sardonic, 'do what you want. Change it if you want to. Personally though, I don't know anyone who does it seven times a night. Do you?'

Leaning over the fridge-top preparing his own drink, he shakes his head, laughing. Throwing a glance over his shoulder, he finds her looking directly at him. At the other end of the line, the piping has grown faster and more excited. Holding him, Crane, in her look, she gives a deep, throaty lascivious laugh, beginning to make small murmuring sounds of sexual innuendo, practised and expert, devoid of all signs of warmth or excitement.

Dragging his eyes back to the drink, he listens as once he had watched, with an uneasy voyeuristic pleasure.

She plays with him, the editor, he can see that. The man is flotsam to her. Perhaps all men are.

It comes to him then, suddenly and with absolute certainty, that one day, probably before too long, she will be sitting in the large black chair from which the little voice now pipes. Except, of course, that it won't be that vulgar over-stuffed monster, it will be something smaller, an Italian design perhaps, discreet, classy, and instead of the black leather jacket draped around it there will be one of wool, like the one she wears now, soft and duplicitously draped, entirely belying the toughness and the intractability of the woman beneath.

Sitting down opposite her with his drink in his hand, he throws her a low guarded look, but she is ready for it. She catches it in the wide clear eyes, her smile wicked and triumphant, as she raises a perfectly shaped eyebrow.

Oh yes, she saw him. She saw him all right, that night in the shadows. Of that he has no doubt.

He smiles at her instinctively, with the realization, shakes his head, raises a glass to her in a toast, in admiration.

Putting down the phone, her own smile is crooked on her lips.

'The editor wants me back early,' she says.

Together they begin to laugh.

Leaning back in her seat, she narrows her eyes at him.

'Well,' she says, her tongue poking gently between her lips in insinuation, 'it looks like I'm going to have to leave you to take care of our Miss Potter.'

Standing a short while later by her car in the car park, he holds out a hand in farewell. 'It's been great working with you,' he says. It pleases him that he means it.

Her eyes are cool as she looks at him, clear and empty once again of all expression. She ignores his hand and, leaning towards him, gives him a light London kiss on both cheeks.

From the way she looks at him, the way she kissed him, he believes that she neither likes nor dislikes him, which, coming from her, he thinks, is most probably a compliment.

'Tell me something before you go,' he says as she is getting into her car, 'something I've always wanted to know. Is the editor mad?'

For the first time since he has known her, a genuine, open-hearted emotion registers on her face. It is simple astonishment.

Her brow furrows. She shakes her head at him as if amazed, once again, at his naïvety.

'Of course the editor's mad,' she says.

2

BELOW HER NOW, Octavia's car disappears from the floodlit car park, out past the two grey stone lions guarding the entrance and into the darkness beyond.

Through the window she watches as Jim Crane stares out after it. Then he shakes his head, shrugs his shoulders and walks, smiling, back towards the hotel door.

Half an hour earlier she had watched from the same spot the most unlikely of scenes: Andrew roaring away in the passenger seat of Gibb the photographer's XR3i. He sat bolt upright, his hands clutching the handle of his briefcase which he balanced, with distasteful precision, upon his knees. The expression on his face said no man should have to face what he was going through.

Poor Andrew. Try as she might, she cannot contain a smile at the memory.

Repugnant as it had been to him to be called in as her official adviser, once so deputed he had been determined to carry out his duties seriously.

When he announced his intention of sitting in on the interview, Jim Crane's face had fallen. She too did not relish the prospect, so she had said hastily, gently, 'Oh that's kind of you, Andrew, but really there's no need. I just needed you to check the contract, and you've done that, so if you do want to get back to London . . . well . . . I'll quite understand . . .'

Andrew, though, did not give in that easily.

'I think it would be best if I stayed somewhere nearby until the interview is finished, Alice,' he persisted pompously, 'just in case any unforeseen problems occur.'

With this in mind he had retired to the lounge to read manuscripts. He returned there again after lunch at which point he had been completely forgotten about by everyone, including herself.

Some three hours later she was lying on the bed sideways, head balanced on one hand and smiling as directed, when there was a light knock at the door and in he walked.

'Oh, Andrew,' she said in some confusion.

Around her Gibb was dipping and rising and making encouraging noises, moving in and out of his arc lights.

'Lean forward, darlin' . . . give us a smile there . . . raise yer head . . . lovely.'

A look of horror stole over Andrew's face as he took in the scene. 'Oh my God,' he said, 'this is all so *tacky*, Alice.'

''Itch yer skirt up a bit more, Alice, could ya?' said Gibb, ignoring him and leaning forward from his waist at a most astonishing angle.

There was a moan of exceptional distress from the doorway.

'I think it's time I went, Alice,' said Andrew. 'I'll get a taxi to the station.'

'Give ya a lift if ya like, mate. I've almost finished here,' said the ever-obliging Gibb.

They had walked together, she and Andrew, along the corridor, saying goodbye. At the top of the stairs she had kissed him gently and affectionately on the cheek. It had astonished her. How easily she did it. How differently she suddenly found herself feeling about Andrew McCartan.

'Thanks for everything, Andrew,' she said, smiling. 'And stop worrying. Of course it's all tacky and vulgar but who cares? You know what they say. All publicity is good publicity. It might even sell some books. At the very worst, it'll make a good subject for a novel.'

She was trying to make him smile but he just looked at her aghast.

'I wait with bated breath, Alice,' he said shuddering.

Turning now from the window, she sees the snapshots of herself and Bernard that Jim Crane and Gibb had been poring over lying scattered on the bed.

'We'll need an old picture of the pair of you together,' Jim Crane had said at dinner last night, and by a stroke of luck she had half a dozen or so lying in her bag.

She'd been carrying them around for several months, since Céline had last come over to London. She, Alice, had found them in a drawer several days before Céline was due to arrive and had put them in her handbag to show them to her, to amuse her.

Céline giggled like a teenager when she saw them, this respectable American matron, with flashing rings on her fingers and designer suits and twin daughters, very Chinese and very serious and growing up fast.

'We look so young, Alice,' she said. 'So young and so sexy.'

The pictures had been taken the day they all went up to the old Peak Café for tea. It was their farewell party. She and Bernard were leaving Hong Kong the next day.

There was Patrick, the delicate mandarin, sitting next to Desirée, holding her hand; beautiful Desirée whom he loved like – what? – a brother, a sister, a lover? Desirée, all high hair and coloured eyes, Desirée who was Jiansheng when he braved the sharks in the South China Sea to swim to freedom, in particular the freedom to wear dresses and grow breasts and have his penis tucked away for ever inside him.

Next to them, Céline, very pert, fringe low over her eyes and the hair like ebony silk, shining in the sun, swinging on to her cheeks; always laughing, always, in every picture, in the middle of doing something, pouring lemonade on someone's head, jumping up, grabbing the camera. And next to Céline, Bud, in every picture staring in absolute adoration at Céline.

Bud booked Céline out the night after she, Alice, met Bernard and, having booked her out, would not rest until he had married her.

She had asked Céline one night not long after they met, 'Do you think you'll get married, Céline?'

It was late. They'd come home in a sampan from a booking. They were drinking a beer and smoking a joint before going to bed.

Céline made the short sharp dismissive puffing noise through her lips.

'Get marry? Who?' Her English was more delicately fractured then.

'I don't know. Some Chinese guy.'

Céline made the blowing sound again.

'Chinese guy want wife stay home,' she said.

'Well . . . an American,' she, Alice, had persisted. 'English . . .'

Céline smiled, an old, hard, truly inscrutable smile.

'*Gwailo* marry Chinese girl want Chinese girl always be grateful,' she said.

But with Bud it had been different. Because Bud had no doubt about who it was who should grateful. He was grateful for Céline from the moment he met her.

As for Céline, she treated Bud from the first more like a mother than a lover, as if, instead of being several years younger than him, she were a million years older, which, of course, to all intents and purposes, she was.

There were members of Bud's family who were not well pleased when first the GI announced his intention of bringing home a bride. Now, of course, a decade on, things were different; now that Bud's one garage had expanded into a small chain, now that he had bought into a motel and part of a shopping mall in which Céline had her boutique selling exclusive French fashions, for which she shopped twice a year in Paris, stopping over to see her old friend Alice Potter in London on the way. Yes, now Bud's family were nothing but grateful to Céline whose motherly nagging and strange affectionate irritation had made Bud the success he had become.

'We look so young, Alice, and so sexy,' Céline had said, looking at the photographs. And so they did. And when Céline said it a small sad pain had crossed her, Alice's, heart.

Crossing to the bed now, she picks up one of the photographs rejected by Gibb. There they were, smiling up into the sun, looking thin and young and brown and carefree and, because of all of these things, overwhelmingly sexy.

Looking up, she catches sight of herself suddenly, unexpectedly, in the mirror. She touches a hand to

274

her hair which is duller now than in the photograph, to her face which is fuller, to a line etching out from her eye she has never noticed before.

The small sad pain snatches at her a second time. Yes. It was true. Where was the surprise? She was growing old. They were all growing old. Even Bernard.

When she saw pictures of Bernard in newspapers and magazines in the early days, it had seemed to her that somehow he was escaping the march of time which was treading, with heavy footsteps upon her. But then recently she had caught him by accident on the *Wogan* show and she had noticed lines that were not there before. He was still beautiful, of course, Bernard would always be beautiful, but there was that certain settling in on his face. Perhaps even Bernard, she thinks now, had realized that we all must grow old. Perhaps that was why, in the end, he had the sense to marry Zoë.

Zoë, too, was on the show. They looked wonderful. They were the couple of the year. About that, there could be no possible doubt.

He wore a fashionably crumpled suit and an open-necked shirt and was very brown from a holiday.

Her shoulders shone smooth and black beneath the lights and the long corkscrewed locks.

Bernard had taken to wearing glasses just like Father Dwyer. They suited him. They made what he had to say sound that much better and what he had to say was astonishingly pleasing.

He spoke movingly of the work they did, he and Zoë, for underprivileged youngsters and drug addicts in the inner cities.

Zoë's upbringing had not been an easy one. Her

stardom was a small triumph. Sitting watching, she, Alice, had seen that there was something fine about the pair of them.

They spoke about the pregnancy. Were they thrilled? Of course they were thrilled. Bernard was particularly voluble. Children changed one's perspective on life, he said, made one realize one had a responsibility to leave the world a better place. That's why he and Zoë were also involved with the various environmental charities.

On the screen, Bernard's brow furrowed beautifully behind his glasses. Would he take a full part in bringing up the twins? Would he? Of course he would. You bet he would. What man, what real man, would waste the opportunity to bring up his kids, to take as equal a part in it as their mother? Wasn't this what being a man these days was all about?

Around the country, in unison, a million feminist hearts fluttered, a million sighs, she could hear them, escaped a million liberated lips.

At first, when she heard what Bernard was saying, she was astonished. But then, watching the titles rise up over their faces, his and Zoë's, she saw what had happened.

Bernard O'Donaghue she saw was, in essence, a beautiful, entirely empty canvas waiting for the best, or the worst, to be painted on him. Father Dwyer, or the scriptwriters who had created him, had painted on that canvas. Bernard O'Donaghue, who to her certain knowledge had never had an unselfish, concerned or meaningful thought in his head during their six years together, had taken on in the two years that he had been playing him the characteristics of the caring, sharing, perspicacious parish priest: a man who saved marriages all about him; a man who leapt in the space of one episode from persuading an armed gunman to give himself up to preventing, almost single-handed, the siting of a toxic waste dump near the school; a man who had found, forgiven and installed in his presbytery the prostitute mother who had given him up for adoption; a man who had sacrificed the love of his life, the lovely neighbourhood lawyer Mercy Hellman, for his loyalty to his sacred vows.

Bernard O'Donaghue, in short, had become his part, had metamorphosed into Father Dwyer and, by way of reward, through the medium of real life, would be permitted to marry the delicious Mercy née Zoë who had been forbidden him on the screen.

The whole thing had an astonishing symmetry about it, she had thought at the time. Indeed, it was perfect. She was not surprised the female population was transported.

'But how Kafkaesque,' she had murmured watching the last of the titles rise.

Absurd really. She was talking to the television.

3

AND SO WITH Octavia gone and McCartan too, and Gibb returned to town to wire his pictures, he and Alice Potter had had dinner à deux again, for the second night.

He ordered champagne.

'Oh why the hell not?' he said in answer to her enquiring eyes.

They were a good way down the second bottle when he raised his glass to her.

'Here's to you,' he said.

'And to you too,' she said, raising her glass back at him.

'And to Octavia too,' he said. He was a little drunk already.

'Octavia,' she said.

'The woman of the future, Octavia,' he said, smiling broadly.

He knew he had made a mistake as soon as he said it.

He groans now, inwardly, outwardly too, reaching for the miniature on the table beside the bed. Outside the hotel window, the wind moans as if in keeping with his mood.

He should have known, of course. How could he have been so beguiled? How could he have forgotten what she was, how, like Janet, she must have those small unseen antennae waving all the time on top of her head, detecting unperceived slights and snubs and general masculine shortcomings?

When he had lifted his glass to Octavia, called her the woman of the future, Alice Potter merely looked at him in a suddenly coldly curious manner.

Feeling the lowering of the temperature, he had tried immediately to cover his tracks.

'What I meant was,' he said, 'she's rather amazing, Octavia.'

'Amazing?' said Alice Potter, her voice too carefully interested, and, at the same time, too carefully flat.

And then of course the problem was that he couldn't really tell Alice Potter just why Octavia was so amazing. In the first place, he couldn't see how you could share with someone you hardly knew the circumstances in which he and Octavia had first met. So he ended up floundering badly, which, he saw afterwards, almost certainly further incriminated him.

'What I mean is . . . the first time I saw her . . . Well, that doesn't matter . . . She's superwoman, that's all. She'll probably end up editor.'

'And that bothers you?'

'No. Not at all. I mean let's face it, I probably won't be there to see it.'

'You mean you'd leave rather than serve under a woman editor.'

It was quite the wrong conclusion and it both hurt and irritated him. He saw no reason why she should have been so quick to misinterpret him in this way.

'No, No. I don't mean that at all. It's just that like I said the other night, they're looking for ways to get rid of me. I approve wholeheartedly of women becoming editors as it happens.'

'Oh good.'

He didn't know where the sarcasm had come from

279

or why it was there but it made him angry. It scraped itself across something in his brain, some fine wires stretched very tautly. He cleared his throat to calm himself. He tried again.

'I've always been right behind the whole . . . women's thing. I mean women should have equality . . . in everything . . . obviously . . . I've always believed that.'

She said nothing. Just plucked a bread stick from the glass in the middle of the table, snapped it in her teeth, continued to smile at him with that awful calm smile. Perhaps that was what did it. The smile. Or the slurp of champagne that he took which winged itself with wicked speed to his brain.

'Although sometimes I think . . . maybe . . . perhaps things have gone too far.'

'Sorry?' she said.

Naturally enough it had been downhill all the way from there.

Before they had been like two fencers circling each other. Suddenly they began to joust and jab.

'Sometimes I think it's time that men fought back. I mean sometimes I think we're the ones becoming the underclass.'

Could he really have said that? But he did say it and the truth was he had wanted to say it for a long time, just like he had wanted before to say 'Stupid fucking bitch' about Alice Potter's friend, and be a man with that moron Gibb. The truth was, again, he had wanted to give vent to something, to be allowed to say something he was not supposed to say.

'Really,' she said, very coldly now. 'That's an interesting idea. You think women are in control now, do you? A scattering of women amongst the country's top medical men, a few female MPs and half-a-dozen women judges and all of a sudden we're in power are we?'

'Well, hey, come on now, we do have a woman Prime Minister.'

It was his last attempt to be jovial. It failed miserably.

'She's not really a woman.'

'Oh yeah well I should have expected that, shouldn't I. The first woman to get power in her hot little hands turns out to be arrogant and dictatorial and compassionless and as bad as any man, and all of a sudden guess what, she isn't a woman any more. Well I got news for you. She wears a skirt. She bulges in all the right places. She looks like a woman to me.'

He heard the sarcasm in his own voice now. It was ugly and unpleasant and he was ashamed.

'She may look like a woman but the fact of the matter is that she does display a great number of masculine traits. Her apparent love of combat in all its forms, for instance.'

'Oh, that's a masculine trait, is it?'

'I think so, yes. The feeling for violence and war is very much a masculine thing, isn't it?'

'No, as a matter of fact I don't think it is. For instance, I would run a mile rather than get into a fight. I'm no good at it, you see. For instance, twice during the last couple of days I have passionately wanted to kick the shit out of two people who totally deserve to have the shit kicked out of them, but on both occasions I've been simply too scared to do it.'

'Well I'm not sure that proves anything.'

That awful superiority again.

'Of course it proves something. It proves I'm a craven coward and not at all up to half the violent things I'm supposed to be up to, given that I'm a *man*.'

He flung the word out at her. He saw her move back sharply as if it struck her and was sorry, but by then it was too late.

'You know what I'm bloody sick of? I'm bloody sick of women treating men as a class, as one big indivisible utterly homogenous lump of humanity, as in "all men are this" and "all men are that". Like, for instance, "all men are capable of rape". Now there's a fucking insult if ever I heard one.'

He hated the obscenity. But it was past now and when she opened her mouth to speak, he would not let her and instead raged on.

'You know what it is? It's the worst sort of racist insult. It's on the same level as "all blacks are stupid" or "all Jews are mean". We don't say that any more because we've grown up. But we can say "all men are bastards", can't we? I'd be run out of town, wouldn't I, if I tried to say all women were feather-brained or all women were lousy drivers. But you? Well you can say what the hell you like about men and get away with it. You can say in your prissy little aren't-we-the-greatest voices, "Well of *course* men don't have *friends* like women do." Or if you want you can say, "Of *course* women are the superior sex," and does anybody challenge you? No. Certainly not. Because it's the right-on thing to say. Just imagine if I tried to say men were the superior sex. God, they'd say I belonged back in the caves and they'd be right. But you, well, you women can say anything. You can say men are stupid, undependable, laughable, violent,

282

bastards, rapists, the list is fucking endless. Let me tell you, something very unpleasant has happened between men and women in the last twenty years.'

They were facing each other, almost nose to nose. She had been trying to speak but he would not let her. Now her face was like flint and her voice, when she spoke, like chips of ice.

'I presume, despite your avowed support for the feminist movement, you are laying this . . . unpleasantness . . . at its door.'

'Yeah, as a matter of fact, yeah.'

It came out harshly like a jeer and he hated it but, again, it was too late. She had jumped to her feet, snatched up her handbag from the table and was clutching it to her before him.

'You want to talk about unpleasantness,' she said. 'Well I'll tell you about unpleasantness. I'll tell you what the women's movement did. I'll tell you the best thing it ever did, the thing it will be remembered for.'

He has a clear vision still of how she looked, her face stiff and white with wrath, her eyes boring into his. As she spoke her teeth bared with the words that were etched now on his brain.

'What the women's movement did was to blow the gaff on a million years of evolutionary secrecy and get out into the open the sheer hatred and disgust that has existed between the sexes since we made the mistake of slopping up out of the sea together.'

And now, thinking over again what happened, the same forbidden thought enters his brain.

God forgive me, he thinks, taking a sip of his whisky, aren't they right really, women. Is this the best I can come up with?

God forgive me, he thinks, swinging his legs off the bed in disgust at himself and walking to the window.

God forgive me, he says to the unseen God outside conducting the storm.

God forgive me for the juvenile, sexist, corny, deeply patronizing, positively heretical thing I am thinking.

God forgive me, he thinks, but she looks wonderful when she's angry.

4

SHE WOKE FROM the dream with a start. She did not know what had done it, what had made her wake up. She wondered if it was the storm, the crack and creak of the elms waving and bending around the car park.

It was a crazy dream. She'd dreamt she was in this office, an architect's office in one of those converted Georgian town houses, in a basement with people's feet passing along on the pavement outside.

The office was bright, high-ceilinged, with stripped pine and pot plants and enigmatic prints. On the side by the wall was a Cona machine, and in the middle a large white slanting drawing board.

By the board was a man, standing, a grey-haired man, handsome, with a good watch and an expensive shirt rolled up at the elbows. He was a decent man, she could see by the laughter lines about his mouth. He was a man who cared, a man who might campaign, for instance, for nuclear disarmament.

She knew this was God.

She saw him stand back, lift a small cigar from a witty kitsch ashtray, and survey what he had drawn on the board. As he did so the door opened and in strolled a languid figure, all flowing kaftan and long drop earring. He clutched a coffee mug which he went to the machine to fill up.

She knew this was the Holy Ghost.

Taking a sip, the Holy Ghost walked to the drawing

board, hitching his kaftan up on his shoulder as he went. Uninvited he stared over God's shoulder.

A look of puzzlement that became suspicion crossed his face.

'What's that,' he said, pointing his mug at it, fingers clasped through the handle.

'That?' said God, refusing to look at him. 'That's love.'

Derision crossed the Holy Ghost's face, then disgust and after that pure, unmitigated dislike.

He looked sideways at God.

'You bastard,' he said.

She had been on her feet, white-faced, staring at Jim Crane across the table when there was a small polite cough to their left. It was the waiter. A call for Mr Crane. Mr Crane said, 'Excuse me,' politely. As he got up, so she sank down, as if they sat, each one of them, either end of a see-saw.

Immediately he had left the room though she pushed her chair back and jumped up. She strode across the floor and out of the door to the foyer, determined to be away from him and in her room by the time he returned.

She had her foot on the bottom stair when she felt a hand on her elbow. She was conscious of a great flood of relief – no, be honest, something more than that. Pleasure.

Her brain scrabbled for something conciliatory to say in response to the effort he was making.

'No, really. It was my fault. I shouldn't have flown off the handle like that.'

She turned with a smile.

And came face to face with Stanley.

He began fluttering about her asking questions about Bernard. He kept dodging ahead of her as she attempted to walk up the stairs. His not being Crane had made her anger return, except that now it was worse than ever.

She warned him. She said, 'Leave me alone,' and 'Get out of my way,' but he did neither. Instead, on the landing as they turned, he said, 'Is it true that Bernard O'Donaghue left you because you were a lesbian?'

That was when she cracked.

He was standing on the step above her looking down. With some surprise she saw her own hand fly up and strike him across the mouth. The action seemed rehearsed somehow, and smooth. It seemed to come from somewhere in the back of her head. The only other time she had done such a thing was with Clive almost twenty years before. It occurred to her, at the time, that slapping men must be like sex or riding a bicycle, something you never forgot how to do.

The blow, which was not hard, caught Stanley off-balance. He reeled a little, then tottered and, sprawling against the wall, cartwheeled the half-dozen steps to the floor. From behind her she heard Jim Crane laughing.

'Oh for God's sake, Stanley,' he said, 'don't you ever give up?'

She did not look back. Instead she strode on up the stairs without turning. In her room, she flung herself on the bed and for no good reason she could think of burst into tears. Then she went to the fridge and found a half-bottle of white wine which she began to drink very quickly.

There was a tap on her door and she went to it, only opening it a crack.

It was him of course. He said, 'I'm sorry about that. I've seen Stanley off the premises. He was after a spoiler I'm afraid.'

'Spoiler?' she said icily.

'Yes. Just a line, a "yes" or a "no" to drum up into a front page nothing to spoil our exclusive. He's a past master at it.'

'I see,' she said.

She could see that he thought he should go but had something else to say. He looked down, shuffled his feet. Then he looked up with a gentle conciliatory grin.

'I thought you'd like to know,' he said, 'bearing in mind our conversation. Stanley was one of the people that I wanted to hit. So thanks a lot.'

He was laughing. He wanted to make up. And she could have laughed too. She could have said, 'Come in, have a drink.' But she did not. Instead she decided, for reasons she could not quite understand, to go on being irredeemably offended.

'Well,' she said, 'I'm sure it makes you feel very superior. Proves your point, I'm sure, that violence is the prerogative of both sexes.'

She made to shut the door.

'Oh Alice,' he said. He said it quickly. Like an apology. Like an appeal, a request for a truce without rancour. In the crack of the door she could see his eyes, watery-blue, bloodshot, but full of a weary ironic determination. They seemed to say to her, 'I know . . . we're too old for this . . . but still . . . nonetheless . . .'

'Goodnight,' she said quickly, closing the door.

Hearing his footsteps pound away down the corridor, she had leant against the door for a long time, shaking. Then she walked firmly to the bedside table calling herself many sorts of a fool — although why, to what end, she was not sure.

She lay on the bed and drank the rest of the wine and then several more brandies. Once she lifted the phone to call him and apologize, but the absurdity of the idea overcame her and she replaced the receiver. Eventually, having drunk so much, she passed out and dreamt the dream from which she had awoken a short while ago, the light still on, still in her clothes.

Getting off the bed now, she walks, cramped and stiff, her head aching, to the window. There she stares out into the night.

She wonders how it could happen so quickly, how she could find herself so suddenly, so easily, sparring under colours not rightly her own.

'Not rightly her own.' The words cause her pain. She draws back from them. As if they touch her. Tar and feather her.

Somewhere, outside the window, in the night, Madeline's face appears.

'Strip your sleeve, Alice,' it says. 'Show your scars.'

And then she sees herself, the latest in the long line stretching back through history, the long line of consorters with the enemy, traitors, whose only crime was to see that all the world's causes eventually become overtaken by the times, and all that is left for those with a desire still to fight is the soul-destroying, life-denying inglorious war of attrition.

Outside the window, dark clouds scud theatrically across the face of the moon. In a moment of light, she makes out the hands of the church clock across the tops of the houses, which tell her it is well after four.

Opposite her, across the small courtyard with the sundial and the pond, another bedroom light still burning catches her eye.

She wonders if it is his and is trying to work it out when, all of a sudden, there he is at the window.

Before she can turn away, he has looked directly at her.

For a moment they stare at each other and then, as she watches, he raises a hand in a wave – no, not a wave, something else, something more dignified, something a little more sad. A salute. Yes, that is it. A small rueful salute.

She raises her own hand, uncertainly, in reply, and then, overcome with something, embarrassment, perhaps even fear, pulls the gold-ringed curtains together, closing off the sight of him with a determined clash.

Undressing she crawls into bed, recognizing the mild despair that always accompanies the beginnings of a hangover.

Saturday . . .

1

HEAD DOWN, ON the towpath, he battles along against the wind. A bundle of bracken torn free by the blast bowls towards him with such determination that he leaps aside to get out of its way. All around him the last of the leaves whirl from the trees like great golden snowflakes.

Where was it, somewhere he had read about, somewhere at the furthest reaches of the planet – Tierra del Fuego, somewhere like that – where the wind blew all the time. Imagine it. All day and all night, wherever you went, whatever you did, a wind howling in your face and in your ears and flattening the grass all around you just like this.

The wind had got worse during the night. He hadn't slept well and each time he'd woken he'd heard it gusting around the hotel, slapping the cords of the flagpole, creaking signs and scuttling stray flowerpots across the courtyard.

He hadn't been suspicious, last night, when he got to the phone and a voice he didn't know said, 'Newsdesk wants a word.' They used so many freelances these days. Sometimes it was hard to find a voice you did recognize.

He'd tapped in irritation on the side of the old wooden telephone kiosk as he waited. As he tapped he thought about Alice Potter. His anger had begun to cool on the way to the phone and he wanted to get back to the table, to make peace or to try and explain.

So he'd shifted from foot to foot, swearing softly into the receiver. When no one came after half a minute or so, he lost his temper and slammed it down. Flinging open the door, he strode out of the box into the foyer, which is where he saw Stanley, long limbs flailing, cartwheeling down the stairs, and where he knew he'd been had.

'Nice one, Stanley,' he said to the pile of limbs at the bottom of the stairs. 'Who made the phone call for you?'

'Got one of the lads on the desk to do it,' said Stanley, picking himself up and dusting down his long dark coat.

'Did you see that?' he said, pointing up the stairs to the empty space where Alice Potter had stood. 'Did you see what she did to me? I could sue, you know.'

'Oh I don't think so, Stanley,' he had replied. 'Think of all the street cred you'd lose. And now, allow me to escort you from the premises.'

'I think I'll have a drink,' said Stanley with offended determination.

'You can't,' he said, trying to put him off. 'The bar's closed.'

'You can't throw me out, Crane,' Stanley said grandly. 'I can stay here if I choose. It's a free country.'

'Really, Stanley,' he said with a sigh. 'Whatever gave you that impression.'

He had to give in, of course, in the end. Buy Stanley a drink just to get rid of him.

'OK, Stanley,' he said, as they settled on their stools, side by side, at the bar. 'I know you're bursting to tell me. How did you find us?'

Stanley's face glowed with self-satisfaction.

'Debbie,' he said.

'Debbie?'

'Debbie. Taxi-firm Debbie. I waited for her after her shift. Knew she'd know where you'd been dropped off. Took her for a drink and to dinner as a matter of fact.'

'Another heart broken I'm sure, Stanley,' he said sardonically.

'No. 'Fraid not.'

'No? Not losing your touch I trust, Stanley?'

Stanley looked crestfallen all of a sudden.

'Took me for a ninety-quid dinner,' he said. 'Ate a filet mignon like it was a hamburger, drank me under the table, then just as I was about to suggest adjourning to my room, she whips out the handbag mirror, plasters on some lipstick and announces she's off dancing.'

Stanley's eyes stared across at him. They were very very hurt. Under the overhead lights at the bar he noticed that the hair over Stanley's ears was very black and it occurred to him, out of the blue, that he dyed it.

'Kissed me on the cheek like I was her father, Crane,' said Stanley.

For a moment, he stared at Stanley. Then he put two fingers on the bridge of his nose and started to laugh.

'Life moves on, Stanley,' he said.

Leaning in at Stanley's car window, some twenty minutes later, he said, pleasantly, 'Do me a favour, Stanley, eh? Bugger off and don't come back.'

Stanley, though, appeared not to be listening.

In the shadowed glare of the car-park floodlights,

295

he, Crane, could see his eyes, misty with thought, as he stared fixedly into the dashboard. Then his face began to brighten. Jerking the car in gear, he began to tease the accelerator noisily. At the same time he pushed his face out of the window.

'I say,' he said. 'Rather attractive our Ms Potter when she's aroused, mmm? Tell me, is she really a dyke then, Crane?'

He, Crane, laughed. He couldn't help it.

'Nice try, Stanley,' he said, giving the car roof a valedictory slap.

It was true, of course. It was what he had thought last night. It was what he thought again now. Yes, Stanley was right, our Ms Potter was extremely attractive when aroused. And she was no dyke, of that he was sure. Not, of course, that it was any business of his whether she was or not. That was her business. Nothing to do with him.

Pushing his way against the wind, he shakes his head.

'Who am I kidding,' he says to Malone. 'And what the hell am I thinking? Lusting after Alice Potter. Let's not fool ourselves here. But it's a job, for Christ's sake. It's a story. I'm a reporter. She's a buy-up. You know what I mean? OK, I know some of them do it. But it's never been my scene, you know that. You don't mix business and pleasure, that's my motto, especially when it's our sort of business. Too many comebacks, if you understand me. OK, a reporter's not a doctor, I know that. I mean if you go to bed with someone you're interviewing, you're not going to get struck off for unprofessional conduct or anything.

'Go to bed with someone? Jesus, Malone, what the hell am I saying?'

296

Seeing the bench ahead of him beneath a tree, he struggles the last few yards in the wind towards it. Reaching it, he drops down, hunching forwards, his arms on his knees.

'Look, last night when I knocked on Alice Potter's door, it wasn't like ... What I mean to say is ... I wasn't after anything ... I mean, you know me, Malone. Mr Nice Guy right? The one who doesn't presume. The one who sleeps on the sofa when the last bus has gone. I just wanted to ... Oh God, I don't know ... make peace ... talk about it ... explain. Explain what ... Oh everything ... Me, Janet, the whole damn business. Because you know, it's a funny thing, but I can talk to her. You wouldn't think that, would you, with what I am, with what she is? But she's a funny mixture you know. She's not what you'd expect. I mean, OK, she's ... well ... way out in some ways ... Like Janet ... I mean she showed that last night when she lost her rag. But she's got a sense of humour too ... which, let's be honest here, Janet didn't have ... and she's been through the mill too, and she's survived, and you have to admire that in someone, Malone.'

An extra strong blast of wind buffets him from the side. He pushes himself more firmly into the bench. Their bench. His and Malone's.

They used to fish from pool to pool, he following Malone downriver. Somehow, though, they had always ended up here. Here, before the deepest pool in the river where they always did best, where they'd take a break, sit on this bench, drink their beer and eat their sandwiches.

He had been rescued by Malone.

When he and Janet had split up, he had sold the house and bought a flat on the Quayside that proclaimed the word 'bachelor'. He bought a couple of new suits too, and took out membership of a club, and partied it for a while, mostly with women much too young for him.

Then one Friday night, when they were having a drink after work, Malone said he was going fishing the next day. In a burst of bonhomie, he, Crane, said he would go too. When they set off the next morning, early, the sky was a cold crystal blue. He borrowed a rod from Malone and from that day forward, as the old pun went, he was hooked.

He was thirty-six then. Over the next six years their friendship, his and Malone's had grown deeper. He went to an opera for the first time with Malone, to the theatre to see Shakespeare. He learnt to appreciate a good malt whisky with Malone.

The last time he was here, sitting on this bench, was his forty-second birthday. His forty-second birthday with a fishing trip to celebrate with Malone.

It was a perfect May day. A cloudless sky, hot, with the river bank gently buzzing.

Lying on his back in the grass in his waders with the sun splattering his face through the branches, it had come to him that his life had become very peaceful, that he was not suffering from that vague longing to be somewhere else that had always afflicted him. He felt, suddenly, a rich sense of contentment, a feeling of having reached some place or state where all of his life he had been striving to be.

As if to set a seal upon his discovery there was a movement from the water. Looking up he caught it again, another movement, another of those wonderful elegant, graceful, curving flashes.

He had seen salmon leap before of course, but somehow never like this. Everything inside him seemed suddenly to leap with it and he jumped to his feet and, calling to Malone, raced along the river bank, still in his waders, to the hotel, returning with champagne and two glasses.

Walking back along the path, he saw Malone sitting on the bench, leaning back beneath the tree. His eyes were closed. The sockets seemed very deep and there was a shadow on his face which he, Crane, thought must be thrown by the tree.

Drawing closer to him, he said his name gently; then, when Malone did not open his eyes, more urgently. He was about to drop down on one knee when Malone's eyelids flickered open.

'Malone?' he said.

But then a shaft of sunlight caught Malone's face. It warmed it, seemed to fill out the sockets again, dissolve the shadow. He, Crane, breathed a sigh of relief, a selfish sigh, the sigh of one who wanted everything to be all right.

He held the glasses out to Malone. 'Champagne,' he said, popping the cork.

'To more of this, Malone,' he said, raising his glass to Malone's in a toast.

'Aye,' Malone said, raising his eyes, unblinking, raising his glass too.

'To much more,' he said.

Six months later the man was dead.

2

IT WAS MORE than a hangover, though. It was one of those grand hangovers.

It was one of those hangovers that would not let you rest, that would not let you lie, or get up, but which *hurt* in a peculiar way whatever you did, not just in your head but throughout your body, and which kept coming at you in waves from the moment the first stabs of pain pushed their way through, prising you from sleep.

She felt so dizzy and so sick when she tried to get out of bed that she had to drop to her knees and crawl her way to the bathroom to take the paracetamol.

Her hands had shaken so much that she was unable to open the container. When the child-proof lid would not lift she began to tear at it, hurling it into the washbasin in a rage that made her head thump even more. Eventually she succeeded in chiselling the lid off with a nail file, cursing obscenely and at the same time weeping, ironically enough, like a child.

She had been too ill to need breakfast. Even the tea, which she made with the kettle and the teabags and the tiny plastic cartons of milk in her room, refused to stay down. She crouched beside the toilet, her arms about it, as it came back in racking dribbling vomits.

All she can face now is water. She sips it delicately, gingerly, from a glass by the bed, sinking back into the pillows to replace the cold damp towel, like a Victorian heroine, on her forehead.

The hangover seems to her to have permeated every inch of her body. It seems mental as well as physical. It lodges in her brain in a dark cloud of misery. To cheer herself up she reaches a hand over to the radio console by the bed and punches in the buttons.

A waltz tinkles out suddenly into the room. She recognizes it immediately. Her fingers scrabble to turn it up, a Satie waltz, one of his strange, sharp, disquieting waltzes, a café-pianist's waltz, a musical picture of an ageing dandy, of an old roué past his time, cynical, world-weary, not a waltz for children, surely, and yet a piece she had heard a thousand times, hiccuping out through the open window, jarring and snagging in young inexperienced hands and accompanied by the harsh rasp of her mother's voice.

'*Valse, valse,*' she hears again and the sharp crack of the ruler on the wood of the piano. A waltz of disillusionment, of disappointed hopes.

After her father, she, Alice, had been her mother's major disappointment. Apart from anything else, she showed no aptitude for the piano, indeed the lessons bored her. At fifteen she pleaded pressure of schoolwork and was allowed to give them up. It added to her mother's bitterness, she saw afterwards, when she not only moved in with Clive but also took up the guitar.

Lately she had found herself thinking a lot about her mother.

Several times she had found herself weeping. She had thought this extraordinary. But then the same thing started to happen to a woman friend whom she met by chance on the street. The woman dabbed her eyes. She said, 'I don't know why. It happens all the time.

'It must be our age,' she said. 'All of a sudden you realize you've become the same age as your mother.'

Behind the towel now, on her forehead, she can see again, quite precisely, every movement her mother made as she played the '*Valse*' that last time. She sees the wasted hands crashing into the chords, the shoulders swinging in dreadful mockery, the lips thin with anger in the mirror above the piano.

'*Valse*, *valse*,' she is shouting, one last time.

Still today the smell of wet macs and wax polish and watery vegetables brought back to her memories of her mother's death.

It was cancer of course. They took off a breast, removed her womb, but all to no avail. The cancer kept growing.

They put her mother and the rest of the women in a hostel close by the hospital while they had the treatment needed following the operation.

The hostel was run by a gaunt, grey-haired former headmistress who ran the place like the school she had left, and so the women, fighting for their lives, had also to fight for small, everyday decencies like the right to a bath when they wanted it, or the right to read a book after lights-out.

Her stay in the hostel though, turned out, by some miracle, to be her mother's finest hour. She organized the resistance. She demanded reading lights and hair-dryers and the right to a pre-dinner sherry for those who wanted it. She organized whist drives and slide shows and she even got a tuner in for the battered old upright piano.

302

And then, each night, after supper, she played for the women.

One night she, Alice, visiting her mother, tapped too softly on the door and, not being heard, let herself into the common room quietly. All about her, faces looked up, hands and bodies stilled for a second at her entrance. One, standing above another seated, twisted a long strand of hair into a roller. Two, sitting on a sofa together, had knitting needles suspended before them. Four had cards in their hands, several more clutched books, while all about them eddied in the air a final note from a thin and fashionable soprano, who cast loving looks upon her mother, one arm draped elegantly across the piano-top.

Staring, she had struggled to put a name to what she saw. Afterwards it came to her. What she had seen in the room, what she had felt, was a simple undisturbed femaleness.

It was this femaleness, she noticed, which dissipated each Friday, when she came to fetch her mother.

The certain gaiety that she felt in the air, that certain lightness, which held the women together like unseen threads, unravelled with the husbands and fathers and sons who came to collect the women, and as a group they fell apart. An awkwardness entered in. Conversation became strained. Those who had laughed and sung and sometimes even danced left clinging, invalids again, on the arms of their husbands.

When the six weeks of their treatment was over, the women parted with tears and kisses and with promises to keep in touch.

They thought keeping in touch would keep their

spirits up but they were wrong. Because one by one they died, and with each death it became harder for those who were left to stay alive. At funerals they stood together, separate, apart, sharers in something special, staring out in a small semi-circle at the rest of the mourners.

Her mother was the last but one to go.

Returning from the funeral of the thin and elegant soprano, she sat down slowly and painfully and lifted the piano-top, beginning to play the piece she had forced so often upon her pupils.

She played it over and over, dipping and rolling, her eyes closed, as if in a trance. With each rendering it became more exquisite, more bitterly ironic. Seeing her mother raise her fingers on the notes again scarcely before the final crashing chords had died away she cried, 'No mother, no!' the tears pouring down her face.

For a long moment they stared at each other in the mirror then her mother, slowly, very slowly, lowered the piano-top.

It was the last time she played. The next day she did not get out of bed. A month later she went back into hospital and two weeks after that she died.

A thin and gentle spinster, a former village shop-keeper, represented the sisterhood at the funeral.

There was colour in her cheeks.

She had put on weight.

3

H E'D MOVED IN with Malone in the end.

He'd shopped and cooked and cleaned for him when he could no longer do these things for himself.

Every lunchtime, he would go round to get Malone a meal. He did it, even after Malone's appetite had dwindled and he could have conveniently left something for him on a tray. He did it for himself more than Malone. He did it because it made Bullerman angry and he liked Bullerman angry. He was angry himself and it suited him to have anger all around.

He'd taken a deliberate pleasure in telling Bullerman he was moving in with Malone.

Once, Bullerman had said to him, that wetness on his lips and in his eyes, 'Always thought Malone was a bit of a . . . you know . . .' He had been outraged at the time, but once he'd moved in with Malone he wanted Bullerman to say it again. This time, though, he wanted him to say it publicly, with the acolytes around his throne. He wanted him to go through one of his pantomimes in the office, have everyone listening as he winked and insinuated on the phone, 'Oh, going home at lunchtime are we, to cook for Malone?' He needed it. He needed Bullerman's innuendo to exorcize his own guilt, because the truth was that he too had once wondered about Malone and wondering, he had come to know, was one of the world's most insidious wickednesses.

There was something . . . masculine about Malone.

Not macho masculine. No, not that at all. Something gentlemanly. Yes, that was it. There was something bookish about him, shy, spare, private. There would be other words, of course. Less kind words. Jargon words. Psychobabble. Words he didn't want to hear. Because there was no mystery. He knew what Malone was. He was a quintessential, old-fashioned bachelor, the sort you read about in novels. Sometimes, to your surprise, you found people in novels also existed in real life. Malone was one of them and that was all. People were people. Malone was Malone. And, like he said, he didn't care to wonder any more.

There were no women in Malone's life, not a mother, not a sister, not even a cleaning lady.

In twelve years of friendship, Malone had spoken little about his background. Sitting beside the bed in those last months, he, Crane, had nudged the conversation gently in that direction, thinking that it was something Malone might want to talk about. But each time the conversation petered away into silence and so he let it rest. If a man wanted to take that privacy, that discretion, to the grave, well then he should be allowed to do so. It was that thought he tried to comfort himself with later, smarting from the discovery that Malone had been married.

All he found out about Malone over the years was that he was an only child, that he had never known his father and that his mother died not long after he started his first job.

He was fourteen years old. The job was dark-room assistant to a portrait photographer with studios in a fashionable square that had long since disappeared beneath the urban motorway.

After three years there, Malone had got a job as a

306

photographer with a weekly paper out in the country. A few years later he came back to the city to work on the old *Evening Echo*. Not long after that, bursting with a young man's pride, he moved on to the paper which thirty-odd years later would inform him in a curt five-line letter that his services would no longer be required.

When he had seen the expression on Malone's face that day as they stood in the secretary's office, he had felt that familiar urge to pulp and blind.

He had wanted to grab one of the Tontons Macoute by his expensive dark lapels, smash him against a wall, scream into his face. 'Doesn't matter what you've done to the paper, doesn't matter that you've turned it into a scabby, scurrilous rag, this man still remembers the day he arrived.'

He wanted to scream, even though he knew there was only emptiness and oblivion behind the dark glasses, 'Guess what. Here's the joke. This man still cared.'

It was impossible, he found, even after he moved in with Malone, actually to acknowledge that he was dying.

Then one night he was helping him to bed, settling his things on the bedside table, his books, his glasses, his radio. He found the small ceremony difficult and so each night was over-jovial, determined to inject into it some pretence of normality. Each night he said, 'OK, Malone?' absurdly, cheerfully, afraid to look at him from the door. But on this night Malone said, 'There is something, Jim . . .' It was the first time he had ever called him 'Jim'.

Malone said, 'I've left you the house.'

He, Crane, sitting on a chair by the bed, looked

away, wanting to drop his head in his hands. He murmured, 'Malone . . .'

Malone said, 'No. I want you to have it. And there's no one else. You'll sell it, of course. But would you do me one favour? Would you keep it, just for a few months, for Uncle Arly, just until he dies?

'He won't last last long,' he said.

'I'd sort of hoped,' he said with a sad smile, 'he'd go before me.'

The lump of grief in his, Crane's, throat had been too large to speak. He turned away from Malone, from the utter embarrassing unmanageability of death. He shook his head. He closed his eyes.

'No problem, Malone,' he said.

There were things that he had done for Malone in the end that he could not have imagined doing for another human being.

The first time he had to place his arms around him, lift him from the chair, he felt a sharp flush of exertion which was part alarm. Helping him up the stairs to the bathroom, they staggered like a drunken couple, Malone jammed against the wall, he against the banister.

Malone had been listening to his beloved *Pearl Fishers*. An aria swirled around them, a baritone and a tenor, two men's voices, swearing in duet an oath of friendship.

The soaring music followed them, like an anthem, as they stumbled, grunting, from step to step, up the stairs.

At the top he, Crane, kicked open the bathroom door with a clumsy foot, half dragging Malone in and easing him down on to the toilet.

As he lowered him, he chattered inanities through

clenched and frightened teeth, turning, without catching Malone's eye, to let himself out. Behind him, though, Malone said, 'I'm sorry, old man, but I wonder if you would mind helping me with my trousers.'

And so, as is the way, he had become too effusive, too hearty. 'No problem, Malone.' He looked away with 'There you are now' and 'How's that now', dropping down on his haunches to down the pyjama bottoms.

From above him he heard, 'I'll probably need some help when I've finished.' He was going to mutter something, crawl out of the door. But then he stopped himself. He straightened, stood up. He looked Malone square in the eye. He said, 'That's fine, Malone. I'll be outside,' and then he went out and closed the door behind him, and sank down on the top step and wept.

When Malone called him though, he went back inside without embarrassment. He pulled up his pyjama bottoms, lifted him from the seat and tied them, all this strangely easier than before.

Yes, there were things that he had done for Malone that he could not imagine doing for another human being, things that lay on the edge of what he had believed himself to be, things from a grey area where the world as a whole preferred not to dwell.

He had held his best friend in his arms, lifted him up, dressed him and undressed him.

Death, he found, was a great liberator.

4

THEY SIT IN the back of the taxi, she thinks, as
if they have drawn themselves away from each other.
They clutch at their straps, a vast expanse of seat
between them. Snatching a glance at him, she sees
him staring out of the window at the windswept
winter-brown countryside and the Roman Wall snaking away into the distance behind them.

Perhaps it was thinking about her mother that had
done it, but suddenly, despite her hangover, she'd
had a deep desire to be away from the hotel and back
home in Tanglewood.

It only added to her determination when he'd tried
to argue her out of it.

'Well you see, there's a small problem,' he had said.

'What's that,' she had asked stiffly.

'Well, we need to keep you under wraps.'

'Why?'

'Well, knowing Stanley he'll probably try again.'

'And you think I'll talk to him, do you, despite the
fact that I've signed a contract with you?'

'No, I don't think you'll do it deliberately, but . . .
well . . . Stanley can be very persuasive. And, like I
said, a paragraph of "no comment" is enough for
Stanley to drum up a lead.'

She had been adamant though.

'You can't keep me here against my will,' she told
him. 'I want to go home. And if you don't call me a
taxi, I'll get Rita to come and pick me up.'

It must have been the threat of Rita that did it. There was an audible sigh from the other end of the phone.

'OK,' he said heavily.

It had been unclear to her, at the time, quite why she was being so unpleasant to him. She saw now, of course.

As she had been clambering into the taxi, a host of young guests were arriving for a wedding reception. The car park was full of dark suits and bright button-holes and short skirts and very high heels. The young men slapped each other on the back a lot and laughed and joked in very loud voices. Their cars, which were very shiny with too many lights and too much chrome, all had stickers in the back windows. One told her to wake up with a young farmer, another said windsurfers did it standing up. A third asked her to honk if she had it last night.

Just as Jim Crane was pulling the door closed, a young man passing cried out to another in a loud voice. 'Hey Malcolm . . . getting any?' She lowered her head and fiddled with her coat buttons in a peculiarly spinsterish embarrassment.

'Getting any?' It was as if the world was involved in some conspiracy, trying to keep up some mythical reputation as the horniest planet in the galaxy.

'Getting any?' Of course. Naturally. Raise the eyebrows. Give an enigmatic smile. Lie if need be. Admit to anything. Sado-masochism. Sex with animals. Necrophilia. But don't, whatever you do, even in this age of Aids, admit to not getting any.

A few weeks ago, looking out of her window, she had seen a couple walking past, holding hands. She found herself staring at them, at their linked hands, as if what she saw was not something normal and everyday, but some ritual, some alien custom from another land. She stared as once, a long time ago, she had stared at men dancing upon swords in their bare feet or burning bodies upon the tops of gaudy funeral pyres, or wheels whirling in the air in pursuit of prayer.

That night, unable to sleep, thinking of the couple again, she had done something she had not done for many years. She had begun to count the number of men she had been to bed with.

It was an old sixties habit, so someone had once told her. As she counted them she found that sometimes she could remember names but not faces, other times it was the face to which she was unable to put a name. Sometimes she could remember neither, and all that came to mind was a place or an occurrence, a strange tapestry upon a wall say or an unusual sexual proclivity. Sometimes it was little more than a feeling, a nameless shape, on top of her, inside her, or beside her in the bed.

It was this last that astonished her most when she thought about it.

She wondered if there could be seven ages of woman quite distinct from those of man. Was it possible that as life threw itself into reverse and set off on that road backwards towards that mewling puking infant, that there came, for such as herself, a second virginity? Because that was how she felt sometimes. Like a virgin again.

She had been celibate for four years now. It was not Rita's deliberate, cool, controlled celibacy, not the celibacy of a collection of finely written essays. It was an accidental celibacy, untidy and undisciplined

312

like herself, a simple slapdash celibacy that had gone on growing, all on its own, like briars around a fairy-tale castle lost in sleep, a celibacy that had gone unnoticed and unrecorded, from month to month, from year to year, until there it was, suddenly, a briar-covered, ivy-clad *fait accompli*.

After Bernard left, there had been a few gently melancholy months. Soon though she became deeply sensible of the pleasure of no longer having him around. And then when Rita moved up, their lives intertwined again. She became suddenly busy. A film here, a meeting there. One Saturday morning, she woke up to the sun on her face and a pleasing sensation which upon examination proved to be contentment.

Like most women of her age and experience, she knew her own body well, how, when the need occurred, to satisfy sexual longing. And if this satisfaction too often left its own residual frustration, its faint disquieting aftertaste, well, that was only to be expected. She consoled herself with the thought, and it was no small consolation, that masturbation, no matter how unsatisfactory, still could not compare with the horrors of tentative, cursory or unenthusiastic foreplay, solipsistic penetration or a boring, snoring body.

And so it was that the years passed. So it was that she had thought little about her celibacy until recently, when, for no reason she could quite divine, it had begun to twitch gently at her and jar. It was this twitching and jarring, she saw now, which had precipitated her into the foolish débâcle with Andrew.

With the recognition of her celibacy had come this new feeling of innocence, this feeling of being a virgin again. When she thought about making love, tried to visualize the act, it seemed to her that all her experience of it had somehow receded. Occasionally, in a moment of blind panic, she wondered if she would be able to remember how to do it. Thinking of performing the act made it seem suddenly very large and very serious and utterly beyond the bounds of spontaneity.

She found it increasingly hard now to cast her mind back, to imagine that bewitched and distant time when it was none of these things, when it was nothing more than a preliminary, this most intimate of acts, an introduction, something that happened before you knew where he lived, or whom he voted for, or even if you liked him.

It was this last that astonished her most, remembering how irrelevant had been the question of liking. You went to bed with someone then, more or less, because it was the fashion, because of that overwhelming social pull that belonged to the times. There were those, Clive was one of course, who liked to call it primeval. It would have been nice to call it that. Nice to dignify it in that way. But it was so much less than that. You went to bed with him because of the way he looked, or the way he dressed, or the way he talked. Or you went to bed simply because you had drunk too much, or you could not get home, or because he was miserable or you were, or, and here perhaps there was something in what the owner of the silver-topped cane had had to say after all, because you felt under some mild obligation after he had bought you dinner.

They were strange times, a time of innocent gratification, no Aids to worry about, a little bubble to press out every day to ensure you could not become pregnant. Strange times, times of great pressure and social responsibility masquerading as relaxed and easy.

So? What was the lesson of the sixties? That the pendulum had swung out too far? Well, where was the surprise in that? Pendulums always swung out too far before swinging back again in the direction from which they had come. For so it had been with her pendulum. It had swung out wildly in her younger days, ending its journey with Bernard, before turning round and coming back on itself, bringing with it the last four years of celibacy.

She ached for sex sometimes. Not just for sex, but for the simple feel of another body, her hands on his, his on hers. She was lonely. Simple words would do at such a time. Yes, she was lonely. That was all.

Watching the couple holding hands in the street, she yearned suddenly to be doing the same herself, to catch fingers with someone and to kiss them, not another woman, not a woman whom she would kiss warmly, lovingly, on the cheek or the forehead, even on the lips, but chastely. No, she longed to kiss a man, to feel that first full sense of firmness, that dryness becoming moist, that sinking in together, that searching and drawing out. Ah yes. You could tell, from that first kiss, whether it would be worth going to bed together.

Staring out of the car window now, she feels herself, to her own embarrassment, growing damp. She asks herself, a little stiffly, why she is thinking these things. She tells herself she does not know. A small curving smile in her face, which she sees suddenly reflected in the driving mirror, tells her she lies.

It was absurd. It would be . . . she searches for the

315

word . . . improper. Yes. That was it. Quite improper. It was a business relationship. She had a contract in her bag to prove it. He was a Sunday newspaperman, for God's sake, she a feminist novelist. He represented everything she most abhorred. Also, apart from anything else, she had only known him for twenty-four hours. You could not count, after all, the three weeks he had been sitting outside the house. Good God, she knew absolutely nothing about the man.

Yes, she did. She knew lots about him. Maybe she knew everything about him. She knew he went fishing and liked cooking, that he read Hemingway and knew something of opera. She knew he could find his way around good wine. She knew he was funny and awkward and a bit of a misfit. She knew because of the way he stroked his hair down that he was embarrassed at its loss; the way he shambled a little that he was unhappy at his weight. She knew that he was sad at the moment because of the loss of his friend. Did she know then that he wasn't gay? Yes she knew, because he had that certain warmth with a woman, that warmth that said he liked them. Gay men had that. Oh yes, they did when they liked women, but their warmth lacked his awkwardness. What had a gay man, after all, to be awkward about with a woman?

Yes he was awkward all right, walking wounded she would guess, probably from his marriage.

Altogether she thought he seemed like a decent human being. She was sorry she had flown off the handle at him. She had been going to apologize when he came to her room to tell her the taxi was waiting, but just at that moment the phone had rung and it had been Rita.

'Alice,' she said, 'I'm just checking. Are you all right?'

She smiled. She knew what Rita meant by 'all right'.

'Of course I'm all right, Rita,' she said.

I'll come out if you like, Alice,' she said.

She sounded, though, a little hesitant. She, Alice, had smiled to herself. Saturday was the day of Rita's big weekly run. She would cover twenty miles or so on a Saturday.

'There's no need, Rita,' she said gently.

At the other end of the phone, she could hear her taking a breath.

'I've got some big news for you, Alice,' she said.

The sound of her, taking breath like that, awakened an old notion. Good God, she had thought, surely this was not the moment Rita was going to choose to step out of the closet? Or perhaps, she thought, it was something else, something quite unimaginable, something to do, say, with Andrew?

'It's a big thing for me,' Rita was saying. 'I'm going to need all the help I can get.'

'You'll get it, Rita, you'll get it,' she said. 'Just tell me what it is, for God's sake.'

At the other end of the phone she heard Rita swallow with the enormity of what she had to disclose.

'I've decided to give up full-time working so that I can train for a triathlon,' she said.

Laughing, she, Alice, had placed her hand over the phone so that Rita should not hear and be hurt as she disclosed, in all seriousness, details of her grim training schedule.

Suddenly there was a small silence. Then Rita's voice again, which, now, was soft and shy.

'It's hard for you to understand, I know that, Alice,' she said. 'But you see it's really important to me.'

A lump came to her throat then. She turned away so that Jim Crane, who stood uncertainly at the door, should not see her face. She wished Rita was there in the room so that she could give her a hug.

'I know it is,' she said, 'and I think it's wonderful and I'll be right there with you all the time. I'll be there to cheer you on. I'll be your support vehicle if you like. I'll do anything I can to help.'

She was still smiling when she put down the phone.

It was only as Jim Crane coughed politely from the door that it occurred to her that she had not told Rita she was coming home.

5

AHEAD OF THEM now, the city is sliding into view.

Leaning forward, he gives the directions to the driver.

Next to him, she turns enquiringly from the window.

'I'm sorry,' he says, with an embarrassed half-smile. 'The cat.'

All things considered, he'd been glad when she said she wanted to come back early. For a start he was worried about Uncle Arly. Of course, he didn't eat much now Malone was gone and he had left three plateloads of food. Still, he'd be glad to get back just to check things were all right.

On top of that, he was glad to get away from the hotel. He was feeling low and dispirited now, and he knew it was because every corner he turned there reminded him of Malone, made the absence of him seem more dreadfully final.

The crematorium had been full for the funeral. Even he had been surprised at the turn-out. It pleased him to see the place packed for a man as quiet and modest as Malone.

The vicar was a woman. A deaconess you called her.

It wasn't uncommon, of course, these days, although naturally enough Bullerman had seen fit to complain.

'Bloody women priests,' he had said when he saw her.

'A theological debate in which I'm sure you're keenly interested, Bullerman,' he had replied with heavy sarcasm.

Crippled with embarrassed grief, he had tried to ascertain before Malone died whether there was anything he particularly wanted at his funeral.

Several times he tried to bring up the subject. Then one day, as he tried, stumbling again, Malone smiled at him, white and tired, from the pillows. 'I leave it all to you, Jim,' he said.

The funeral director was plump with pudgy hands and a very red face and looked so much like a funeral director that he might have been an actor chosen for the part.

Malone was not a church-goer and neither was he, so in the end it was the funeral director who supplied the name of a vicar.

When he called the number, he found the man was away on a week's retreat. 'I'll give you the deaconess's number,' said his wife.

Replacing the phone he had stared at it for a moment, confused, wondering if it would be right, having Malone sent on his way, as it were, by a woman. Then he shrugged and picked up the receiver.

'I leave it all to you, Jim,' Malone had said.

Her voice on the phone was young and friendly. When he called round and she opened the door, he said her name hesitantly, not sure it was her. To put it bluntly, she looked too young and too pretty to be a priest.

'Times change, Malone,' he had found himself saying.

She made him some coffee and sat down the other side of her desk. She asked him if there was anything he would like to make the bare crematorium service a little more personal. When she said it, he felt a small sharp stab of *déjà vu*. At first he could not think why, then he realized they were almost the same words as the woman registrar had used when he and Janet were arranging their wedding.

Perhaps that was why he'd been determined to think of something for Malone. Milestones, he thought. Milestones in our lives. The further away we got from the caves the more we steam-rollered out the milestones. Primitive societies burnt their bodies on funeral pyres, sailed them down the Ganges, dug them up after they'd been buried and reburied them halfway up a cliff. They celebrated, we civilized with crematoria and convenience formalities designed to flatten out as far as was possible this, our most fundamental rite of passage.

Seeing his furrowed brow, the deaconess began to prompt him gently. Was there something of which Malone was especially fond? Afterwards he saw that she meant a hymn or a psalm. Misunderstanding her though, he said the first thing that came into his head.

'Fishing,' he said, and she smiled.

'Well, we're not short of fishing stories in the Bible,' she said.

She picked a good one, as it turned out. Couldn't have been better.

When she announced the reading from the Gospel of St John, chapter twenty-one, it didn't mean a thing to him. But once she started in on it, well, he thought, yeah, that was just about right.

He picked up a Bible on the ledge in front of him to follow it, feeling Bullerman staring in surprise.

Peter the fisherman wanted to go fishing. It was after the crucifixion. He was sick, you could tell. Well, who wouldn't be? With his leader banged up on a cross.

It was evening. He could imagine him, edgy, roll-up in hand, pacing up and down the beach in the dark, then tossing the cigarette away half-smoked and saying, 'I'm going fishing,' and striding down the shingle to shove out the boat.

He listened with the rest of them, hearing, all night, the eternal, empty poop and suck of the water. He saw the sea, still like glass, and then across it, in the early morning, the dark shape on the shore. He could hear the nets rattle out again on the other side as directed, see them sinking and sinking and growing heavier.

Twenty-five years he had in the business. With twenty-five years behind you you got a smell for the truth, for that little something that told you it was a story you could believe. And he believed this one. Why? Well, man, because of the tally. Because the story didn't say they caught 'over a hundred fish' or 'around a hundred and fifty' or 'nearly two hundred', neat easy phrases to camouflage the lack of information. No, it said they caught one hundred and fifty-three. A precise figure. A figure counted out and passed from mouth to mouth in surprise, till eventually it got to John who wrote it down. Yeah, an exact figure, a fisherman's figure. Once he had caught a monster salmon with Malone. Twenty-one pounds thirteen ounces. Never forgot the weight. Fishermen didn't make mistakes about catches. Forget anglers' yarns. Figures like that stayed in a fisherman's mind.

He thanked her with all his heart as she read it. A hell of a catch. A hell of a catch. A hell of a good story.

'This one's for you, Malone,' he said.

6

HE KNEW SOMETHING was wrong the moment he opened the front door. It was that certain . . . silence.

It was not that Uncle Arly was the sort of cat who ran up at the sound of the door opening to rub himself against your legs. No, he was much too dignified for that. A lazily extended paw, a yawn, a bored stare from the amber eyes was all you could expect from Uncle Arly.

He found him curled up on his favourite chair, a perfect circle of orange. He did not need to touch him to tell that he was dead. He sank down on the sofa and let his head drop back.

'I'm sorry, Malone,' he said.

In the doorway now there is a movement.

'I sent the taxi away,' she says.

He opens his eyes very slowly, scarcely troubling to raise his head.

'I should have left the heating on,' he says. 'Uncle Arly's died of cold.'

She walks over to the chair, kneels and touches the cat.

'No,' she says. 'Not with this fur. With this fur he could sleep out on Everest.'

But he persists, belligerently, like a little boy.

'He died cold and hungry,' he says.

She rises to her feet, walks over to the kitchen the other side of the room divider.

'There are three plates of food untouched,' she says.

'He was old,' she says. 'He died peacefully in his sleep, at home, on his favourite chair.

'We should all be so lucky,' she says.

'Come on,' she says. 'Let's bury him.'

They wrap him in a white damask tablecloth in a strange old hat box they find lying in the loft.

The wind pulls at his mac and tears at the bare branches of the apple tree as he digs a hole beneath it.

Watching him smooth out the last shovel of earth, she recites softly:

> 'On a little heap of Barley
> Died my agèd Uncle Arly.

'A small funeral oration,' she says.

Back in the house, he says, 'Those two lines you recited . . . over the grave.'

'Lear,' she says.

They are sitting in Malone's study by this time, with a whisky each to warm them up.

'What did you mean,' he says, 'do you remember, in the car on the way up to the King's Head on Thursday night, about it being love poetry?'

'Well, Lear, was a sort of buttoned up Victorian. He was an epileptic, last child of a huge family, brought up by his sister. He was shy, possibly gay, but anyway he fell in love with this girl but somehow wasn't able to do anything about it. His poetry used to be thought of as nonsense stuff written for children, but now we've come to see it could be more than that, that beneath the nonsense could be serious love poetry written by a man who, because of his problems, was unable to express his emotion in ordinary language.'

Then she recites some more lines for him.

> 'You shall have my chairs and candle,
> And my jug without a handle.'

'But that's what's written in the front of Malone's book,' he says, jumping up and scrabbling in the drawers for the poems.

'Tell me about Malone,' she says.

He'd gone on talking to Malone right up to the end, even after he knew Malone could no longer hear him.

He had this idea that if he kept talking, Malone might not go, that he might chivvy him somehow into staying, as once he would have chivvied him into another drink. 'Just one more, eh Malone? Just one more for the road, Malone.'

Sometimes he joked with him, joked with the eyelids, grey and closed and crinkled against the pillow. 'The pub, Malone,' he would say. 'Me in the kitchen, remember, you behind the bar.'

Once when he could think of nothing more to say, when he'd been driven into silence by the strained and empty breathing, he leant forward and put a hand through the bars of the cot, laid it on the bedclothes, stroked them and whispered, 'Don't go, Malone, don't go.'

But then, as it lay there, he heard the door open, and so he pulled it back quickly and raised it in the air, the other one too, throwing his head back in an ostentatious stretch.

It was a nurse, a sister, moving on rubber-soled feet. She squished around the bed, taking Malone's pulse, making marks upon a clipboard, twitching the bedclothes back into place.

He started to talk to her to cover his embarrassment and from that day forward they began exchanging pleasantries.

Some days later, when Malone was very near the end, she invited him into her office, late at night, for some coffee.

He found himself entertaining her, name-dropping, telling anecdotes which he could see that she liked. About the ward she was stiff and brisk, but there, in the pool of light from the lamp on her desk, she unbent, became girlish, even coy, as he teased her about her choice of daily newspaper.

The paper that she read was old-fashioned, conservative, like her he thought. From their conversation he found that they were the same age, which surprised him. He had thought her older than himself, less for her appearance than for a tight, closed-up look she had about her, as if she had been too careful with herself and was now, too late, beginning to realize it. He could see, as they talked, that she was lonely and that she was hoping something might come of their meeting.

When he went to fetch Malone's things the day after he died, she took some time finding the key to the locker. Her movements were slow and he could see that she was making time for them to talk. Embarrassed for her, he began to gabble, praising her and her staff too effusively.

Behind the tight white skin of her face as she held

out the black plastic bag, he saw the hope beginning to drain away. Her voice lost its familiarity and became formal again. In the end she nodded curtly to him in farewell and, turning away from him, squished back down the corridor.

Watching her go, he knew she was disappointed and in some way dishonoured and he knew it was his fault and he was sorry.

But there was something else, something that happened on that last night, on the night that Malone died.

He, Crane, had been working late. It was after twelve when he got to the hospital.

He'd arrived in a terrible rage. A trawler had been lost with a father, two sons, and an uncle on board. London told him to leave it to a freelance. Instead they wanted him to doorstep some woman who'd been married to a soap star.

'It was the first time I came round to your house,' he explains to Alice Potter.

He was sitting telling Malone all about it. His teeth were clenched, his knuckles white and tight by the bed.

He told him, 'I get taken off the trawler deaths, Malone, to sit on the doorstep of some stupid woman whose only claim to fame is she was once married to this . . . Father Dwyer.

'You'll have to forgive me, Alice,' he says. 'I was very angry at the time.'

They'd told him Malone was in a coma, that he could hear nothing now, but it didn't matter. He'd stormed on just the same.

'That's it, Malone,' he said. 'It's official now. People who don't exist are more important than those who do.'

He was hunched over the bed in his wrath. He'd closed his eyes, pressed his fists into the sockets with his anger. He was sitting like this when he heard the faintest of movements from the bed. Opening his own eyes, he saw an eyelid of Malone's flickering open. It was a slit, nothing more. Then the voice came, a voice that sent shivers down his back, very hoarse and very distant, from somewhere on the edge of the grave, repeating for him their maxim, their motto, their toast to which they had clinked their glasses on a thousand occasions together.

'Crane . . .' it whispered one last time, 'this is no way for a grown man to make a living.'

7

SHE CAN SEE that he thinks he is telling her with a wry smile on his face. She can see that he thinks he is joking. She can see that he thinks he is laughing, gently, affectionately, whereas he is, in fact, weeping.

'Oh God,' he says, discovering the tears on his cheeks. 'I'm sorry.'

'Where's the big deal,' she says, 'in weeping?'

Which is when he realizes that she's crying too.

'It's the strangest thing,' she says. 'This morning, just by chance, I heard some music on the radio. It made me think of my mother.'

She says, 'Why do we think it's so terrible to lose someone when you're young? It's the old who need the sympathy. The older you get, the harder it is to bear. Because the older you get, the more you realize that death is so utterly final.'

She says, 'I know now there's only one tragedy in life. Love isn't tragic. Having someone walk out on you or be unfaithful or fall in love with someone else. That's not tragic. Bernard taught me that. You can get over all of those things. There's only one tragedy in life and that's death. It's all so simple. Death is the tragedy of life.'

And so, both leaning their heads back, closing their eyes, they had continued to weep for a moment, separately, but also together in a curious, spontaneous conjunction.

They wept for those who had died before them

and those who would die later, and for themselves too, for they too would die.

He wept for his friend Malone and she for her mother. They wept for the might-have-beens of life and the never-could-bes and last of all for the sheer hopeless wonder of being alive.

Raising her head, some time later, and wiping her eyes, she finds the last of the day draining away into night.

Reaching down she picks up the book of poems which he had let slip through his fingers on to the floor.

Turning the pages idly she lights upon some lines which stare out at her through the gloom.

> I am tired of living singly,
> On this coast so wild and shingly.

Struck with a faint feeling of embarrassment, she closes the book with a small snap.

'I think it's time to go home,' she says.

Saturday Evening . . .

1

S HE WATCHES HIM from the window, surprising
herself by how much she likes him.

Below her she can see him easing himself awkwardly out of the taxi door, a carrier bag bulging in
each hand. Pushing open the gate, he turns away
from the wind which lashes rain in his face and
catches his mac, flapping it wildly.

'Good God,' he says, dumping the carrier bags on
the hall floor as the front door clashes closed with a
bang behind him.

'What a night,' he says, head down, shaking himself
like a dog.

The bland look of good humour on his face as he
lifts it to greet her changes to one of incredulity.

'Good God,' he says, a second time.

'I decided to dress for dinner,' she says primly.

Rising to his feet at Malone's he'd said, 'Look, I
haven't broken the bad news to you. I'm supposed to
stick with you all day, in case Stanley tries again.'

She had smiled up at him, a funny crooked smile.

'Well,' she said, 'that doesn't seem like such bad
news. I'm sure neither of us fancies being alone at the
moment.'

'We could go out to dinner,' he said.

At that moment a handful of rain hit the window
like gravel.

'It's such an awful night,' she said doubtfully.

'Well . . .' he said, hesitantly. 'If you like, I could cook.'

Outside her house, in the taxi, she said, laughing, 'I'll be here all alone and unprotected till you return. Supposing Stanley reappears.'

'Lock all the doors,' he said dramatically. 'Don't answer the bell or the phone till I return.'

'But how,' she said in a throaty voice, 'shall I know it's you?'

'I'll use the password,' he said.

'The password,' she said. 'What's that?'

'The same as the Famous Five's,' he said.

'Remind me,' she laughed.

' "Adventure",' he said with an awful leer.

Three times as she got ready she'd taken the dress out of the wardrobe and put it back.

It wasn't her usual sort of dress. It was silk, black silk, cut like a wisp of nothing. It clung around her breasts and her waist and then flared from her hips, and its neck was cut wide so that it kept slipping, of its own accord, down off her shoulders.

'Ooooh, it makes you look soooo sexy, Alice,' Céline had said.

Céline always insisted on buying her something when she came to London: a pair of shoes, a handbag, once an exquisite hat.

'But I can't, Céline. I really can't,' she said, lifting the price ticket.

'Oh poufff,' said Céline. 'Bud so rich now he thinks he run for mayor.'

'But when will I wear it?' she persisted.

Céline clicked her teeth and raised her eyebrows in exasperation.

'You wear it when you want to look sexy, Alice,' she said.

In the kitchen now he unpacks the carrier bags upon the bench-top.

'I was queuing at the meat counter,' he says, conversationally, 'when I realized you were probably a vegetarian.'

'No,' she says, with a small edge to her voice. 'I can understand why you might think so. But there is still one tiny recalcitrant corner of my life not entirely sound.'

'Well it doesn't matter anyway,' he says, a little surprised at her sharpness. 'I got some fresh pasta and I decided to make this asparagus sauce I've been wanting to try for a while. And I thought I'd do syllabub for pudding.'

'Oh *pudding*,' she says, mollified, her eyes wide with awe.

Sitting at the table, the hanging light making her wine glow deep red, she watches him cooking.

'I'll need a knife,' he had said.

'Over there,' she said, pointing at a drawer.

Scrabbling around inside among the rusting old-fashioned kitchen implements, he had pulled out the best he could find. It was an old bone-handled affair with a very blunt blade.

'You don't cook much do you?' he said, smiling.

'I gave it up,' she told him, grimacing. 'After Clive.'

Leaning her chin on her hand, she follows his movements with pleasure.

He is not clumsy like her in the kitchen. His actions are smooth and deft and economic. There's a neatness in the way he chops and pulps. He sweeps the vegetables with a flourish from the board into the pan, spilling nothing. His gait, she notices, has lost all its awkwardness. He seems smaller somehow, less bulky, as he moves gracefully between the bench and the stove.

Oh God she was a joy to cook for.

He watches her now with satisfaction out of the corner of his eye as she lifts the tagliatelli slowly, savouring it as she chews. Sucking a piece in, she licks a dribble of the sauce off her chin like a child. God how he hated people who picked at their food, women worried about every inch, or gluttons, stoking it in like fuel, like Bullerman.

Taking the first forkful of pasta into her mouth, she had closed her eyes with delight. Opening them again, she looked at him with undisguised admiration.

'Unbelievable,' she said in hushed tones, shaking her head.

Laying down her fork, she lifted her glass to him in a toast.

'To the chef,' she said.

'I'm sure you're very good at what you do,' she said, 'but for myself I can't help feeling you're wasted as a reporter.'

And now, dinner over, he wanders around her

study, touching the strange objects reverently – the bird cage, the wind-up gramophone, the tailor's dummy.

'I've lit a fire in the study,' she had told him. 'I thought it would be cosier than the lounge.'

The fire crackles comfortingly now in the dark marble fireplace.

It was such a beautiful room, the sort of room you saw in one of those features in Sunday supplements, stamped on every corner with her personality – the rugs on the stripped floorboards, the pot plants, the wonderful deep old sofa, and the books, rising from floor to ceiling either side of the fireplace.

Tilting his head, he reads the titles and, halting, pulls an old orange Penguin from the row.

Carrying in the coffee and the brandy, she sees him reading it and looks at him enquiringly.

'*Catcher in the Rye*,' he says.

'You know I think for sixties people there are moments,' he says.

'Moments?' she says, putting the tray down on the coffee table.

'Well, like where you were at certain times.'

'Oh, you mean like when Kennedy was shot?'

'Yeah. And John Lennon.

'Where you were,' he says, 'when you first read *Catcher in the Rye*.'

It was the end of term, that time like no other. It was after his 'O' levels. He lay on his blazer in the long grass at the end of the sports field. Tadger Hughes turned up, Tadger Hughes whom he hated, of whom he was frightened because he was a bully. Tadger had the others with him too and he was menacing. He said, 'What you doin', Craney?'

He looked Tadger Hughes straight in the eyes for the first time in his life. He said, 'Fuck off, Tadger, I'm reading.'

It astonished him at the time. His own courage. It was the first time he had used the word. And the miracle was that Tadger Hughes went away.

It was very hot. First he read on his stomach and then he turned over and held the book in the air. Occasionally he took breaks because of the wonder of it. He put the book down on his chest and stared up into the clearest, the bluest, the most incredibly beautiful sky.

'It was the most amazing sky,' he says.

She read it in Nepal, on a hillside in the sunshine, with the Himalayas stretching out before her. All around her was a freedom she could have reached out and touched. Somewhere someone was playing a guitar. There was a smell of hash in the air and something good cooking. Somewhere, a long way away, the world she knew was working because it was a Monday afternoon and that was what the world she knew did on a Monday afternoon. People sat at desks and rushed around with files, and typed and picked up phones. But she read a book looking out on the Himalayas. She lowered the book and stared up into the sky.

Her eyes are misty as she tells him.

'The sky was always blue,' she says. 'The first time you read *Catcher in the Rye*.'

*

It surprises him, how much they have in common. He wouldn't have thought it, him and her. Not just books but music too. Now the floorboards are covered in album covers. 'You must hear this' . . . 'Wait . . . remember this one?'

They play them all. Elvis and Dylan, the Everly Brothers, Dusty Springfield, the Beatles, Carole King, Joni Mitchell . . .

He sings along with them. It delights her. He sings well and he knows all the words. Soon they have rolled back the rugs and are dancing, very drunk.

They dance like those of their time, inexpertly but with an excess of enthusiasm. They wave their hands in the air and bump and grind with old out-of-practice hips.

Their faces are flushed with too much brandy. Their eyes sparkle. They laugh and mock. Stumble and slip a little, and all this without embarrassment.

They have forgotten the worries about awkwardness that plagued them earlier on as they got ready, she lying out in the old claw-foot bath, he across town in his cubicled shower.

They have forgotten that only a few hours ago they questioned, each one, whether or not to part with a handshake would have been better, whether or not it would have been wiser, at their age, given all that they knew, not to attempt the impossible.

They are both drunk. By the grace of God, they don't care. He thinks wryly he can't drink like he used to. In Northern Ireland he could do twelve hours at a stretch on a bar stool. She remembers Hong Kong where she and Céline could keep going all night.

And now suddenly they are silent, slumped back upon the sofa, overcome by their exertions.

341

Outside the wind howls and thumps and rattles the ivy against window. Tired, it says. Not me.

It occurs to him that perhaps he should be offering to go. Not that he wants to. But perhaps, he thinks, she is waiting for him to make a move so that she too may rise and say, politely regretful, 'Yes, I suppose we'd better call it a day.'

He isn't, after all, he thinks, the type to presume.

At the other end of the sofa, the same thing is occurring to her. Perhaps she should make it easy for him, for the pair of them. Perhaps she should yawn and say, 'Ah well . . .' in the usual, accepted, self-explanatory fashion.

There's a small disappointed jar in his heart as she rises to her feet. He struggles up a little himself. But she says nothing, merely walks to the window and pulls back the curtain.

'What a night,' she says, by way of excuse.

In the street the elm trees sway and bend in the wind which rolls the brambles in the front garden like waves. The smirking cherub turns sightless eyes up to her begging to be brought into the warm. Down the back alley somewhere a dustbin lid breaks free and bowls emptily away.

She knows suddenly, without a shadow of doubt, that she does not want him to go.

More music, she thinks. He can't leave while the music is playing.

She begins to scrabble among the records. Taking his cue, he uncorks the brandy.

'Top you up?' he says.

'Why not,' she says.

She pulls out an album, any album, and slips it on to the turntable. The Satie waltz tinkles out into the room.

She begins to sway to it, advances a few steps and turns. The dress has slipped off her shoulders. Her hair, carefully caught up, is falling down in large wisps.

He jumps to his feet, stands before her.

'Miss Potter,' he says. 'I think, if you check your card, you will find this dance is mine.'

'Indeed, Mr Crane,' she answers demurely, 'I do believe it is.'

She is intensely aware as she steps into his arms of the pressure of his hand upon her waist, the sudden proximity of his face to hers.

'They tell me, Mr Crane,' she says, turning her face away, 'that you work for one of our Sunday periodicals.'

'Indeed so, ma'am,' he answers precisely.

'I do not believe I know it. I do not believe it is one of the periodicals which Papa takes,' she says, searching for something to say.

'Indeed, all things considered, I think not, ma'am,' he replies with a smile.

Drawing back from him without warning, she finds herself caught in a look which he is casting upon her. Held in it, unable to withdraw her eyes, she feels a deep blush creep slowly up over her naked shoulders to her face.

'It must be a hard life, Mr Crane,' she says, stammering softly.

'It has its compensations, Miss Potter,' he murmurs in reply.

Moving gently in his arms, she considers the look which he cast upon her. It was one of regard certainly, but more, oh so much more than that. It seemed to take in everything she was, everything he thought himself too, everything that they might be together.

It cried out her name. It cried out, 'We two . . . We two.' It spoke of fresh beginnings and scarcely dreamt-of possibilities, of strange new bedfellows – love, say, and comradeship, respect and desire. It drew her to him and whispered, 'What bodes this?' It answered, 'Why peace it bodes. And love. And quiet life.

'Here,' it said. 'My hand is ready.

'May it do you ease.'

It seems to her then that turning and turning, faster and faster, they become one with the music, that it takes them over, bewitches them, spinning them together like a top. She can feel him drawing her closer to him, as if afraid she may fall. She feels small suddenly in his arms and very light, too frail to survive this glorious whirling without him.

As they spin, the walls seem to melt away and the room becomes suddenly vast with branched candelabra on the walls that draw circles of light about them. She feels the wide skirt of her crinoline fling out wildly behind her, sees the tails of his top-coat flying.

Beneath their feet, the polished floorboards become ice so that they skate and then fly, their feet seeming to leave the ground altogether so that all that binds them to the earth, it seems to her, is the firm determination of their embrace.

And then, just as she thinks they can keep going no longer, when the world has become a spiral into which they are disappearing, they hear the last triumphant chord crashing around them.

Released, she staggers a little, overcome with dizziness.

'Oh Mr Crane,' she says, laying a hand upon her bosom.

'Alice!' he cries; no, not a cry, a shout a cheer a triumphant moan.

He snatches her to him, feels her for one dazzling moment against him before he dips his head and, in a moment of unsurpassed courage, plasters full upon her lips a kiss of pure and unadulterated passion.

Below them, as they are so enjoined, the impossible happens. They feel the earth begin to tremble. Something moves beneath their feet. There is a great rushing in their ears, a rumble, a sound of rending as something crashes away about them.

Separating their lips at long last they look up and see the stars. Together.

2

I T WAS THE gable end, of course.

For a moment they had stood there, their arms still round each other, the wind rushing about them, staring in disbelief at the gaping hole.

Then sheets of papers began lifting from the desk and whirling around, several of them disappearing out through the hole.

'Oh my God, the novel,' she screamed.

As they scrabbled, catching the fluttering paper and some album covers skittering across the floor, black smoke, sucked out by the wind, began belching out of the fireplace.

The crash brought Gerald to the back door.

Together the three of them went outside, sheltering beneath their macs, to survey the damage. The gable end lay in a crumpled heap of stone and plaster, dust still rising from it in a vortex. As it had fallen away, it had torn with it the ivy, and a great snake of it hung in the air waving wildly.

It took them an hour or so to come up with a temporary repair. Gerald found an old piece of tarpaulin in his garage which they secured with rope and nails over the hole in the study wall. They cleared away all the loose books and papers, put out the fire, stacked the furniture away from the holed wall and covered everything they could with sheets. Then they came out and she locked the door behind them.

Sitting around the kitchen table over mugs of tea,

Gerald said, 'I think you should spend the night at our place, Alice.'

'Oh I don't think that will be necessary, Gerald,' she said hastily. 'It's very kind of you. But I think I'd rather stay here.'

His farewell at the door was rather stiff. He did not look at Jim Crane.

'If you're quite sure, Alice . . .' he said.

'Quite sure, Gerald,' she said firmly.

Closing the door behind him, she began to laugh.

At the table Jim Crane pulled a face.

'Oh dear,' he said, 'I don't think Gerald approves of me.'

She walked across the kitchen towards him feeling suddenly awkward. In the long mirror on the wall above the table she caught sight of herself.

'Oh God, look at me,' she said.

There was white plaster on the dress and smudges of smoke on her face and her shoulders. Her hair, originally on top of her head, had slipped halfway down the back, and trailed about her in long wisps.

'You look pretty good to me,' he said.

He got up from the table and stood before her. There he took both of her hands in his. He started to laugh.

'Now where were we,' he said.

His lips were good and strong and firm, warm too, and tender and gently enquiring.

As they drew apart he took a small step back, keeping her hands in his.

'Would you like me to go home?' he said.

'No,' she said, knowing it to be the truth.

*

347

What surprised her afterwards was the ease of it, this thing she had imagined would be so difficult.

By the side of the bed, as she slipped off the dress, he lifted her hand and kissed the fingertips.

'I suppose we should . . .' he said.

'I guess so,' she said, 'bearing in mind the times.

'Although to be honest,' she said, looking up at him, 'I haven't been to bed with anyone since Bernard.'

He pulled her gently to him. Laid his forehead upon hers.

'I haven't exactly been busy myself,' he said.

In bed, she said, 'I know I'm supposed to be able to put this thing on in a sexy fashion but I'm a sixties person and I've never had to use them.'

She managed it though in the end.

'Oh yes,' he said, smiling up at her. 'Sixties person, eh? Don't know how to do it?'

She tapped her forehead.

'Racial memory,' she said.

She liked his body, the chunkiness of it.

'Some might say fat,' he said.

'No,' she said, softly drawing the word out, drawing a hand, at the same time, across his stomach.

He spent a long time enjoying her body. Once he drew a hand over her forehead.

His eyes had stared urgently down into hers.

'You must tell me,' he said, 'what you want.'

'I know,' she said. 'And I will. But such things take time.' And he nodded.

She was surprised, after that, how the complications had melted away. No, not melted away. That

348

was too simple. How they'd become less important. How she'd been able, as it were, to adjourn them. Just for this moment, it was good to have him inside her, that was all. She moved beneath him, enjoying the sensation, enjoying the feel of his body on hers, his hands about her head. She liked the way he said her name softly as he drew nearer his climax, and when he said it she felt, as she always felt, strangely maternal. It was often that way, she found. It was why they were frightened. Why they wrote what they wrote. If there were a difference, she thought, the difference was here, in this fear of abandonment. Women had no such fear. They welcomed abandonment with open arms. When they got it, they were glad. But men needed reassurance. To abandon themselves to their own satisfaction, they needed to be certain that what was so near to them as to be indivisible, was experiencing the same abandonment in the same absolute way.

In the end he came slowly and quietly, as if aware of a need for restraint, and she liked it, this quietness, this stately, faintly methodical conclusion.

Some men came loudly, exploding in your arms, calling a name that vanity told you was yours.

When you were young, you were proud of the noise. You kissed his eyes and his forehead in gratitude at the exclamation of such pleasure.

But when you grew older you learnt the truth, that they could come this way all the time, sad or happy, drunk or sober, for a passing fancy or full of love, their explosion detonated by the mystic remote control that was the masterstroke of a caring but over-ambitious God.

Thinking all of these things, slipping into sleep, she thinks that almost certainly there will be other times, different times, times in which they will make love differently, knowing each other better.

Thinking all of these things, she pushes her body in strange new self-conscious contentment into his.

Her buttocks feel very warm against his loins.

The last thing she remembers is his hand on her belly.

Sunday . . .

1

H E WAS AWAKENED by a ringing.

At first it seemed to be in his dream. He said to the people, who were waltzing around him and whom he did not know – all save Malone, who was dancing with a woman in a silk kimono and who smiled but said nothing – 'The phone,' he said, 'the phone.' But they just went on whirling around him.

He had dropped to his knees and was scrabbling around their moving legs for the telephone wire when he began to surface through the dream like a diver to find his hand, of its own accord, a quarter of a century of experience behind it, shaking off sleep and crawling like a drowsy, well-drilled sentry across the covers to the phone.

He had dragged the receiver to his ear and said, 'Mmm,' his eyes tightly closed, before he remembered where he was. By then, though, it was too late.

At the other end of the line a female voice spoke a curious, faintly querulous, 'Alice?' He had no doubt who it was.

He took a breath, passed a tongue over lips dry from too much brandy, and said, 'Mmm?' again, this time with a questioning inflexion.

There was a small silence, then the voice said, 'Damn,' unceremoniously, as if talking to itself, and then, suddenly, as if remembering its manners, 'Sorry. Must have the wrong number,' whereupon there was a sharp click and the burr of the dialling tone.

'Good morning,' a voice said next to him.

Turning, he found her eyes, sea-green like rock pools beside him on the pillow.

'I'm sorry,' he said. 'I answered the phone without thinking. It's something I do automatically now.'

'It's OK,' she said. 'Who was it anyway?'

'I have a feeling,' he said, 'it was your friend Rita.'

'Oh *dear*,' she said laughing.

She took the receiver from his hand and stretching over him replaced it on the cradle. With a flourish, she pulled the telephone plug out of the wall. Sliding herself over him, she put both arms about him and, leaning forward, whispered in his ear.

'Now where were we?' she said.

And that was how it was. The eroticism of her.

She was more experienced than him. He had guessed that she would be. He felt no shame in it. He was glad. The way she touched him made something curl up inside him, made him want to say things, do things he had never done before. He felt no embarrassment at his own pleasure. He felt his fingers in her hair and heard his voice on the air and didn't care.

'That was wonderful,' he said, holding her face in his hands.

'But you have to tell me . . .' he said again.

She said, 'I will.' She said it gently, she stroked his face. 'Telling someone what you want is the hardest thing in the world.

'Like I said,' she said, 'it takes time.'

He got dressed and went to the shop for eggs and bacon for breakfast. At the same time he bought the papers.

They had made the front page of course.

There was a picture of Alice stretched out on the hotel bed. She looked sexy but at the same time very grave.

The headline down one side of the page said, FATHER DWYER IN MARRIAGE SENSATION, which of course it wasn't at all, but that was the way of these things, he thought with a sigh.

Over the top, in white on grey, it said, TV PRIEST WENT TO BED WITH THE LODGER SAYS WIFE. The strip along the bottom read, MY CHAMPAGNE NIGHTS OF LOVE WITH BERNARD O'DONAGHUE: TURN TO CENTRE PAGES.

He carried it back to the house with trepidation.

He laid it on the kitchen table and began cooking the breakfast. She came down, still in her dressing gown, rubbing her eyes. The type they used for the first paragraph was so big he could read it from the stove.

The wife of TV's 'Mr Holy', it said, *has told how she came home unexpectedly to find him in bed with the sexy young lodger.*

'*TV's Mr Holy*,' she said, picking up the paper.

'Yeah, well,' he said, shamefaced, the spatula in his hand, 'you know how it is.'

She lowered herself to the bench seat, the paper in her hand, and began reading. He snatched looks at her as he cooked but her face gave nothing away.

When she raised her head eventually she was smiling.

'It's OK,' she said, 'you did a good job. Mind you, I still can't believe it's worth thirty thousand pounds.'

'You're going to need it,' he said, jerking a head at the pile of plaster outside the window.

As they'd stood in the garden last night, gazing up at the damage, he had spotted a piece of paper caught in the ivy. He reached up and pulled it down. It was a page from her novel. He handed it to her and she read it, pulled a face and, scrunching it up, hurled it away from her.

'An omen,' she said dramatically. 'Possibly an Act of God.' More quietly she said, 'It never was a good novel.'

It was a beautiful morning. Surprisingly warm. The sun was shining. The wind had dropped. What little remained blew scudding clouds across the sky.

They walked in the Dene, hand in hand, to get rid of their hangovers. They wandered around the stalls selling bric-à-brac. He found a good kitchen knife and he bought it for her.

'As long as you promise I don't have to use it,' she said.

Just by chance she found a *Catcher in the Rye* among some books and bought it for him.

He was curled up on the sofa in the lounge reading it when she flicked the television on. It was the omnibus edition and suddenly there he was on the screen.

'It's a peculiar thing, isn't it,' he said. 'A priest being a sex symbol.'

'Not really,' she said. 'We have a prurient interest in priests. We like our vicars dirty. You of all people should know that. We like scandal about the clergy, it keeps them in their place. Prevents us having to take them seriously.'

He thought she was right. He thought of Bullerman. 'Heard the one about the two nuns, Crane . . .'

Soon, he thought, there would be one about female priests.

She poured the pair of them a glass of wine and settled down on the sofa to read the *Observer*.

Some time later, with her lying in his arms, he had turned her face and kissed her.

Which is how they ended up where they lay now, naked again, limbs entangled. Back in bed.

Monday . . .

1

H<small>E HADN'T LEFT</small> in the end till this evening.

The leaving was a little frosty. He left saying nothing more than, 'Well then . . .' when the truth was he had wanted to leave saying so much more, saying something like, 'Well . . . I'll call you then . . . tomorrow . . .'

He couldn't remember exactly how the argument started, how the evening had taken a turn for the worse.

It had been a good day. It started in the usual way. His lips turn upwards with the remembrance. He aches from it still, the love-making.

'Getting old, Malone,' he says with a rueful smile. 'Can't stand the pace.'

She excused herself lightly, although she didn't need to for his sake.

'I've got a lot of time to make up for.'

'Good,' he had told her.

Staying a second night should have been difficult, instead it was easy.

She'd said, with a sigh, 'I'll need to reorganize a study tomorrow. I think I'll use Madeline's old bedroom.'

All he had to say then was, 'I'll give you a hand if you like,' and there it was, all settled.

They'd taken care of the formalities by getting drunk again and stumbling off to bed so that for a second time he woke up next to her in the morning.

Today he'd helped her to move her stuff, her old

desk, books, papers, typewriter. He'd even helped her to put up some shelves. Him! Putting up shelves, with a drill borrowed from Gerald who continued to glower at him disapprovingly.

They were so tired after they finished that they had a take-away from the Indian around the corner. They were sitting eating it with a bottle of wine when it started.

She had been reading him out bits from some dumb feature in the *Guardian*, something about the New Man being entirely sound but unfortunately not as sexy as the Old.

'I mean what the hell do women want?' he had said. He thought it was reasonable under the circumstances.

'Oh God,' she said sarcastically, 'not that old chestnut again.'

'Well,' he said, 'it's a reasonable question.'

'Who knows what they want? Who knows what anyone wants? Life is just finding out what you don't want. Eliminating options. Striking out the choices. Maybe on your deathbed you get somewhere near knowing, who knows?'

She was right, of course. It was a crazy question. What did he want?

He didn't even know if he wanted to stay with her another day. He knew he didn't want to leave and at the same time he knew staying caused a flit of panic in his stomach.

He liked everything she was but arguing with her caused an irritation in him. He wanted her to be complicated and simple at the same time.

'Oh, men,' she said, in that special voice she had for saying the word. 'Men are just little boys.'

'Oh yeah,' he said. 'And speaking of old chestnuts.'

'It's true,' she said. 'They're not like women. They don't have the same openness. The same upfront approach to life. They hold their lives like cloaks around them to protect their nakedness. They don't give like women do.'

'It's not true,' he said; thinking, at the same time, there was some truth in what she said.

'It is true,' she said. She was looking away from him, out into the garden.

'Men,' she said. She sounded suddenly as though she hated them. 'They're like plump little smirking cherubs, covering their little-boy's cocks with their little-boy's hands.'

'I'd better go,' he said.

When he got home the light on the answer machine was flashing.

He thought probably it was his mother. One of her Jewish momma calls: 'We just thought we hadn't heard from you for a few days.'

It wasn't true, of course. He had rung her . . . when was it? He could hear his father somewhere in the background, 'The lad's busy, Lillian.' Ah, the joys of parenthood.

Or he thought maybe it was one of those crazy calls he got occasionally from a devoted reader who wanted to tell him exactly what he would like to do with the scarf discreetly draping the naked loins of Sunday's Page Three girl. But it was neither a reader nor his mother. It was Octavia.

She left her home phone number. Oh oh, he thought. Trouble.

When he rang her though, there was no such inflexion in her voice. It was cool, humorous.

'How are you, Crane?' she said.

She didn't wait for his reply. She said, 'Crane, it seems you're speaking to the new features editor.' So now here it comes, he thought. Get rid of Crane. Show your executive potential. What came next, he wondered. You've had three warnings, Crane. And now we've paid thirty thousand for that crap.

'There's going to be some changes, Crane,' she said, laughing and confirming his worst suspicions. 'There's some dead wood around that has to go.'

Then she said, 'You'd be amazed, Crane. There're people here keeping their heads down in corners who haven't done a decent day's work in years.' That was when he'd begun to be confused.

She said, 'I need some people around me I rate, Crane. I like the way you work, the way you operate. We don't need district men any more anyway. It's cheaper to have freelances do day-to-day stuff. I suggest a six-month trial. See how you get on.'

He said, 'Hang on, Octavia, hang on. You've left me. Are you suggesting me coming down to London?'

'Of course,' she said impatiently.

He was too confused to give her a coherent answer.

She said, 'Think about it. Call me by the end of the week.'

He said, as she was about to hang up, 'By the way, what happened to . . .' He realized then he didn't even know his old features editor's name.

'Exactly,' she said. 'Who knows? Left by the back door after clearing his desk with a cheque in his hand, I imagine. That's the usual way, isn't it?'

'Live by the sword, die by the sword.'

'What?'

'Just an expression,' he said.

He showered and sat down by the window with a cup of coffee which is where he sits now, looking out on the river, his river; on his city, a small city, a manageable city; a city where you could go shopping and be certain that you'd always see someone you knew; a city where you knew you belonged. Not a city like London.

Things were changing. Suddenly he could feel them. There was Malone's house for a start. He would sell that. For the first time in his life he would have money in the bank. Freedom. And then, of course, there was Alice Potter.

What did women want? She was right. Life was just eliminating options. How did anyone know what they wanted? Go to London? Stay here? Have a life, a little lonely certainly, but safe at least and pain-free, or one short on loneliness but long on the dangerous complications of love?

Love?

Ah, love was it now?

Well, no point in fooling himself. A man could get serious about Alice Potter. Which meant, of course, given the nature of the game, a man could also get hurt.

So what did *he* want?

He shakes his head. Drains his glass. God he was tired. He wanted his bed, that was what he wanted.

He lingers at the window one more moment.

He wanted something else too. He wanted her to see this view. He wanted her to see the traffic ploughing over the bridge at night, the lights flickering through the great soaring arch. He wanted to cook her one of his specialities – a fillet steak say with one of his fancy sauces – to serve it here in this window. He wanted them to sit here drinking good wine from his fine glasses. He wanted them to talk, to argue if necessary. He wanted them to get up and yawn and stretch and embrace by the window and slope off to bed.

He would take a chance.

He would give it a go.

He would ring her in the morning.

'After all, Malone,' he says. 'She can only say no.'

2

S HE WAS SORRY now that they had argued.

She would like to ring him, to tell him so. One more brandy and she might even do it.

Relationships. God. When you were lonely, when you saw a couple walking hand-in-hand in the street, you longed for one, and you thought about all the good things, forgot about the bad.

They could be so beastly, relationships. So entirely bloody. So ridiculously run through with complications. An absurd system, this men and women thing. She wasn't surprised people tried other permutations: men/men, women/women. It was a dumb experiment, one that could have been strangled at birth if only Adam and Eve had had the sense to say, 'Not likely,' or, more acutely, 'You must be joking,' when the Eternal Architect confronted them with the masterplan.

It was at times like these, she thinks now, when Rita's determined celibacy appeared the less extreme, when it seemed to have certain attractions.

She called Rita up. She said, 'I'm back, Rita.' She had to raise her voice over the electric drill.

Rita said, 'What's that noise, Alice?'

She closed her eyes and took a deep breath. She said, 'Well, it's like this, Rita . . .'

When she'd finished, Rita said pretty much what she thought she would say, which was, 'I really can't imagine what's come over you, Alice.'

It was a good point. She wasn't entirely sure what had come over her either.

The pain involved in relationships, she thinks now, is like the pain of childbirth. Hold a new lover in your arms and the pain of past loves was quite forgotten. Which, there again, was like the pain of writing. For what did one stroke of a new novel's cover do but erase all the angst that produced it?

Andrew phoned.

He rang, with immaculate timing, just as they were sweating and straining getting the desk here, up the stairs.

A small pang strikes her heart. He had been wonderful, Jim. She says the name out loud. Strange how awkward it feels in her mouth.

Andrew said, grudgingly, 'I suppose, all things considered, Alice, the piece probably won't do us any harm.'

He said, 'When you've finished the final draft, Alice, I think we should talk about money again.'

She said, 'That might be quite a while, Andrew. I'm intending to rewrite it. In fact I'm thinking of chucking the whole thing out and starting again.'

He said, 'For heaven's sake why, Alice?'

She said, 'It's a long story. I don't want to talk about it now.'

It was reading *his* damn story that had done it, his damn story in that damn raggy gutter-press newspaper.

Sighing, she leans back in her chair and lifts the paper from the desk-top.

It was absurd. It was her damn story, the same damn story she was trying to tell in her novel, only he had told it better.

The wife of TV's 'Mr Holy' has told how she came home unexpectedly to find him in bed with the sexy young lodger.

Against her will, her lips lift upwards.

That damn flat journalese.

Jubilee Square's Father Dwyer is seeking a 'quickie' divorce from wife Alice so that he can marry co-star Zoë Fairley, Jubilee's beautiful black lawyer Mercy Hellman, who is expecting his twins.

Soap star Bernard O'Donaghue was a penniless actor when he bedded luscious student Madeline Tarrant whose father is a fourth cousin of the Queen.

Said attractive Alice, 42, 'I was paying all the bills and supporting him when I came home one day unexpectedly and saw him coming out of her room naked. He'd had other affairs during our marriage and it was the last straw.'

The TV priest walked out on her the same day with 24-year-old Madeline, now New York's 'Whipping Queen', who has told of their wild affair.

She said the sexy Father Dwyer, who turned down an affair with Mercy Hellman on the screen rather than have sex with her and break his vows, told her his wife was a lesbian.

Said writer Alice: 'Bernard would say anything when he wanted to get someone into bed. He really was a terrible rogue.'

Brunette Alice says she went broke paying for his playboy lifestyle during their six-year marriage.

'It was champagne all the way,' she said. 'It cost me a small fortune. Although it was four years ago I'm still recovering.'

But she says she bears no grudge against the womanizing priest.

'He was worth every penny,' she says.

Beneath the story, a long strap ran along the bottom of the page. It read, MY CHAMPAGNE NIGHTS OF LOVE: TURN TO CENTRE PAGES.

No. She would not bother to turn. Not this time. She had read enough. She sighs. Who was 'attractive Alice, 42' anyway? Not her, surely? Surely this story wasn't hers. It was too exciting to be hers, dammit. Reading it, she had forgotten all about her embarrassment, she had almost forgotten that it was her there, stretched out on the page. It seemed like it was someone else's story, someone more interesting than herself.

Yes. It was her life but his was the better version. A better story, better told, which was all a novel was, after all, a story told. It was fuller, his version, for all its crude tabloid-speak. It had more guts to it. More life. It made the page that he plucked from the tree seem precious and bloodless and – worse than both of those things – self-indulgent.

Yes. Face up to it. Self-indulgent. Self-complacent. There was something almost masturbatory about her writing. That first person. Always that bloody first person. Always the 'I'. Always that single solipsistic point of view. That itsy-bitsy, cutsy-tricksy narrative voice. That female voice. Face up to that too.

'But that narrative voice is your great strength, Alice.' That's what Andrew had said.

'Well perhaps I'm tired of the voice,' she had replied mutinously.

'I'm thinking of trying the third person again,' she said. She wasn't thinking of it at all. She didn't know why she said it, but as soon as she had said it, she felt a longing for it, for the third person, washing over her like a long cool silver stream.

The third person. Possibilities. Other people's points of view. Which is when suddenly she remembered. And felt that surge of fear shading into despair.

'What do women want?' he had said to her.

It was how the argument had started.

Parting at the door, she said, quietly, a little bitterly, 'I'll tell you what women want. It's something quite simple. They just want some vague idea, some faint notion, of what the hell's going on in men's heads.'

Ah, there's the rub. There was the problem with the third person. Male characters.

'Thinly drawn and unconvincing,' a reviewer, unkind she had thought at the time, had said about her men. And she couldn't argue. Only mitigate.

Standing on the step, he had turned his face away from her, looked out into the garden.

'There could be,' he said, 'a simple explanation of what's going on in men's heads. It could be fundamentally the same as what's going on in women's.'

She'd pulled a face. Refused to catch his eye as he looked back at her.

'Well,' she said, in her superior itsy-bitsy cutsy-tricksy sophisticated woman's voice, 'we must discuss that sometime.' Which, as a matter of interest, if the truth were told, was what she wanted to do, but she'd said it flatly and coldly with a belligerent air of farewell.

She gets up with a sigh. Walks to the window. Down below her the fallen cherub smirks up at her.

It was a nice idea, that suggestion of his. The case

against it, however, appeared to be proven. The evidence, after all, was empirical. All about them. Out there in the world. That men and women did not seem to think the same way was pasted, like Orlando's love letters, on every tree.

Looking down, she is infused suddenly with a strange emotion. It is unfamiliar. Upon examination, it occurs to her it may be hope.

Why not do it? Why not do what so many had done before her? Why not purely for the sake of argument, assume that men and women – make that *certain* men and women – beneath the fashion and the philosophy and all the other -ologies that made up modern life, beneath the social attitudes and the cultural constructs that hemmed them in and laced them about and grew up over them like ivy on a wall, why not assume that beneath all of this, these certain men and women thought much the same?

Yes, why not? Why not do it? What did it matter if it didn't work? The list was long and distinguished, after all, of those who had done it already and failed.

She would take a chance.

She would give it a go.

She would introduce another character, a male character, a male character with equal billing. She would tell *his* story as well as *hers*, and she would tell them, the pair of them, in the cool, neutral, scrupulously fair terms of the third person.

Probably the whole idea was absurd. More than likely it was wrong. But it would be a start. That was all. It would be a start.

She moves back abruptly towards the desk.

She picks up a piece of paper to roll into the

typewriter but then pauses with it suspended in the air before laying it back down again on the desk-top thoughtfully.

Reaching out, she pulls the phone towards her and lifts the receiver.

FOR THE BEST IN PAPERBACKS, LOOK FOR THE

In every corner of the world, on every subject under the sun, Penguin represents quality and variety – the very best in publishing today.

For complete information about books available from Penguin – including Puffins, Penguin Classics and Arkana – and how to order them, write to us at the appropriate address below. Please note that for copyright reasons the selection of books varies from country to country.

In the United Kingdom: Please write to *Dept JC, Penguin Books Ltd, FREEPOST, West Drayton, Middlesex, UB7 0BR.*

If you have any difficulty in obtaining a title, please send your order with the correct money, plus ten per cent for postage and packaging, to *PO Box No 11, West Drayton, Middlesex*

In the United States: Please write to *Dept BA, Penguin, 299 Murray Hill Parkway, East Rutherford, New Jersey 07073*

In Canada: Please write to *Penguin Books Canada Ltd, 2801 John Street, Markham, Ontario L3R 1B4*

In Australia: Please write to the *Marketing Department, Penguin Books Australia Ltd, P.O. Box 257, Ringwood, Victoria 3134*

In New Zealand: Please write to the *Marketing Department, Penguin Books (NZ) Ltd, Private Bag, Takapuna, Auckland 9*

In India: Please write to *Penguin Overseas Ltd, 706 Eros Apartments, 56 Nehru Place, New Delhi, 110019*

In the Netherlands: Please write to *Penguin Books Netherlands B.V., Postbus 3507, NL–1001 AH, Amsterdam*

In West Germany: Please write to *Penguin Books Ltd, Friedrichstrasse 10–12, D–6000 Frankfurt/Main 1*

In Spain: Please write to *Alhambra Longman S.A., Fernandez de la Hoz 9, E–28010 Madrid*

In Italy: Please write to *Penguin Italia s.r.l., Via Como 4, I-20096 Pioltello (Milano)*

In France: Please write to *Penguin France S.A., 17 rue Lejeune, F-31000 Toulouse*

In Japan: Please write to *Longman Penguin Japan Co Ltd, Yamaguchi Building, 2–12–9 Kanda Jimbocho, Chiyoda-Ku, Tokyo 101*

A Woman's Guide to Adultery

Rose's love life is governed by one simple law: 'thou shalt not make another woman unhappy.' And that, of course, rules out adultery. But since all the desirable men are almost by definition attached, the choice seems to be between sin and celibacy. And where does love fit into that?

'Erotic, compelling, painful and elating by turns, heady yet everyday, exquisite in its sensibilities, piercing in its perceptions ... Ms Clewlow certainly knows her territory, not to mention the hearts and minds of women' – Fay Weldon